# THE SECRET - VIOLET'S STORY

(BOOK 3 IN THE LIFE ON THE MOORS SERIES)

ELIZA J SCOTT

Copyright © 2019 by Eliza J Scott

All rights reserved.

Eliza J Scott has asserted her moral right under the Copyright, Designs and Patents Act of 1988 to be identified as the author of this work.

No part of this book may be reproduced in any form or by any electronic or mechanical means, including information storage and retrieval systems, without written permission from the author, except for the use of brief quotations in a book review.

This book is entirely a work of fiction. Names, characters, places and incidents are either a product of the author's imagination or are used fictitiously. Any resemblance to actual people living or dead, events or locales is entirely coincidental.

This book has been edited in British English (BrE) and therefore uses British spellings.

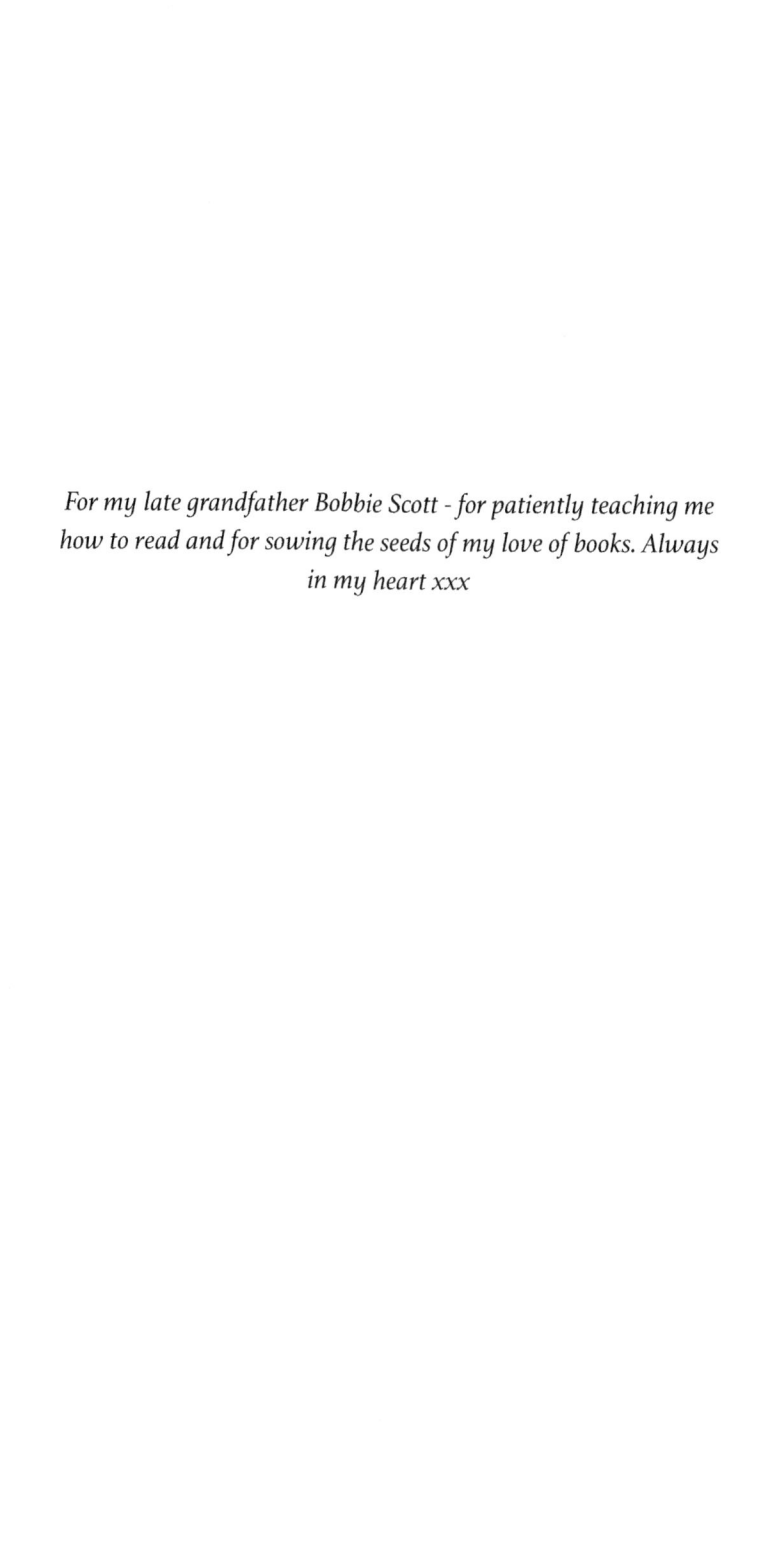

*For my late grandfather Bobbie Scott - for patiently teaching me how to read and for sowing the seeds of my love of books. Always in my heart xxx*

## CHAPTER 1

MAY

'So are you really not going to tell me where you're taking me?' Violet turned to Jimby, taking in his easy smile, the dark stubble of his chin glinting in the sunshine and his mop of chocolate brown curls that were only just on the right side of unruly. He was looking summery in his pale blue shirt with the fine white stripe down it, the cuffs rolled back revealing strong forearms, the "v" of a white t-shirt peeking out at the open collar. They'd left Sunshine Cottage in Lytell Stangdale late that morning and had been driving along the twisting, turning roads of the North Yorkshire Moors for the last hour, and yet she was still no wiser as to their destination.

'Nope. You'll find out when we get there.' Jimby changed gear and turned to her, flashing one of the trademark broad smiles that triggered his dimples. Even though his chocolate brown eyes were hidden behind a pair of aviator sunglasses, Vi knew that they'd be sporting their familiar twinkle. The one that made her heart do somersaults.

'That's so not fair, Jimby.' Though she huffed, there was

a smile playing around her full lips. 'What harm can it do to tell me now? You've kept it secret for ages.'

'If I told you now, it would spoil your birthday surprise and, like you just said, I've managed to keep it secret for this long, so I might as well keep it for that little bit longer. Not that it's been easy, I can tell you. You can be one fierce interrogator when you put your mind to it.' He briefly took his eyes off the road and caught a glimpse of his girlfriend as she pouted. He threw his head back and laughed.

'Hey, you. It's not funny!' She gave him a gentle prod in the ribs, which merely served to make him laugh even louder. 'Have you any idea how difficult you've made it by only telling me to pack a case with enough clothes for two nights and a variety of occasions? No wonder my mind's going into overdrive with what you've got planned. I've practically had to pack my whole wardrobe.'

'Really?' Jimby raised his eyebrows. 'From the pile of luggage I've had to force into the boot and onto the backseat, no one would ever have guessed. Thought I was going to have to resort to a tub of butter and a couple of shoehorns to get them all in.'

Vi couldn't help but giggle. 'Well, you've only got yourself to blame for that. Just promise me you haven't booked us on a course to go mountaineering or white water rafting, or anything else equally horrible and scary.'

'I'm afraid I can make no such promises. Anyway, I thought you liked cycling?'

'Cycling? Please tell me you're joking. I'm sure I'd hate cycling, all that wobbling about, and the risk of falling off into a prickly hedge or worse. I can tell you this, if you've booked anything like that, you'll be doing it on your own, buster. There's no way I'll be ruining my make-up or getting my hair wet, especially when I've just spent a fortune getting it done.' Vi pulled down the visor and peered over her cat-eye sunglasses to check her reflection in the mirror, smoothing the waves of her glossy, deep-purple hair.

'And very lovely you look, too.'

'Honestly, Jimby, I'm warning you, if you've booked us in for anything like that, payback time will involve you coming to one of my burlesque classes and being used to demonstrate how not to do it.'

'Sounds fun, I've always fancied having a nosy in the village hall when they're on.'

Vi was a trained burlesque dancer and taught a class in the village once a week, which was something she always looked forward to. It not only kept her hand in at the art, but it was also great fun. The women of Lytell Stangdale and the surrounding villages who attended didn't take themselves too seriously and the class was always a bit of a giggle.

She sighed noisily. 'Oh, Jimby, please tell me. I think I'm going to burst if you don't.' She moved closer to him, giving her best pleading expression and fluttering her sooty eyelashes.

'Hmm, let's think ... er, nope!'

'Argghh! James Fairfax, you are so annoying! This is killing me. I've no idea why everyone's being so tight-lipped about it. Trying to get information out of Kitty and Molly was like getting blood out of a stone. They reckoned they knew nothing about it when I asked them, but I could so tell they did.'

Jimby was practically hunched over the steering-wheel with laughter. 'Look, Vi, you might as well accept it, I'm not going to spill. So, I suggest you just sit back and enjoy the glorious scenery until we get there.'

'And you might as well accept that if I get soaking wet, covered in mud, or injured in any way, I'll never speak to you again.'

'Every cloud ...'

Vi, knowing when she was beat, huffed again, and turned her attention to the scenery as Jimby had suggested, her almond-shaped green eyes taking in the countryside that had suddenly sprung into life as the heat of the May sunshine beat down in the year's first glimpse of an early summer. *What a beautiful weekend to be celebrating a birthday,* she thought, hoping she could trust Jimby not to have planned anything she wouldn't like. She flicked the radio on and music blasted out.

'Oh, I love this song,' said Jimby. He turned up the volume and started singing along at the top of his lungs, tapping his fingers on the steering-wheel.

Vi gave him a sideways look and wound her window down.

'That's more like it, Vi,' he said taking a break from his vocals and breathed in deeply. 'Get the windows open and let the fresh, country air in.'

'Actually, I've opened it to let your foghorn of a voice out, before it causes permanent damage to my ears or shatters the windscreen.'

'That's hurtful.'

'That's noise pollution.'

'Point taken.' He grinned at her. 'I'll tone it down.'

Violet smiled back and returned her attention to the stunning scenery that rolled by, the sun warming her as its rays reached in through the windows. The moors had enjoyed a week of glorious, sunny weather, putting an end to a vicious cold snap that had had a firm grip on the area for a good month. How quickly that was forgotten. Now, frothy pink and white blossom dripped from the trees, while a host of wildflowers burst out of the verges like brightly-dressed showgirls. The sky was cloudless, and Vi couldn't remember the last time she'd seen it such a perfect shade of cornflower blue. A cluster of fluffy, white lambs caught her attention as they darted off, running about the fields in high spirits, playing games of chase, kicking out their hind legs in sheer joy.

Her mind turned to her best friends, Kitty and Molly, and how she'd quizzed them mercilessly about where Jimby was taking her.

'Honestly, chick, that brother of mine has told me nothing,' said Kitty. Vi scrutinised her friend's elfin features for any tell-tale signs that she knew more than she was letting on. The three of them were sitting at the table in Molly's sunny kitchen at Withrin Hill Farm, having one of their regular catch-ups over a pot of tea.

'Forgive me if I'm wrong, Kitts, but I could've sworn you had your fingers crossed just then.' Vi arched her deep-purple, sculpted eyebrows at her friend.

'I don't think she did, Vi,' said Molly. Refusing to make eye contact, she brushed a tangle of stray curls off her face, then smoothed an imaginary crease in her skirt. 'Jimbo hasn't told any of us anything.'

'You are such a bad liar, Moll. In fact, I know you're both a pair of rotten fibbers, but I can see I'm not going to get anything out of either of you, so I'll let it drop.'

The look that passed between the cousins didn't escape Violet's attention, and she was about to pounce on it when Molly's three-year-old daughter Emmie, roused from her afternoon nap and called downstairs. A cuddle with her god-daughter was always a welcome distraction for Vi.

'Not much further now.' Jimby's voice brought her thoughts back to the car.

'Oh, right,' said Vi, taking in the name of the village on the old black and white sign.

**CHAPTER 2**

'Kirkbythwaite? Isn't this where that fancy hotel is? The one that's just been given five stars and had that big write-up in Yorkshire Portions? And wasn't the head chef a finalist on some cookery show?' Vi's mind was racing with excitement as they made their way past a cluster of well-maintained Georgian houses with equally neat gardens set prettily around the edges of a village green. Two ancient oak trees stood side-by-side in the centre, their gnarled branches intertwined, a dense cluster of bluebells huddled at their feet.

'It is, and I do believe he was,' replied Jimby. He stopped at a junction and contemplated the road sign opposite, laughing as he read the words.

'What's funny?'

He nodded towards the sign which informed them that the village was divided into two parts: "East End", which was left, and "West End", which was right, though the "s" in "West" had been painted over. 'I like the sound of the left option best; I think I'm going to take that.'

Vi read the words aloud, 'The Wet End.' The penny

dropped and she flicked him on the arm with the back of her hand. 'You're horrible, I can't believe you bring me all this way and take me to somewhere that has the words "wet end" in its address. It sounds disgusting.'

'Well, I think it sounds like a bloody lovely place. I'm going to go and investigate.'

Vi tutted and he roared with laughter until the driver of a car who had been waiting patiently behind them beeped his horn for them to move along. 'Alright, keep your knickers on,' Jimby called to him.

'Come on, Jimbo, seriously, which way?' said Vi.

'Like I said, left sounds the most promising, so I think we'll give that way a try first. And, if my reckoning's right, the hotel should be just down the end of this road.' He made his way down a twisting lane, edged with estate fencing and shaded by the branches of tall, overhanging trees of mixed variety, all in full leaf.

'Oh, wow!' Vi gasped as the car nosed its way through a grand pair of wrought iron gates, overseen by two large stone eagles perched on gateposts at either side.

'See, I was right, my inner compass served me well.' Jimby nodded to a tasteful, hand-painted sign announcing their arrival at The Kirkbythwaite Hall Hotel. 'We're here.'

They followed the well-maintained sweeping drive lined with lime trees, punctuated by weather-worn statues, where a herd of deer roamed free. Jimby's car crunched over the gravel as they approached the impressive former stately home built of butter-coloured sandstone. A flag flapped in the light breeze atop a tower on the far right, while small panes of glass set in broad mullioned windows glittered in the sunlight.

Vi shivered with excitement, her mouth falling open in awe as Jimby eased them into a parking space between a pair of stylish sports cars, both having been buffed to within an inch of their lives. 'I can't believe you wanted to bring us here in your scruffy old Landie,' she whispered.

'Er, why are we whispering? And there's nothing wrong with my lovely, lickable Landie — I was only teasing about bringing it, actually.' He gave her a cheeky smile as he removed his sunglasses. 'Listen, just grab your handbag, I'll see to the rest of the luggage once we get settled into the room.'

Vi had a quick rummage about in her aubergine designer handbag, pulling out her make-up bag and giving her pout a quick swipe of glossy, crushed berry lipstick. She followed that with a spritz of her signature floral fragrance. Once done, she stepped out of the car, smoothed down the full skirt of her fifties-style white summer dress covered with a blowsy rose print, then threw a shrug cardi over her shoulders. She looked every inch a young Elizabeth Taylor. Still tingling with excitement, she followed Jimby, being careful to avoid her new heels from sinking into the gravel.

At the entrance, a noble-looking coat of arms sat above the sandstone arch of the doorway and the broad oak door was propped open, offering up a squat entrance hall lined with stone benches. Beyond this was a closed, inner half-glass door. Jimby pushed it open to reveal a magnificent oak panelled reception area, where stags' heads kept company with grand portraits of previous occupants of the house. 'Oh, this is gorgeous,' Vi whispered.

While Jimby dealt with checking-in and organisation of luggage, Vi gazed around her, inhaling the heady scent of the flower arrangement that filled a huge copper cachet pot in one of the windows.

'Here's your key, you're on the second floor, take a right when you come out of the lift and it's the second door along on the left.' The receptionist, whose name-tag informed them she was called "Jodie", gave a friendly smile. 'Bob, here, will show you how to use the lift, but if you need anything else, just let me know. Now all that's left for me to say is, have a lovely stay.'

'Thank you,' replied Vi. Her heart was fluttering. She and Jimby had never stayed anywhere as sumptuous as this together before; but, then again, he never usually seemed bothered about having a night away. Not that she was complaining, it just made the surprise all the more special.

The pair followed Bob along to the lift. 'Is this it?' asked Jimby.

'Yes, sir, this fine piece of Art Deco engineering is the hotel lift,' replied Bob. He pulled back the small, highly polished wooden door and launched into a clear, well-rehearsed set of instructions, before indicating for them to step inside. Vi could feel his eyes wander over the delicate floral tattoos that adorned her ankles and wrists. 'Any problems, just holler, I'll be able to hear you.'

'Well, that's alright then,' said Jimby. He winked at Vi, pulled the metal grille across, then selected their floor. 'Thanks, Bob.'

Feeling a hint of anxiety creep in, Vi asked, 'Do you think we'll ever get to our room?'

At that, the lift gave a shudder. 'I think we're just about to find out.' Jimby put his arm around her, and grinned as the lift set off at a considerably quicker pace than she was expecting, making her stumble.

'Oh!' She grabbed hold of him to steady herself, sticking her tongue out when he laughed at her.

'Can't say I'm sorry to get out of that,' she said as they walked along the wide landing.

'I thought it was sweet; quirky.' He stopped outside a

door with a polished brass plate boasting the words, "The Gardenia Suite". 'Looks like this is us,' he said.

'You booked us a suite?' Vi's eyes were wide and Jimby replied with a smile that dimpled his cheeks, making her heart flip. He really was full of surprises today.

The large key turned with a solid "clunk". Slowly, he pushed the door open. 'After you, madam.' His grin deepened as he took a low bow.

'Oh, wow!' Vi kicked off her heels as soon as she stepped into the room, her bare feet sinking into the deep pile of the cream-coloured carpet, the aroma of essential oils washing over her. 'Jimby, this is stunning, it's even decorated in my favourite colour.' Her eyes roved over the bedroom where, centre-stage sat a super-king-size bed, looking every bit as noble as its name would suggest, with its large velvet headboard in a deep shade of plum. A sumptuous throw in complementary shades of purple and gold lay across it, and neat contrasting cushions rested against plump pillows in crisp, white Egyptian cotton pillowcases that matched the sheets.

Along one wall were three large oak doors. Vi pulled the first one open to find a generously-proportioned en-suite bathroom, complete with walk-in shower at one end and a large copper bath in the centre. She ran over to the toiletries set out along the marble top of the sink. 'They've got their own branded aromatherapy products!'

'I take it that's good?' Jimby smiled at her enthusiasm.

'It's very good.' She twisted the lid off one of the bottles and inhaled the contents. 'Oh, that's heavenly.'

'I wonder what's behind here?' He pulled open the next door which revealed a large walk-in wardrobe. 'At least there's plenty of room to hang all of that stuff you packed into all those suitcases the porter's bringing up as we speak

– poor sod.' His gaze followed Violet who clearly hadn't heard him and was making her way towards the lounge area.

'Oh, Jimby, come and look at this view.' She was standing at the large mullioned window, taking in the stunning garden, lined with neatly clipped box hedges, archways laden with the large blowsy heads of spring-flowering clematis, and a spectacular fountain at the centre. Directly in front of the hotel was a patio area where all-weather wicker tables and chairs were set out for guests to have afternoon tea and sip champagne. A cream gazebo trimmed with soft pink roses was set out for those wanting to take shelter from whatever the weather decided to throw at them. To the right of this was a sympathetically built extension that housed a heated swimming pool, sauna and jacuzzi. Beyond the garden, halfway along the deer park, was a small folly topped with a gold-leaf coronet that glittered in the sunlight. 'I don't think I've ever stayed in such a romantic place.' Vi sighed.

Jimby went over to where she was standing, draping an arm around her shoulder. 'I read that the gardens had an overhaul about five years ago. The new owners brought some award-winning garden designer in, and he transformed the place. I must admit, it looks pretty amazing.'

'It does, as does the room, or suite, should I say. Thank you for bringing me here, Jimby.' Vi reached her arms around his neck and kissed him firmly on the mouth.

'Mmm. My pleasure Miss Smith.' He nuzzled her neck, inhaling her perfume. 'If you're looking for a way to show your appreciation, I can think of a couple of things ...'

'Oh really, Mr Fairfax?' Vi found his lips again, pressing herself against him, making him groan.

They were interrupted by a discreet knock at the door.

# The Secret - Violet's Story

Jimby rested his forehead against hers. 'That'll be the luggage.' He strode over to the door, opening it wide. 'Ah, excellent timing, come in,' he said, not quite convincingly, to the young porter, who looked no more than sixteen and couldn't take his eyes off Vi.

~

'CAN WE STAY HERE FOREVER, PLEASE?' Vi snuggled into Jimby's arms as they lay in a tangle of the finest Egyptian cotton. The window was open slightly, and a delicious whisper of a breeze floated through it, caressing her skin.

'As long as you carry on doing the things you've just done, the answer's yes.' He ran his fingers up and down her arm, then placed a kiss on top of the silky waves of her hair.

'I can't see that being a problem.' Vi giggled, as her hand disappeared under the duvet, smoothing its way along the ripples of his toned abs.

'You saucy little minx.' Jimby grabbed her hand and propped himself up on his elbow. 'Much as I would love you to continue, I'm afraid we've got plans this afternoon and, looking at the time, we need to get cracking.' He dropped a kiss on the tip of her nose. 'Come on, there's no time to lose.' With that, he threw the duvet back and leapt out of bed.

'Oh, should I be worried? I thought you were joking about mountaineering and stuff like that.' Violet looked momentarily crestfallen, making Jimby laugh.

'No need to be worried. I've reserved us a table on the Moorland Express; we're off for afternoon tea.'

'What? You mean the one that runs between Pickering and Skeltwick?' Violet had seen a brochure advertising the newly restored vintage train a couple of months ago and it looked amazing. Come to think of it, she could have sworn she'd mentioned it to Jimby at the time, but he hadn't seemed interested. *He was obviously paying attention*, she thought as she felt her excitement levels rise.

'The very one. Now come on, chop, chop, young lady, or we'll miss it.'

**CHAPTER 3**

'Cheers, beautiful. Happy birthday.' With a wide smile, Jimby clinked his glass of champagne against Violet's.

'Cheers, Jimby.' Vi beamed back at him before taking a sip, wrinkling her nose as the bubbles danced their way up. 'I can't believe you've actually booked us a table on here, as well as booking us a suite in the best hotel in the area. I'm feeling very spoilt.' She looked around the immaculate wooden interior of the train carriage at the other tables. There were six in total – one side with seats for four, the other side with seats for two. Each table was covered with crisply starched white cloths, set with silver cutlery and tinkling white china, while a silver vase of freshly cut flowers had been placed in the centre. Brass luggage racks gleamed above the seats alongside brass- armed lamps with fluted glass shades, evoking the glamour of a forgotten era.

'It's nice to have a treat every now and then,' he replied.

He was looking at her intently, and Vi was struggling to read his expression. 'It's not a special birthday, or anything, you do know I'm only thirty-eight – same as Kitty – don't you? I'm not celebrating the big four-o yet, you know?' She was beginning to think that he'd planned all this to celebrate something big.

Her words triggered a low, rumbling laugh from Jimby, one that made his shoulders shake and his eyes crinkle at the corners. He reached across and squeezed her hand. 'Oh, Vi, of course I know it's not your fortieth. I know you're the same age as our Kitty. But you should've seen your face when you said it. You looked outraged.'

'Well, I was preparing to be offended. Not that there's anything wrong with being forty, and I won't have a problem hitting that age, as long as everyone thinks it's the year when I'm meant to.' She smiled, showing him she was taking it in good spirits.

∽

As the miles trundled by, the pair dined on neatly cut triangle sandwiches and the fluffiest scones Violet had ever tasted. 'I feel really naughty, eating this,' she said, slathering clotted cream onto a piece of scone and topping it with raspberry jam. She took a bite and groaned. 'Mmm. That is so good – naughty but nice.'

'Yep, which is, in fact, just the way I like my women.' Jimby waggled his eyebrows at her.

A women at the next table stifled a giggle, and Vi glanced across at her, amused. 'You do know you're in danger of sounding like a right old male chauvinist-pig, don't you, Jimby?'

'Just as well you know I don't mean it then, isn't it?' He popped a piece of scone into his mouth and winked at her.

'Hmm.'

∽

Back at the hotel, the pair were heading to their suite when Vi decided to take a look at the garden their room over-looked. With Jimby behind her, she headed through reception and followed the signs that delivered her to a large oak-framed patio door. She opened it and stepped out onto the terrace where a variety of stone, terracotta and lead planters brimmed with brightly coloured bedding plants. 'Oh, this is just beautiful. Look at that fountain, Jimby.' She pointed to an ornate carved structure about two hundred yards away.

'Wow! That's what I call impressive. And look at those peacocks.' He pointed towards the males who had suddenly fanned out their tail feathers and begun strutting about like a couple of Victoria's Secret models, basking in the admiring glances their display attracted.

'How come all males are such big-heads with massive-yet-fragile egos?' asked Vi.

'I've no idea what you mean.'

'Well, just look at those two strutting around, they remind me of the lads at school when they were showing off in front of us girls, you included, Jimbo.'

'I doubt that very much, I was two years older than you, so I'm sure I won't have been doing much strutting around you and your friends.'

'You still are, actually – two years older. And you most definitely did strut, I can remember seeing you in your full-strutting force.'

'Ah, so you had the hots for me even then, and couldn't take your eyes off me, could you?' He put his arm around her and gave her a squeeze.

'Daft arse.' Vi giggled. 'Come on, I need to get changed if we're going to walk that afternoon tea off in time for me to feel hungry for dinner.' She took his hand and led him back to the hotel.

~

'That was lovely, just what I needed,' said Vi. They were heading back from their walk, making their way along the path from the deer park in the grounds of the hotel, hand in hand. Vi had changed into a pair of deep plum ankle grazers and a pink gingham shirt, tied at the waist, swapping her usual heels for a pair of black ballet flats.

'Yep, it certainly did the trick.' Jimby ran his fingers through his curls. 'And I know we see plenty of deer in the wild at home, but they're usually just in small groups or on their own. Seeing so many together is something else.'

'Mmm. They're magnificent creatures,' said Vi. 'But my favourite part was seeing the kingfishers darting about along the path by the stream.'

'Yep, you had to be quick to spot them; a quick flash of electric blue, and they were gone.'

'It's been lovely today, Jimby.' Vi sighed, snaking her arm around his waist and leaning her head on his shoulder.

'It has, beautiful.' He wrapped a muscular arm around her, kissing her cheek.

Vi couldn't remember when they'd last been able to spend so much uninterrupted, quality time together. Though she'd sold Purple Diamond – her PR company – and moved from York back to her home village, other commitments seemed to keep them rushed off their feet. Romantique, the new company she'd set up with Kitty, designing and making burlesque costumes, vintage-style lingerie and now wedding dresses, in a timber-framed extension in the garden of Sunshine Cottage, had really taken off. So much so, they were considering taking on another member of staff. And it didn't help that she and Jimby lived between two houses: Sunshine Cottage – the property she'd bought on her return from York, and Forge Cottage – Jimby's barn conversion. But whenever she tested the water with him about them moving in together, he always seemed non-committal, so she didn't push it, thinking he'd lived on his own for so long, he liked having somewhere to go to when he needed his own space. Not that he'd done much of that.

∽

'Oh, how lovely. Jimby, look at this.' Back in the room, Vi ran across to the bed, where a large gift-box, brimming with aromatherapy goodies had been placed. 'It's got everything in, even some massage oil.' She held the bottle up to show him.

'Massage oil? Now you're talking.' He gave her a cheeky grin and waggled his eyebrows.

'Not on this expensive bedding, I'm not.' She patted him on the chest and made her way to the lounge. 'Oh,' she gasped, pressing her hand to her mouth. On the table before her was a huge bouquet of cabbage roses in a vintage shade of lilac. 'Who? Have you got anything to do with these?' She turned to Jimby, whose wide smile answered her question. 'They're gorgeous, thank you! Oh, and look, there's a box of chocolates from my favourite chocolatiers in Middleton-le-Moors. How did they know? You again, Jimby? Thank you so much, you're so thoughtful.' Violet rushed over to him, kissing him deeply.

'You're very welcome.' He pulled back, pushed her hair off her face and kissed the tip of her nose. 'How do you fancy a cheeky little glass of fizz?' He walked over to the ice bucket where a bottle of pink champagne was chilling, beads of condensation peppering the glass. Jimby eased it out of the ice-cubes, setting them rattling.

'Ooh, that sounds lovely, but you can't open it in here, can you? What if it fizzes everywhere?'

'Hmm. Good point. I'll open the window a bit wider, and aim it out into the garden. You have the glasses ready for me to pour it straight into.' He wrapped the white cloth napkin around the neck of the bottle and started to ease the cork out.

'Good plan, but be careful where you aim it.'

'"Careful" is my middle name.'

'I'm not so sure about that. Anyway, I've lost track of the amount of "middle names" you're supposed to have had. Wasn't it "Quiet" last week – which, incidentally, you weren't, and never, actually are?'

'How about "Sex God", then?'

'What?'

'James "Sex God" Fairfax; has a certain ring to it, don't you think.'

'In your dreams, buster.'

'Suit yourself.' Jimby pulled a face as the cork offered up considerable resistance. 'Jesus!' he said, as it flew off with a loud pop and was propelled out into the garden towards a small gathering of guests. Violet and Jimby looked on in horror as the cork tore across the back of a tall man's head, taking with it what appeared to be his toupee.'

'Oh. My. God.' Vi clamped a hand across her mouth in an attempt to stifle her giggles. 'Quick, get away from the window!'

Jimby bobbed behind the curtain, then threw his head back and roared with laughter.

'I can't believe you just did that.'

'What a shot! I couldn't have aimed better if I'd tried.' Tears of laughter had started to trickle down his cheeks and he wiped them away.

'Please don't make me laugh anymore. My face is hurting.'

'I can't help it, that was so funny.'

'That poor man, though. He must be absolutely mortified.' Vi was doing her best to hold her laughter in, but she was finding it too much of a struggle, and started giggling all over again.

'Well, at least I didn't spill any champagne on the furniture.' Jimby looked pleased with himself. 'Hand me those glasses, Vi, before this loses its fizz.'

**CHAPTER 4**

After enjoying a languorous bubble-bath together, Vi and Jimby were heading down to the restaurant. Vi, glamorous as ever in another fifties-style dress, this one was in figure-hugging amethyst satin that skimmed over her voluptuous curves. Her glossy hair was swept back at the sides and fixed with a pair of vintage marcasite grips in the shape of butterflies. On her feet were a pair of eye-wateringly high heels that still kept her a good five inches below Jimby's towering height of six foot two.

'Looking rather gorgeous, Miss Smith.' His eyes roved over her, his pupils darkening. 'I could very easily be tempted to take you back to the room and have you for dinner.'

Her heart soared; she loved that he appreciated her curves, that she could be herself and not have to deprive herself of sweet treats or watch her figure. 'You don't scrub up so badly yourself.' She stood before Jimby who was looking handsome, his usually unruly curls momentarily tamed, his jeans swapped for a pair of smart dark blue chinos and a newly purchased finely woven tweed jacket.

'But my stomach's rumbling after that walk, and it would be rude to cancel our reservation this late in the day.'

'Spoilsport.' He grinned. 'I'll catch up with you later.'

'Promises, promises.' With a lopsided smile, she took his hand and led the way along the corridor, passing the lift. 'I think we'll take the stairs,' she said, making him laugh.

The restaurant was as tastefully decorated as the rest of the hotel, with hand-printed wallpaper in shades of pale yellow and off-white lining the walls above mellow oak panelling. The level of lighting from burnished brass wall lights was set to create an ambient atmosphere, and gentle music blended with the discrete hum of conversation. To add to the mix, mouth-watering aromas of food permeated the air.

They were seated at a table overlooking the garden – Jimby had asked for a window view when he'd made the original reservation. 'Mmm. Everything sounds so delicious,' said Vi. They were perusing the extensive menu that had a heavy emphasis on seafood. 'I think I'm going to have to go for the hot smoked salmon starter – it sounds so yummy – followed by the monkfish wrapped in Parma ham.'

'Hmm, it does sound good, I'm finding it hard to choose, but I think I'm going to have the crayfish cocktail starter, then it's got to be lobster thermidor for me.'

The starters were every bit as good as expected and the couple were soon tucking into their main courses. 'Mmm, this is scrummy. You've got to have a taste, Jimby.' Vi pushed a chunk of monkfish onto her fork, followed by a small amount of crushed potato dipped in the roasted red-pepper sauce, and offered it to him.

'Mmm.' He nodded, his eyes betraying his feelings. He

finished his mouthful and spoke, 'Oh, man, that's seriously good. That sauce ...'

'I know.' Vi giggled.

'Here, try some of this lobster.' He reciprocated Vi's gesture, which was received in much the same way as the monkfish.

'Well, I'd heard good things about this place, but it's outdone every single one of my expectations.' Jimby took a sip of his crisp white wine.

'Me, too. Thank you for bringing me here, Jimby. I feel very spoilt.'

'You're welcome. It's nice to have some time just the two of us.' His smile set his brown eyes twinkling.

The couple had asked for a break before their puddings, and had chatted away non-stop in animated conversation, blissfully unaware that the evening was slipping away. It was only when they noticed a waitress, armed with a couple of menus, hovering in the periphery that they realised it was time to order.

Vi opted for a sumptuous chocolate fondant with Chantilly cream and a zingy raspberry coulis, while Jimby couldn't resist his all-time favourite pudding, treacle sponge, served with liquorice ice-cream and a crisp tuile.

～

VI PRESSED a hand against her stomach. 'I can't remember the last time I ate so much.'

'Probably the last time we had a meal at the Sunne.' Jimby smiled, picking up his cup of coffee and taking a sip.

'I think you're right.' She gave a contented sigh and turned to the window where the sun was disappearing behind the trees. 'Look at how beautiful that fountain is. It reminds me of the Trevi Fountain in Rome, all lit up like that.'

'I'll have to take your word for that since I've never seen it.'

'Mmm. It's stunning,' she replied dreamily.

'Well, if it's anything like this one, it must be.' He drummed his fingers on the table while his leg jigged up and down.

'Are you alright, Jimby? You seem a bit distracted all of a sudden.'

'No, no, nothing's the matter, I'm absolutely fine.'

'You're not concerned the man with – or without – the toupee is going to confront you and demand an apology, are you?' she said, a smile playing over her lips.

Jimby laughed. 'Oh, lord, no, nothing like that. I was just wondering if you fancied having a last walk around the garden, you know, take a closer look at the fountain while it's all lit up.'

'Okay, that sounds nice. I could do with stretching my legs a bit.' There was definitely something on his mind, she thought. He'd been like a cat on hot bricks since halfway through their desserts.

Outside, Vi slipped her arm through his. The heat of the day had all but disappeared and it had turned chilly. Droplets of dew were already beginning to glisten on the grass. Vi, shivered and snuggled in closer to Jimby.

'We don't have to stay out long,' he said. 'We can take a look at the fountain and head back indoors, if you like.'

'Okay.' *He's definitely not himself.*

Up close, the fountain was even more spectacular, with jets of water shooting high into the air before crashing down into a frothy mass of bubbles, illuminated by an alternating hue of lights. Vi dipped into her clutch bag for her mobile phone. 'This is just absolutely stunning, I just need to take a photo.'

Jimby turned towards her and cleared his throat. 'Vi, I, er ... can I ask you something?'

'Yes, Jimb ...' Vi had pulled her gaze away from the fountain to see Jimby down on one knee in front of her. Her heart began pumping faster and butterflies took off in her stomach, swirling around frantically. 'What on earth are you doing down there?'

'Violet, beautiful Violet, the woman who stole my heart, I was wondering if you'd do me the honour of becoming my wife?' Though he was wearing his trademark grin, Vi couldn't help but think it wasn't quite as self-assured as it usually was.

She was conscious of her mouth hanging open as Jimby produced a small box from his jacket pocket. He opened the lid and presented it to her. A large purple stone, flanked by two smaller white diamonds sparkled back at her. Vi gasped and clasped a hand to her chest. 'Jimby,' she whispered.

'It's a purple diamond, cushion cut apparently,' he said. 'A right bugger to get hold of, and the reason I didn't offer you my jacket when you were shivering, because it was in the pocket and I didn't want you to find it before I did this.'

'Oh, Jimby!' Vi thought her heart would burst with happiness. 'I don't care about you not offering your jacket, of course I'll marry you!'

'Well, that's a relief.' He got to his feet and eased the ring onto her manicured finger, before kissing her deeply.

'You like it?'

'It's absolutely gorgeous. I can't believe you've gone to so much trouble to find me a purple diamond. It's my absolute favourite stone.'

'I know, I remembered. Had the jeweller in Middleton-le-Moors using all his contacts to find it, he was hunting around for a good few weeks before he found this one.'

'Well, it was definitely worth it; I love it.' Vi took a moment to admire the diamond on her finger; it glittered and flashed in the changing lights of the fountain. She hadn't noticed that Jimby had climbed up onto the edge.

'She said, "yes",' he called across to the hotel, waving his arms above his head.

There was a cheer and Vi turned to see a cluster of staff on the patio, waving back at them, words of congratulations floating across the garden. In the next moment, she heard Jimby cry out, 'Arghh!' It was immediately followed by a loud splash that needed no explanation: accident-prone Jimby had done it again.

'Jimby!' With her hand clamped over her mouth, Vi stood for several seconds, her mind processing the sight of her new fiancé flailing about in the water, which, at chest-height, was deeper than she expected; him, too, by the look of things. Her mind was wrestling with the urge to burst out laughing or to shout for help. 'Oh, shit, Jimby, what have you done?' She ran over to him. 'Hang on, I'll give you a hand.'

He squirted a jet of water out of his mouth as he heaved himself over the side, water cascading from him. 'S'alright,' he spluttered. 'I can manage.'

Vi couldn't contain her laughter any longer and in a moment, she was bent double, placing her hands on her knees to steady herself. 'Oh, Jimby, how come you can never be near any water without actually falling in it?'

'It's a gift,' he replied, wringing out the sleeve of his jacket.

In a moment, a handful of hotel staff had joined them, one armed with a blanket that Vi helped drape over Jimby's shoulders. Words of congratulations for the pair mingled with words of sympathy for him, peppered with hoots of laughter.

∼

LATER THAT NIGHT, in the vast expanse of their super-king-size bed, Jimby lay sleeping beside her, his arm thrown across her stomach, his breathing slow and regular. Vi gazed up at the darkness. It had been an amazing day, full of surprises. Who knew Jimby could be so romantic? All the thought and effort he must have put into planning everything. *Oh, Jimby, you lovely, lovely man.* Of course, such a day was bound to include one of his accident prone moments. She couldn't help but smile as the image of him splashing about in the fountain played out in her mind.

It had been a perfect day, but one thing had begun to prod at her happiness, reminding her that she had a little secret tucked away at the back of her mind. A secret that any decent woman would share with the man she was going to marry. It could, after all, have the potential to be a game-changer. But she hadn't shared it with anyone. Not her mum and dad, not even Kitty and Molly. Her brow prickled with sweat and her stomach lurched. *Oh, God,* she thought as her conscience quickly reached in and glimpsed at the memory of that horrible day. The day that she relived every year. She shuddered. She would have to tell Jimby, she knew she would. It was only right. Maybe it wasn't a game-changer. She was sure he would take it well, understand, believe her. She'd never met anyone like him before. She felt good around him, everyone did. He was a man comfortable in his own skin, happy with his lot and completely without arrogance. He had a real zest for life, and faced the world with enthusiasm that couldn't help but rub off on you. It would be fair to say that he wasn't just a glass half-full type of man, his was so full, it was brimming over. He tried to see the positive side of everything and everyone – well, everyone except that tosser Dan who Kitty had been married to. Surely he would understand what she'd done. Wouldn't he?

**CHAPTER 5**

The following day, with the sun still pouring its rays over the county, the pair headed off to explore the surrounding villages. Vi was eager to go to an exhibition of vintage clothes at a nearby stately home, where she took copious photos as inspiration for wedding dress designs for Romantique. She'd found herself admiring her engagement ring all day, not just because it felt strange to have something on that finger, but because the stone was so captivating. 'Thank you, Jimby, I love it,' she'd told him countless times, pressing hot kisses to his lips.

'According to the jeweller, it's from Australia, and it's colour's classed as "fancy intense". And you can have another one, if this is the reward I get.' He pulled her in close, nuzzling her neck.

Vi held out her hand and gazed at the ring, though Jimby's kisses were proving to be more than a little distracting. 'It's such a beautiful deep colour; I'd heard that the darker the stone, the more precious it is.'

'Mmhm.' His kisses found their way from her neck to her lips. 'I wanted to show you how much you mean to me.'

He parted her lips with his tongue and with a groan, she felt herself melt.

Reluctantly, he pulled himself away from her. 'I think I'd better get you back to the hotel before I drag you off into those woods and have my wicked way with you.'

'Don't let me stop you.' Vi wouldn't have objected if Jimby had been serious.

'Ordinarily, I wouldn't think twice, but I've just seen a group of bird watchers disappearing along the path and I think doing what I have in mind might not look too good through their binoculars.'

'Ooh, I take your point.' She giggled as he took her hand.

'Come this way, Miss Smith.'

They headed back to the hotel, relaxed and happy, giving themselves plenty of time for a romantic bath and a delicious moment between the crisp, cotton sheets.

Vi couldn't remember a time when she'd felt so happy, until later that evening at dinner, when the laughter of a fellow diner triggered an unwelcome memory. She froze, the hairs on the back of her neck standing on end. That pompous laugh could belong to only one person. She looked across the softly-lit dining room and a bolt of panic shot through her as her eyes landed on a man she hadn't seen for sixteen years. He'd aged, his hairline had receded – though he was trying to disguise the fact – and he'd filled out a bit, but it was definitely him. Mike Williamson – or *Professor* Mike Williamson, as he preferred to be known. He was sharing a table with a woman much younger than himself. A woman who wasn't his wife. *He clearly hasn't changed.* Last she'd heard, he'd moved to Spain. Something had clearly brought him back to the area. As if sensing the weight of her gaze upon him, he looked up and a beat passed before a flicker of recognition crossed his face. Vi snatched her eyes away. 'I'm ready when you are, Jimby,' she said. Her heart was pounding; she needed to get out of the room. Out of *his* way.

'Yep, I'm done.' He set his napkin down on the table. 'Can't wait to get me back to the room so you can rip my clothes off with your teeth, can you?'

'Got it in one.' Vi hoped the laugh she gave wasn't too shrill.

'And who am I to stop you?' He tucked his chair under the table and flashed one of his cheeky grins.

By the time they were back in the room, the look in Jimby's eyes told Vi he knew something had rattled her. 'You okay?' he asked.

She nodded and made her way over to him, wrapping her arms around his neck. He'd put so much effort into making this weekend special, there was no way she was going to let that creep from her past spoil it for him. He didn't deserve it. 'I'm absolutely fine. Just a bit tired after such a wonderful couple of days, I think.' She kissed him tenderly and began to unbutton his shirt.

'Well, funny you should say that, but I know the perfect remedy for it.'

'I think you'd better hurry up and show me then.'

Vi lay awake until the early hours. Why, after all this time, did she have to see *him*? The timing couldn't have been worse, intruding on a weekend Jimby had made so special. He had no right. *No!* she thought. She wouldn't let him worm his way into her mind, she'd wasted enough time and energy in the past, thinking about him. *But, it's odd, isn't it* a little voice niggled at her, *how he should be here on the very weekend Jimby proposes, and only last night you were thinking you should have to share your secret with him?*

Vi scrunched up her eyes, squeezing the voice out of her mind. *Go away! I'll tell Jimby as soon as we're home.*

NOT WANTING to run the risk of bumping into Mike Williamson, Vi had suggested breakfast in bed. 'Just so I can savour every moment of snuggling-up beside you, Jimby,' she'd said. 'And make the most of staying in this gorgeous room. The time we'd waste waiting for our breakfast to be cooked, we can use to enjoy another bath together.'

'Sounds like a bloody good idea,' Jimby had agreed.

'SO, HAVE YOU ENJOYED YOUR WEEKEND?' Jimby asked as they made their way along the country roads leading home.

'It's been wonderful.' Vi turned to him, smiling.

'Good.' He glanced across at her and squeezed her knee. 'Just, you've seemed a bit quiet on and off. Like you've got something on your mind.'

'Have I? Sorry.' *Shit!* She hadn't thought of her secret properly for years and now it kept jumping back into her mind, throwing a bucket of icy cold water over her happy thoughts. She needed to tell Jimby, and sooner rather than later. But not now. She didn't want to spoil this weekend, especially when he'd put so much effort into making it special, been so romantic. But when? And how? She was struggling to work out how could she throw it into the conversation after all this time.

The last thing Vi wanted was for Jimby to think she was being miserable. 'I think I'm just in shock that you've actually proposed and how romantic you've been. It's totally out of character.'

'Hey, never let it be said that Jimby Fairfax doesn't know how to romance a woman properly.'

'Well, they couldn't now.' She held up her left hand, gazing at the perfect ring he'd chosen for her; it glittered in the sunlight, casting rainbows around the car. She reached across and rubbed his back. 'And is there anything else you're keeping hidden from me under this tough northern man exterior?'

He grinned. 'Ha! That would be telling, it's what's known as classified information. Mind you, we could have a game of spin the bottle tonight and we could whittle secrets out of one another. How do you fancy that?' He didn't notice Vi's smile drop.

**CHAPTER 6**

'Come on then, share all the details of your romantic weekend with us, Vi,' said Molly. The following evening they were sitting in the low-beamed bar of the Sunne at their usual table in the corner by the large inglenook fireplace where an open fire was crackling merrily away. Though the days had been sunny, it was still early in the year and the evenings could be surprisingly chilly, so the fire was always lit in Lytell Stangdale's quaint thatched, fifteenth century pub.

'Well, maybe not all of them,' said Ollie. He was Jimby's best friend and Kitty's husband.

'Quite,' said Kitty. 'Though I am keen to know more about how my brother ended up falling into a fountain late in the evening after proposing.' Quiet and reserved, Kitty was the opposite of her confident, bubbly brother, though her heart was as warm and tender as his.

'Yep, only Jimby could manage to do something like that,' agreed Camm, his dark eyes glittering in amusement.

'I'll have you know it was a carefully choreographed

moment,' said Jimby. He picked up his beer and took a sip. 'I still can't believe Vi's agreed to have me, mind.'

'Neither can we.' Molly laughed as Jimby gave her a feigned hurt look. The cousins' large brown eyes ensured no one was left in any doubt that they were related. The same could be said for the dark, curly hair, though Kitty's was clipped into a short elfin crop.

'Congratulations the pair of you. It's absolutely wonderful news.' Bea, landlady of the Sunne, bustled over with a bottle of champagne in her hand. Husband Jonty was close behind armed with an ice bucket, his half-moon glasses perched in their usual place on the end of his long nose. 'This is from Jonty and me,' she said, pressing a kiss to Vi's cheek.

'Oh, thank you, that's so kind.' Vi beamed up at the pair.

'Yes, many congratulations to both of you. You make a perfect couple.' Smiling broadly, Jonty took the fizz from his wife and jabbed it into the ice bucket. 'I'll just go and get some glasses,' he said in his plummy accent.

'And I've got some nibbles I'd like you to try out for me,' added Bea. 'Two ticks.' She headed off in the direction of the kitchen. She regularly asked the group of friends to sample potential dishes for the pub menu, all of which were enthusiastically received.

Bea was back in a flash, carrying a large platter of bite-size nibbles. She was closely followed by her rescue dogs of indeterminate breed, Nomad and Scruff, who'd picked up on the delicious aromas of the food. 'This isn't for you two rascals. You go and lie down. Go on!' The two dogs obeyed and flumped down in front of the fire, their eyes never leaving the table.

'So when's the big day?' asked Jonty. He popped the champagne cork with a practised hand, filling the flutes and passing them round the friends. Vi caught Jimby's eye and smiled as they shared a private moment, remembering the last time a champagne cork was popped.

'Oh, they won't have had time to think about that yet, darling,' said Bea. She pushed her tortoiseshell glasses up onto her head, securing her smooth blonde bob out of her face.

'Well, I'm keen to make an honest woman of Vi sooner rather than later,' said Jimby. 'So, we've agreed it's going to be this year.'

'Yes, we quite liked the idea of a summer wedding, but thought that would be pushing it a bit, so we're thinking early September,' said Vi. Her heart leapt with happiness at the thought. 'And we wondered if the Sunne could do the catering, like you did for Kitty and Ollie?'

Bea clasped her hands together, her eyes shining. 'Oh, we'd love to, wouldn't we, Jonty?'

'Absolutely.' He smiled across at the couple. 'We have very fond memories of your wedding, Kitty and Ollie, and it would be wonderful to do it all again. Now, enjoy your fizz, folks, I'll have to get back to work, looks like there's a queue forming.' He nodded in the direction of the bar, where Bill Campion and Tom Storr were waving their empty beer glasses at him.

'And I'll have to get back to the kitchen, but enjoy your evening, darlings,' said Bea.

Almost as soon as she'd left, Rosie and Robbie Webster arrived, looking breathless.

'Ey up, here you are at last,' said Jimby.

'Sorry we're late,' said Rosie. She tucked her shiny auburn bob behind her ears. 'The babysitter's only just arrived.'

'And I had some last-minute tweaks to do to some plans,' said Robbie. He was a freelance architect.

'No matter, it's good to see you. I'll just go and get another couple of glasses so you can share this fizz with us,' said Jimby.

'Oh, yes, congratulations, both of you. Rosie kissed Vi on the cheek. 'I can't wait to hear all about it.'

Jimby was back in a flash and the friends dived into the nibbles, devouring them appreciatively and declaring them to be delicious. Jimby and Vi filled everyone in on how Jimby had proposed and how he'd managed to end up in the fountain, with Vi sharing photos of the aftermath on her phone.

'Hmm. I'm still not quite sure how I feel about the future Mrs Fairfax taking photos of me while I was in the middle of drowning.' Jimby gave Vi a side-long look.

'Because it was priceless, Jimby, plus I knew you'd be alright,' she replied.

'I'm bloody glad she did, these are hilarious,' said Molly, giggling. 'Look at these, Camm.' Vi smiled as Molly passed her phone to the man who had helped her friend through her heartbreak. It was good to see her looking happy and relaxed again. Camm was a good man, and he was good for Molly.

'Ha! I can see what you mean, Vi.' Camm brushed his black curls from his eyes, his shoulders shaking with mirth as he passed the phone to Robbie.

'How come sympathy always seems to be in short supply with you lot?' Jimby rubbed the stubble on his chin.

'Because you're so funny, that's why, Jimbo,' said Molly. 'And we're always too busy laughing at you to give sympathy as well.'

'Moll has a point.' Vi giggled. 'Anyway, moving on from

Jimby and his many escapades, and on to the subject of bridesmaids. Ollie, we'd love Noushka to be chief bridesmaid, if that's okay?' Anoushka was Ollie's nineteen-year-old daughter from an earlier relationship.

'I'm sure she'd be over the moon to hear that. She loved being Kitty's.' Ollie's eyes shone with pride.

'Ooh, she'll be thrilled. She loves your sense of style, Vi. Only the other day she was calling you her style icon and saying if you ever get tired of the clothes in your wardrobe, she'd be happy to take them off your hands,' said Kitty.

'The way Vi's wardrobe's bulging, I think that would be a good idea.' Jimby sniggered into his pint.

Vi ignored him and turned to Kitty. 'Bless her, that's so sweet – I'll have a rummage and see what I can sort out for her. Anyway, Kitts, we'd love it if Lily would be a bridesmaid, too – but we wondered if Lottie might be just a smidge too young?'

Kitty nodded. 'Lils will be so excited, and, yes, I think Lotts is a bit small to be a bridesmaid, don't you, Oll?'

'Mmm, she'd probably cause havoc,' said Ollie. 'She's at that inquisitive stage and would probably wander off as she's walking behind you down the aisle.'

'Ah, bless her. We'll still make her a pretty dress so she doesn't feel left out.' Vi turned to Molly. 'And we'd love little Emmie to be a bridesmaid, too. We thought, being three, she'd be fine to do it, and look so cute, too.'

Molly beamed. 'Thanks, Vi, she'll be so excited to hear that. You know how she loves her pretty dresses. Mind, she can be a right headstrong little madam at the minute, stamping her feet and giving me a load of sass.'

'Can't think where she gets it from, Moll,' said Camm.

'Yeah, Molly, isn't that a bit like the pot calling the kettle grimy arse?' Jimby chuckled.

'Don't know what you mean,' Molly replied but her smile told them she couldn't argue with their observations.

Vi turned to Rosie, 'And we couldn't leave little Abbie out; we'd love her to be a bridesmaid, too.'

Rosie beamed. 'Oh, thank you, Vi, she'll be so excited, won't she, Rob?'

Robbie nodded. 'I think you'll find that's an understatement, especially when her and Lily get talking about it.'

'Hah! I'm sure there's nothing more than eleven-year-old girls like than the thought of being a bridesmaid, plus it'll take their minds off being anxious about moving up to secondary school,' added Kitty.

'Perfect.' Vi clapped her hands together. 'With Kitty's help, I'm going to design and make all of the dresses, so we need to get started pretty sharpish.'

'Ooh, I can't wait,' said Kitty.

'And, if you like, I can do the wedding make-up,' added Rosie. A trained beautician, she ran the Manor House Sanctuary from her home, an imposing timber-framed building with a heavily thatched roof.

'So how come you're keen to get married so soon after getting engaged?' asked Camm.

'Well, it's not like we don't know each other really well.' Vi set down her glass of fizz on the table. 'I've known Jimby all my life, he's always been in my circle of friends, and we've been practically living together for the last couple of years.'

'And there is, of course, the fact that Vi's always had the hots for me.' Jimby winked at her.

'In your dreams, buster,' she replied.

'More like the other way round if I remember correctly,' said Molly.

*The Secret - Violet's Story*

'Yeah, wasn't it you who kissed Vi in the playground all those years ago?' Kitty gave her brother a knowing look.

'Actually, now you come to mention it, I think you're right.' Jimby nodded. 'Got a kick in the nuts for my trouble, I seem to recall.'

'Didn't put you off, though, did it, mate?' Ollie laughed.

'Well, actually, it did for a while, until that summer when Vi transformed from a pesky school kid into a sizzling hot babe.' He gave a low wolf-whistle which caused heads to turn at the nearby tables. 'Ouch,' he said as Vi gave him a quick dig in the ribs with her elbow.

'Shh, Jimby,' she said.

Molly and Kitty looked at their friend, fondness shining in their eyes. It was clear they remembered it too, and the amazing boost it had had on her confidence. Not to mention the affect it had had on the boys at school.

'And I'm keen to start a family as soon as possible. I'm desperate to be a dad.' Jimby beamed around at his friends as he threw his arm around Vi's shoulders.

'Ahh, you'll be a great dad, Jimbo,' said Ollie. 'All our kids love you to bits.'

'And the feeling's bloody mutual,' Jimby replied.

No one seemed to notice Vi freeze or that her smile didn't quite reach her eyes.

Except for Jimby.

**CHAPTER 7**

Earlier that morning, Vi had called in on her parents at Rowan Slack Farm – the tenanted farm that had been her childhood home – to share her news.

'Oh, lovie, that's wonderful, isn't it, Ken?' Her mum hurriedly wiped her floury hands on her apron, and flung her arms around her daughter, rubbing her back furiously.

'About time,' said her dad. His ruddy face was wreathed in smiles. 'I was wondering when that lad was going to get round to it, I mentioned it to your mother just the other day, didn't I, Mary?'

'You did that, love. We're absolutely over the moon for you, aren't we, Ken?'

'Aye, lass, we are. Are you going to stick the kettle on, Mary? We need to celebrate with a cuppa.'

'In a minute, Ken, lovie. And you're going to get married at the local church, not some registry office, aren't you?' Mary's expression said that the thought of getting married in a registry office horrified her.

'She wouldn't get married in some boring old registry

office, would you, Vi? She'll want a proper wedding at St. Thomas's, isn't that right, Violet?' said her father.

'Don't worry, we're having a church wedding here. Which reminds me, we need to make an appointment to see Rev Nev, set the wheels in motion. We're hoping for Saturday the sixth of September.'

'And what about bridesmaids? Are you having Kitty and Molly?' Mary went to fill the kettle.

Vi shook her head. 'No, I'm having Lily, Emmie and Abbie, with Noushka as chief bridesmaid.' She watched as her mum mulled this over.

'And Jimby will be having Ollie as best man?' Mary's question was obviously rhetorical.

'Course he will, lass. The lads have been best friends all their lives, who else would he ask?' said Ken.

'Well, I was just checking. You never know, our Jimby might've asked Camm; help make him feel part of the family.'

'Give over, don't talk daft, Mary, why would he need to do that? Camm already feels like part of the family. Anyroad, where's this tea you promised us?'

'It's on its way. I can't make it till the kettle's boiled.' Mary batted Ken's impatience away. 'And any road, Camm's a lovely lad, and Jimby might've thought it would be a kind thing to do, you know what he's like.'

'Jimby's asked Ollie to be his best man, and Camm's going to be a groomsman with Molly's twins as well as Lucas – he's fourteen so should be good to do it.'

'And you're not going to invite them awful Mellisons, are you? They look down their nose at everything and I wouldn't want them to do that at your wedding, lovie.'

'Course she isn't, Mary,' said Ken. 'She won't want their

sort at the wedding, and neither will young Jimby. Kettle's boiled, lass.'

'I have got ears you know, Ken.' Mary took the kettle off the stove and poured the boiling water over the teabags in the pot. She gave them a quick swirl around with a teaspoon and poured a mug for her husband. 'There you go, it hasn't had time to mash properly, but it'll shut you up. We'll wait a couple of minutes for ours, Vi, chick.'

'Thanks, Mum.' Vi pressed her lips together, trying not to laugh at her parents' banter. 'And don't worry, there's no way I'd invite the Mellisons to anything, never mind my wedding.'

It was rare for Vi to hear her parents say anything bad about anyone, but they did have a point about the Mellisons – a family of incomers who had done nothing but ruffle feathers since their arrival in Lytell Stangdale in an air of superiority and arrogance. Aoife, whose Teesside accent she annoyingly tried to disguise with affected Queen's English, had quickly proved herself to be the worst sort of snob and competitive mother, thinking her two obnoxious children, Teddy and Evie, were perfect and the best at everything. Her husband Dave, with his severe case of small man syndrome, was nothing more than a bone idle-layabout who spent most of his time knocking back beer at The Fox and Hounds in neighbouring village, Danskelfe. Their popularity – or lack of it – hadn't been helped by a series of incidents that had the Mellison's hallmarks all over them, but the family had managed to manipulate their way out of any blame – at least in their eyes, the rest of the village thought otherwise.

'I told you our Vi wouldn't do owt like that, especially after how that woman treated Kitty. Nasty piece of work, she is. And all that business with the sheep worrying, not to mention the fire, I mean, we all know it was them who were responsible.'

'You're right, love. And all I can say is, it's a relief their sort won't be around to spoil anyone's day,' said Mary. 'I'd have to give her a piece of my mind if she did anything to upset our Violet.'

Vi smiled at the fussy way her parents went about things, it was cosy and warm and full of loving intentions – even though it did drive her absolutely bonkers at times. And she couldn't imagine her mild-mannered mother saying anything confrontational to anyone – except, of course, her dad.

'And how about Granny Aggie?' said her father. 'Isn't it going to be embarrassing for the vicar if you invite her, what with all the mucky text messages she's been sending him?'

'Your dad's got a point, love. Only last week I heard Molly complaining in the shop about how she was having to apologise to Rev Nev about her again. Apparently, what Aggie had put in a text was enough to make your eyes water. Her in her eighties as well!'

'There's nothing new there, Mum; she's always doing it.'

Mary put three slices of homemade Victoria sponge onto a plate and took it over to the table. 'Poor Molly, she's had a lot to deal with since Pip passed away.'

'Aye, not least leaving her with his difficult old grandmother,' said Ken.

'Trust me, Moll's always had to sort Granny Aggie out; even when Pip was alive; the old bat would never listen to him,' said Vi.

'Aye, I can imagine that; he was a soft-hearted lad. Anyroad, how about that man eater woman? Will you be asking her?'

'Ooh, good point, Ken; that one'll be chasing all the men if she goes, won't she?'

'You mean Anita Matheson – or Maneater, as everyone calls her?' said Vi, before taking a bite out of her slice of cake.

'Aye, that wrinkly old bird who wears her skirts halfway up her arse.'

'Ken!'

'I'm just stating the obvious, Mary, that's all.'

'Well, you just watch yourself with her if she does go,' said Mary. 'And it's not funny, Violet; I've seen the woman in action.'

'Me, too; she's bloody terrifying.' Ken's expression said it all.

Vi was struggling to contain her laughter. 'Oh, Mum, I don't think she'd trouble Dad, she usually chases younger men. And we haven't had time to draw up a guest list yet, so you don't need to worry about her.' She loved that her parents were so funny without them even realising it.

**CHAPTER 8**

To say that Violet's arrival into the world was a surprise to her parents could very easily be described as an understatement. Total shock would be more fitting.

Mary and Ken Smith had given up hope of having a family several years earlier. Having accepted that they were never going to be blessed with children, they were content to spoil their nephews and nieces, something they did with great enthusiasm.

On the day of their twentieth wedding anniversary, Ken had arranged for himself and Mary to have a rare night away to celebrate at a hotel just outside of Middleton-le-Moors - a thriving Georgian market town, set around a pretty market square, ten miles away from Lytell Stangdale. He'd organised help to do the milking and take care of the farm for the short time they were away.

Mary had woken early that morning, not quite feeling herself. She glanced in the mirror to see her usual ruddy complexion had taken on a pale, slightly waxy hue. 'Typical,' she muttered, rubbing a nagging ache in her back and deciding that nothing was going to spoil a night away with her husband. She couldn't remember the last time they'd been out together, never mind had a night away. The farm had always taken priority, not that she minded.

Mary had even treated herself to something new to wear – well, more out of necessity really. She'd been steadily putting on weight since she'd turned forty and had cursed her age when she'd tried on her usual failsafe best dress the week before. It had steadfastly refused to budge over her stomach. As for her boobs, 'Uhh!' she'd prodded them in dismay.

Later that morning Ken and Mary climbed aboard their trusty old Landie and trundled their way across the moors, with Mary gritting her teeth as they bumped and bounced over the numerous pot-holes in the roads. She couldn't think what she'd eaten the previous evening that would have given her such a gripping stomach ache, but she wished it would bloomin' well go away.

'You alright, lass?' Ken asked in his broad moorland accent.

'Aye, just excited, lovie,' she replied. 'And I could do with stretching my legs a bit.'

'It's not like you to be so quiet. You're normally chatting away, ten to the dozen.'

'Oh, don't mind me, I'm fine.' She shifted uncomfortably in her seat, hoping to ease the ache in her back. *Landies definitely weren't designed for comfort*, she thought.

Ken gave her leg a hefty pat, the sort he usually reserved for the back end of a cow. 'Nearly there, now, missus,' he said. 'We can have a wander round the gardens when we get there, if you fancy?'

'Mmm. Sounds good.' Mary did her best to smile back at him, gritting her teeth while a spiteful pain squeezed at her insides.

*The Secret - Violet's Story*

∼

Later that evening, Ken checked the knot of his one and only tie in the full-length mirror of the wardrobe, before rearranging his thinning fringe. 'You nearly done in there, Mary? If you hang around any longer, you're going to come out looking like a wrinkly old prune.' He chuckled at his own joke.

On the other side of the door in the en-suite bathroom, Mary was enjoying a soak in the large bathtub, the warmth of the lavender-scented water doing a good job of soothing the aches away from her back. 'Coming, lovie,' she called back. What she'd give to have another hour lying there, topping up the hot water. Reluctantly, she heaved herself up and wrapped a towel round herself.

'What time is it?' She poked her head round the door.

'Half six, we've got half an hour before we need to head down to the restaurant.' He glanced across at his wife. 'You sure you're alright? You definitely look a bit peaky.'

'I'm fine, honest. Just got too comfy in that big bath, that's all. I'll be right as rain in a minute.' She hoped her voice sounded more convincing to her husband than it did to her.

∼

'We should do this more often.' Ken reached across the table and squeezed Mary's plump hand. They were in the cosy restaurant, sitting at a simply laid table, waiting for their starters to arrive. 'I should make more of an effort to have a break from the farm so thee and me can spend some quality time together.'

'That would be nice.' Mary smiled back at him. He

worked so hard, long hours, whatever the weather. She did, too, helping with milking, looking after the hens and the geese, and making preserves to sell at the stall at the end of the lane to their farm. 'It's easier said than done, though,' she added. 'And we just end up getting stuck in our usual routine – not that I'm complaining. I love my life, I wouldn't swap it for the world. Well … there's maybe just one thing I'd change … but it's a bit late now …'

Ken saw the wistful expression in her eyes and squeezed her hand a little tighter. 'It wasn't meant to be, Mary, not for us anyway. Kids were obviously never part of the plan, but we've got each other, and I'm more than content with that.' The smile he gave Mary was genuine, and made her heart swell with love for him.

'Me, too.' She smiled back at him.

They were interrupted by the young waitress bringing their starters. 'Two prawn cocktails?'

'Ow!' gasped Mary, suddenly clutching her stomach.

The waitress's face dropped and she froze to the spot. 'Oh, er …'

'Mary, love! Are you alright?'

'Mmm,' she nodded. Her face grew more and more puce as she did her level best to keep the pain under control. 'I'm fine.'

The waitress looked on, her face a picture of confusion. 'Shall I leave your starters?'

Mary nodded. 'Mmm, thanks, lovie.' The waitress set them down and scurried off.

'Well, you don't look fine,' said Ken.

'I am fine, stop fussing.'

Ken didn't look convinced as they tucked into their prawn cocktails. And he was right not to be, as not ten minutes later, Mary cried out in pain again.

## The Secret - Violet's Story

'Ouch!' She doubled-up, her face distorted by pain.

'Mary, you're not fine.' Ken looked distraught.

'I think it's a bad case of trapped wind. Must be them peas I was podding last night. I ate a good half of them, knew I'd be sorry later.'

'Oh,' he replied. 'Can I help you to the toilet? S'probably best you don't let one go in here, it being posh and all that.'

Mary shot him a look. 'I'm fine, thanks. It's trapped. It's not coming out. That's the problem. And I wouldn't dream of trumping in here. What do you take me for?'

'I was just saying ...'

'Well, don't!' As Mary spoke, even she was aware that it wasn't like her to be so snappy.

∼

JUST THEN, the waitress returned, looking distinctly uncomfortable. 'Was everything alright with your starters?'

'Delicious, thank you,' said Ken.

'Very nice,' said Mary. 'Arghh!'

Ken pushed his chair back and hurried round to his wife, who by now had eased herself off her seat and was on all fours on the floor. 'Mary, love, are you okay?'

'No.' She shook her head, beads of sweat peppering her brow. 'I've wet myself.'

'You've what?' He took a step back, glancing at the floor.

Before Mary had the chance to reply, a fellow diner who'd been watching events unfold, hurried over. 'Hello there, my name's Violet Armstrong, Dr Violet Armstrong. I'm a retired GP, and I'd like to help.'

'Oh, thank God ... argghhh!' Mary was gripped by a stronger pain this time. 'I thought I had trapped wind, doctor, but the pain's so strong, I think it must be appendicitis.'

'You can't have appendicitis, Mary, you had your appendix out twenty years ago,' said Ken. He gave the doctor a worried look. 'She can't have two can she?'

Dr Armstrong was crouching down on the floor next to Mary, she looked up at Ken and shook her head. 'It's highly unlikely – though I have heard of it.' She turned to Mary and asked discreetly, 'Did I hear you tell your husband you'd wet yourself, Mary?'

Mary nodded. 'Yes ... oh ... ow! Please help me, I'm in so much pain and I'm getting a really funny feeling down there.'

'Okay,' said Dr Armstrong. 'Do you think you can get up and walk anywhere?' Her voice had a soothing tone.

'No, I can't move.' Mary, who'd by now rolled onto her back, looked terrified.

'Don't worry, we'll stay here; you'll be absolutely fine,' said the doctor. After taking a moment to feel Mary's stomach, she turned to the waitress who was still standing next to the table, empty prawn cocktail glasses in hand. 'Things appear to be moving quickly, I think it's best we clear the restaurant.'

'What do you mean, things are moving quickly?' Ken looked worried sick, even the smattering of broken capillaries that threaded across his face had paled. 'And why do you need to move everyone out of the restaurant? What's wrong with my wife? Mary's never ill.'

'Your wife's not ill.' Dr Armstrong turned back to the waitress. 'Can you bring me a large bowl of hot water and heaps of clean bath towels, please? As quickly as possible.'

The waitress nodded and hurried off out of the room. Dr Armstrong turned back to Ken. 'Your wife's in labour.'

## The Secret - Violet's Story

'She's wha ... she's ... labour ... isn't that ... well ... how?' Ken loosened his tie and pushed his fingers through what was left of his hair. 'Bloody hell, Mary, you're in labour, lass.'

'Arghhh!' Mary cried, squeezing onto Dr Armstrong's fingers, making her wince. Just then the waitress hurried back into the room armed with a large bowl of sloshing hot water. Hot on her heels was the housekeeper, peering out from behind a pile of fluffy white towels.

'Perfect,' said Dr Armstrong. 'Right, Ken, get yourself up to this end, and I'll take over proceedings at the other. Can we have a nice soft towel to put at the back of Mary's head please?'

Fifteen minutes and a tirade of foul-mouthed abuse hurled at Ken by his wife later, Mary was delivered of a baby girl, who was quickly swaddled in a soft towel and whose gusty cries took the place of her mother's.

Despite the depths of their shock, both parents manage to pull themselves together sufficiently to declare that their little bundle should be named after the woman who'd brought her into the world: Violet.

Mary's life was now perfect.

**CHAPTER 9**

Violet had grown up being swathed in love and positively doted on by her mum and dad. But, despite having such an idyllic childhood, as she grew older she became more aware of the consequences of having older parents. And to make matters worse, Ken and Mary had the mindset and style of an age bracket older, even, than their own. Once Violet arrived at secondary school in Middleton-le-Moors, this suddenly made a tangible difference. At home, no one noticed nor cared that her home-made clothes were slightly old-fashioned. It was quite the opposite at Middleton Secondary. Having what was mockingly described as a 'frumpy' name didn't help either. Violet was teased mercilessly; her skirt was the wrong shape, the wrong length, the wrong fit, her shoes were for ten-year-olds, her coat was for grannies and her haircut was decades out of date. It didn't help that her intelligence had marked her out as being a nerd, too. By the age of fifteen, she'd had enough.

She'd gone home at the start of the summer holidays, relieved at the prospect of having six weeks without being the butt of somebody's cruel jibes, but with a steely determination that things were going to change. She just needed to know how.

It was a rainy afternoon, sitting in Kitty's bedroom at Oak Tree Farm when inspiration struck. After pouring her heart out to Kitty and Molly about how she was fed up of being teased and didn't know how to make it stop, the friends were flicking through the channels of the television. 'Hey, Molly, turn back to that last channel,' said Kitty. Molly obliged. 'Look, Vi, you look like that actress, doesn't she, Moll?'

'Ooh, you're right, Kitts, she does.'

'I do? Let's see,' said Vi. She sat up on her haunches, peering closer at the TV, taking in the nineteen-fifties movie that was playing out on the screen. The young woman was stunning, and as for her clothes, *wow*!

'Look, you've got the same shaped nose and chin,' added Kitty.

'And your eyes are a similar shape, too, though aren't Elizabeth Taylor's supposed to be violet coloured?' asked Molly.

Both friends turned to look at Vi. 'Are you thinking what I'm thinking, Moll?' asked Kitty.

'Well, if it's that we've found the perfect solution to Vi's problem, then yes, I bloomin' well am.'

'I'm thinking exactly that!' replied Kitty.

Vi tore her eyes away from the screen and took in the expression on her friends' faces. Their eyes were dancing and they were wearing huge smiles. 'What? You think I look like Elizabeth Taylor?'

'Yes,' her friends chorused, their enthusiasm bouncing round the room.

'And you think I should start dressing like her?'

'Well, at least do your make-up like her,' replied Kitty. 'She's gorgeous, and so are you, Vi.'

'Kitty's right,' Molly agreed.

Vi was quiet for a moment, turning her eyes back to the beautiful Hollywood actress on the television. Suddenly, the cogs started whirring as her creative mind kicked into action. She could model herself into a contemporary version of Elizabeth Taylor, take bits of her look and use them for herself. She should get her hair cut at that smart salon in Middleton, instead of using the mobile hairdresser her mum had round every six weeks and whose repertoire only included granny sets and perms. Vi reached a hand up to her thick, wavy chestnut hair. And what if she had it dyed her favourite colour: purple. A smile spread across her face. She would make purple her signature colour, wear it all the time. She'd become known for it, and for looking glamorous.

'What do you think, Vi?' asked Molly.

'I love the idea! Have you got a pen and paper, Kitts? I'm going to make a list of everything I need to do for my transformation.'

'Ooh, fab, this is so exciting.' Kitty scrambled over to her desk.

'Where's your make-up bag, Kitts? I could practice doing cat-flick eyeliner on you, if you like, Vi?'

'Let's do the list first,' said Vi. She caught Kitty's eye, reflected in the mirror and they exchanged a knowing look. Only last week they'd let Molly do their make-up, and her heavy-handed application resulted in them looking like they were ready for some sort of zombie horror show. Less certainly wasn't more for Moll, but neither of them wanted to hurt her feelings.

With her list complete, Vi spoke to her mother about

how she'd been feeling, being careful not to offend her. Mary listened patiently, sorry – and not a little guilty – that her daughter had suffered at the hands of such cruel girls, but determined that it was going to stop. A gifted seamstress, Mary could run up clothes without the need of a pattern. All Vi had to do was show her a picture of what she wanted and she would rustle up a new wardrobe of fifties-inspired dresses for her. A shopping trip to York had followed, where they'd picked up swathes of sumptuous fabrics in shades of purples and greens. Once home, Mary had set to work immediately, Vi watching intently as her mother transformed bales of fabric into stunning dresses.

Next up was Vi's appointment at the salon in Middleton-le-Moors. She went in an awkward, plain-looking schoolgirl and emerged looking every inch a Hollywood movie star, her beautifully sculpted fifties-inspired short bob in a sumptuous shade of aubergine, shining in the sunshine. 'Perfect!' she'd declared when she looked at herself in the mirror. She was used to standing out for being different at school, but purple hair would be a cool kind of different.

By the end of summer, Vi's newly emerging curves had filled out into a stunning hour-glass figure. And, on the first day of the school term, she'd sashayed into the building with a clickety-clack of her kitten heels, her pert bottom wiggling in her tight-fitting pencil skirt, oozing confidence. She slung her school bag over her shoulder and sauntered off, linking Kitty's arm. The boys watched, mouths hanging open, while the girls who'd previously made her life a misery looked on with envy and not a little admiration.

Vi was going to embrace her name; she would never be called frumpy again, and she was going to prove that you could be brainy and be cool, too.

**CHAPTER 10**

'I hear congratulations are in order.' Lucy greeted Vi with a smile as she headed towards the counter of Lytell Stangdale's village shop, the delicious aroma of home baking seeping in from the adjoining teashop and filling the air. Together with the Sunne, it was the heart and hub of the village, where news was exchanged and local gossip caught up on.

'Yes, congratulations to you both,' added Lucy's husband, Freddie.

'Thank you.' Vi beamed back at them. 'I have to say, it came right out of the blue, I totally wasn't expecting it.'

'How romantic,' said Lucy. 'Let's have a gander at this ring then.'

Vi obliged and held her hand forward. 'It's a purple diamond.'

'Oh, it's absolutely gorgeous, Vi. I've never seen a real purple diamond before,' said Lucy.

'I didn't even know they existed,' said Freddie, peering at the ring. 'It's a beauty.'

'Thank you. Jimby totally surprised me with everything.

He even managed to get the size right, but I think that had a lot to do with Kitty and Molly.'

Just then, the bell above the shop door jangled as Little Mary stepped in. 'You be a good boy, Pete. Mummy won't be long,' she said to the plump dachshund she'd tethered outside. She closed the door and smoothed her neatly set curls, her face lighting up at seeing Violet. 'Oh, hello, chick, and congratulations. It's wonderful news. You make such a lovely couple, you and young Jimby, don't they, folks?'

*News sure travels fast round these parts*, thought Vi.

'They do,' said Freddie.

'Perfect,' agreed Lucy.

'And let's have a look at this ring I've been hearing so much about.' Little Mary set her huge shopping bag down on the floor and took Vi's hand in her own, which was tiny and peppered with liver-spots. 'Oh, lovie, it's just beautiful, goes with your hair. And he's a lovely lad is Jimby, you've got a good 'un there, Vi. He's so kind hearted.'

'He is, Mary, he's the best,' said Vi.

'Yes, chick, they broke the mould when they made him.'

'You're not wrong there, Mary.' Vi laughed.

'Too right,' said Freddie.

'Now, tell me all about how he proposed. I hear it was a big surprise for you. Did he get down on one knee?'

Vi was in the middle of telling Little Mary about their weekend away when the door-bell jangled once more, and Lycra Len bounded in. For once, he wasn't in his usual Lycra cycling gear. 'Morning, all. Am I alright to jump the queue? I'm off to York for breakfast at a cafe with the ex-wife – don't ask – and she'll have my balls for earrings if I'm late.'

'Goodness me!' said Little Mary, her eyes wide.

'Wowzers, I don't want to be responsible for that,' said

Vi. 'We were just having a chat, so feel free to get what you need.'

'Thanks, Vi, and congratulations to you and Jimby.' Len grabbed a packet of chewing gum and handed the money to Lucy.

'Thanks, Len,' said Vi. 'Hope the suit does the job. With your wife, I mean.'

'Yes, you're looking very dapper, young man, I hope she appreciates the effort,' added Little Mary.

'Thank you, ladies. Just pop the change in the charity tin, Luce.' Len raced out of the shop with cries of good luck following him.

'Poor man, I hope it goes well for him. I always think he looks a bit lonely,' said Little Mary. 'Anyway, I'm in a bit of a hurry myself. I need to get to the mobile library and change my books before all the good ones go, so if I could just have my bread, please, Freddie, then I'll be off.'

'There you go, Little M.' Freddie handed Mary a small brown loaf. 'I hope none of them racy reads find their way into that big shopping bag of yours. I know what you're like.'

'Get away with you.' Little Mary flushed to the roots of her pure white curls. She had a reputation for reading steamy novels and sharing them with Granny Aggie. 'Right, I'll be off. See you all later.' She hurried off out of the shop.

Once she'd left, Vi released her giggles. 'Ahh, bless her.'

'That was wicked, Fred,' said Lucy, laughing despite herself.

'I didn't mean to embarrass her, I thought she'd see the funny side. Anyway, it's reminded me that I've always want to ask why there are so many women called Mary in Lytell Stangdale?'

'Well,' said Vi. 'Little Mary – who's related to my mum on her dad's side – was the only Mary until my mum came along; my mum was named after her and they have the same surname. At the time, people referred to her as "Big Mary" and my mum was "Little Mary" until she hit her teens and grew taller than the original Mary, which isn't difficult, when you consider the current "Little Mary' is five foot nothing. Following, Freddie?'

'I think so.'

Vi wasn't totally convinced, but she continued. 'Anyhow, when Mary Ramsbottom moved here, she became known as "Big Mary" on account of her being so tall. So, you see, we've got Mary, Little Mary and Big Mary, just to avoid confusion. Bet you're glad you asked.' Vi couldn't help but laugh at Freddie's bemused expression.

'Don't worry, Vi, he'll catch up in a minute,' said Lucy.

Just then, Molly's mum Annie breezed in, looking a good decade younger than her years. Always well-groomed, she was dressed in a pair of camel slacks and a white short-sleeved blouse with a lacy collar. The broad smile on her gentle face was strikingly similar to her daughter's, though she was in possession of a much milder temperament. 'Oh, Violet, lovie.' She pulled Vi into a warm hug. 'Our Molly told me the news and I couldn't be happier for you both. I bet your mum and dad are over the moon.'

'You could say. Mum's already started with her fussing about who's coming to the wedding and who's not, who's sitting where at the reception, what food we're having. You name it, she's on it.'

Annie patted her arm and gave a sympathetic smile. 'They'll be excited, their only child's getting married to a lovely village lad.'

'You're right,' said Vi.

'Listen, lovie, if you need a hand with anything, just shout up, Jack and me will be more than happy to help.

What are you doing about catering? If you like, I could always make a batch of sherry trifles for you? Or, if you'd prefer, I could help with the flowers?'

'I've heard you're good with flower arrangements, Annie.' Freddie set her usual order of bread and the local daily newspaper on the counter.

Vi caught Lucy's eye and a knowing look passed between them. Her heart sank at the thought of Annie having a hand in any of the catering. Her food was legendarily horrendous and regularly only just on the right side of being safe to eat, though no one had ever had the heart to tell her. But she was a kind-hearted soul – as was Molly's dad, Jack – and with Jimby's parents no longer with them, having been killed in a car accident several years earlier, it would be nice for Jimby to have his aunt's involvement, so Vi leapt at the offer of help with flowers. 'The way you did Kitty's flowers, I'd be chuffed to bits if you'd do them for our wedding, Annie, and I know it would mean a lot to Jimby, too.'

Violet notice a dark shadow momentarily cross Annie's face. She was clearly thinking of her sister, but it was soon replaced with a warm smile. 'Flowers it is, lovie. I'm guessing there'll be a purple theme?'

Vi laughed. 'Of course!'

'Right, well, there's no time like the present, I'm going to head home and do my research on flowers in shades of purple. I'll go on that Pinterest thingy, then I can give you some ideas of what you can have. But first, our Molly's asked me to pop in on Granny Aggie and have a word with her. Apparently she's upset the vicar again, sending him mucky text messages.'

'It'll be all those racy books her and Little Mary read. And Little M's getting stocked up with some new ones as we speak,' Freddie said

## The Secret - Violet's Story

Vi pulled a face. 'Oh, no. She's not still doing that, is she, Annie?'

Annie nodded. 'Yes, she is, and she still blames it on predictive text or the arthritis in her fingers, but I'm not so sure. This one was something to do with butt plugs – whatever on earth they are.'

Vi heard Freddie snort; she hardly dared make eye contact with him or Lucy as she struggled to hold in a laugh that was forcing its way up inside her.

'Anyway, I'd best be off.' Annie hurried to the door. 'See you later, folks.'

She'd barely closed the door behind her when the three of them collapsed into fits of laughter. 'Oh, Lord above. I don't know how I kept a straight face,' said Freddie.

Vi gasped for air. 'Oh, it was so funny hearing Annie say that.'

'The village would definitely be a quieter place without good old Granny Aggie.' Lucy wiped tears of laughter from her eyes. 'She's so funny.'

'I'm not so sure Moll would agree with you,' said Vi.

'And, in all her excitement, Annie's gone and forgotten what she came in for,' said Freddie.

Just then, Jonty burst into the shop, his eyes filled with panic, bringing their laugher to an abrupt end. 'Does anyone here know how to give CPR? It's Gerald, he's collapsed, and he doesn't look too good. Big Mary thinks he's stopped breathing.' His words came out in a tumble and he stood in the doorway, gasping for breath, looking from one stunned face to the other.

'Oh my God.' Vi's hand flew to her mouth.

'Has anyone called an ambulance?' asked Freddie. He snatched up the shop phone.

'Yes, there's one on the way.' Jonty swallowed down the

worry that was blocking his throat. 'But it could take a while.'

'Where is he?' asked Lucy.

'In his front garden at home,' said Jonty. 'I heard Big Mary shouting and ran over to see what was the problem. Poor Gerald was lying there on the floor looking very badly, she said he was trying to get an old tree stump out then just collapsed.'

Octogenarian, Gerald Ramsbottom and his wife and muse, Big Mary had moved to the village from County Durham several years ago, and their kindness together with their quirky eccentricities had quickly endeared them to the residents of Lytell Stangdale.

'Jimby knows how to do CPR, he trained as a first responder years ago. Ollie, too, but he's on a job over at Middleton somewhere.' Vi's heart was thudding in her chest. 'Jimby's at his forge. I'll call him.'

As soon as Vi had explained the situation to him, Jimby tore along the road to Damson Cottage where the artist and his wife lived. He knelt down beside Gerald, whose rainbow-coloured hair and beard stood out in contrast to his face which was a pale, mottled colour. 'Gerald, Gerald, can you hear me, mate?' He felt for a pulse in the old man's neck before gently pinching at his ear lobes in an attempt to generate a reaction. 'Has he got his teeth in?' he asked Mary.

She shook her head, an expression of fear in her eyes. 'No, pet, they're in his pocket.'

Her response, in her soft Geordie accent, would normally make Jimby roar with laughter, but not today. He turned back to Gerald. 'Right, I'm just going to loosen your shirt, Gerald, make you feel a bit more comfortable. Then I'm going to do a few compressions on your chest. Okay? Stay with me, Gerald, the paramedics won't be long.'

Vi put her arm through Mary's. 'He'll be okay, I'm sure of it,' she said. She'd followed Jimby, and was trying to comfort Big Mary, while he performed compressions on Gerald. She was relieved to see Jimby's earlier training had come back to him in an instant.

Before long, the whirr of helicopter blades could be heard overhead as the Air Ambulance searched for somewhere to set down. The large flat field at the back of the Sunne, where Kitty and Ollie had held their wedding reception, was the most suitable and in moments Violet was relieved to hear the thunder of feet racing up the trod.

As soon as the paramedics reached them, Jimby stepped back while they attached the defibrillator wires to Gerald, with cries of, 'Stand back,' before administering an electric shock.

Big Mary looked on, her face wan, dabbing the tears that streamed from her eyes with a raggy paper handkerchief. 'Please be okay, Gerry, love,' she sobbed.

'I'm sure he will.' Vi rubbed Mary's arm. 'He's in good hands.'

'We've got a pulse,' one of the paramedics said. 'Let's get him onto a stretcher and into the helicopter.'

'Oh thank God,' cried Mary.

∽

LATER THAT EVENING, Jimby and Vi were sitting on the sofa in the small, cruck-framed living room of Sunshine Cottage, her legs resting on his lap while she flicked through a magazine.

Though the exterior of the quaint, chocolate-box pretty cottage was typical of Lytell Stangdale, with its thatched roof, thick, lime-washed walls and slightly wonky lean-to, the interior décor of the house could almost be described as contemporary. Carefully positioned table lamps and the warm glow of the flames from the wood-burner cast a soft light over the room, creating a cosy atmosphere. Vi's fixation with purple was evident in the soft furnishings and feature wall on the chimney breast in the living room, which added a quirky feel of luxury to the three-hundred-year-old property with its low ceilings and exposed oak beams. It was a far cry from Forge Cottage which, despite being tastefully done, had a distinct air of bachelor pad about it, and lacked the cosy extras Sunshine Cottage had, thanks to Vi's creative talents.

From the corner of her eye, Vi noticed Jimby looking distant. He'd been quiet since Gerald's collapse. 'You okay, chick?' she asked.

He dragged his hand down his face and sighed. 'Yeah, I'm fine. S'just the last time I had to give CPR was when Pip, you know … It just brought it all back.'

'I did wonder,' she replied, rubbing his arm. 'It can't have been easy for you, but you did your best for both of them. You mustn't beat yourself up over it, Jimby.'

'I know,' he sighed. 'You're right.' He didn't sound convinced.

Earlier that day, before Gerald's collapse, Vi had toyed with the idea of gently introducing her secret, maybe if they had a quiet moment that evening. Since the night Jimby proposed, the thought had caused a regular flurry of butterflies in her stomach, and she was keen to get it out in the open. But after what had happened to Gerald, it wouldn't be right to share it tonight. Inside, Vi breathed a sigh of relief.

Jimby's voice snapped her out of her thoughts. 'You know, we really should have a defibrillator in the village. Lots of places out in the sticks have them now.'

'Yeah, I've seen them, they're usually fixed to village halls, aren't they?'

'They are. I wonder how they get them? No doubt they'll cost a bloody fortune.' He gnawed on his bottom lip, an idea germinating in his mind.

'You're right, they won't be cheap, and if I remember correctly, I think it's been Women's Institutes who have done the fund raising for them; I seem to recall reading an article about it somewhere.'

'Fund raising, eh?' Jimby rubbed his chin, and Vi could almost hear the cogs whirring in his brain.

'Oh, heck, that sounds ominous.'

**CHAPTER 11**

The following day, Violet made her way out of the backdoor of Sunshine Cottage and followed the neat gravel path that led to the timber-framed workshop that housed the Romantique studio. Jimby had headed off to the forge early, with the intention of popping in on Big Mary to see how Gerald was doing.

Vi had woken that morning with her mind skittering all over the place, her secret seemingly growing in size as the days passed. The need to tell Jimby what had happened sixteen years earlier jostled with the fear that it could change their relationship forever; there would be no going back. Whenever a moment appeared for her to tell him, she'd fortify herself, assemble the words, prime her mouth but at the last minute, something would happen to make it impossible to share. Or did it really? Could it be that she was just making excuses? Backing out, taking the coward's way. Whatever the reason, it was making her feel unsettled and she hoped getting stuck into the order of vintage-style underwear she had from a burlesque dancer in London would take her mind off things. Kitty wouldn't be in for a while, and Vi hoped the time by herself would give her chance to iron out her thoughts.

She was concentrating hard on a fiddly bit of hand stitching when the pitchy tune of her mobile phone rang out from the corner of her workstation. The image on the screen told her it was James. 'Hi, Jimby.'

'Hiya, gorgeous.' Vi could hear a smile in his voice, and judging by the background noise, and the distinct boastful crowing of his cantankerous cockerel Reg, he was outside somewhere in the village. 'Thought you'd like to know that I've just spoken to Big Mary and she says Gerald's doing fine. He's had a heart attack, like we thought, and he's got to undergo further tests. She said something about a heart bypass, but to be honest, she was gabbling that fast, it was hard to keep up with what she was saying. Anyway, it looks like he's going to be in hospital for a while – but on the bright side, at least he won't be painting any pictures of Mary in the nude.'

Vi giggled. 'There's always that.'

'And, the main thing is, he's still with us.'

'Bless him, it is. I bet a lot of that's down to you, you know, Jimby.'

'Well, I don't know about that, Vi, but it's definitely got me thinking a bit more about our conversation on defibrillators. Oh, and while I remember, I saw Hugh Heifer on his usual walk with Daisy; he said I had to pass on his congratulations. Apparently he'd been wondering when I was going to get round to making an honest woman of you.'

'Really? I'm amazed he gave it a second thought. And don't tell me he was still dressed for winter, wrapped up in that old tweed coat and grubby flat cap.'

'I'm afraid so, I suspect they'd have to be surgically removed, his wellies, too – by 'eck, I bet it's interesting in them. Sweat was absolutely pouring down his face, I swear Daisy smelt sweeter than him. Anyway, on that happy note I'd best be off. Speak later.'

'Yep, speak later, Jimby.' Vi set her phone down, her thoughts lingering on retired farmer Hugh, who'd looked the same as far back as she could remember. Though since his retirement from dairy farming at Tinkel Top Farm, and move to Dunmilkin Cottage, he'd always kept a pet heifer – always named Daisy – and the pair had become a regular sight walking steadily through the village. Vi smiled to herself, before her mind jumped to wondering what exactly Jimby had in mind about defibrillators.

A moment later Kitty arrived wearing a faded denim jacket over a blue and white Moroccan print dress in her usual Boho style. Vi was pleased to see she was armed with a batch of Lucy's handmade chocolate-dipped flapjacks.

'Morning, Vi. I hear our Jimby's the hero of the hour.' Kitty hung up her jacket and headed over to the kitchen where she flicked the kettle on.

'Hiya, Kitts. News travels fast round here. But, yes, poor old Gerald took a bad turn – heart attack, the doctors say – and Jimby looked after him till the air ambulance arrived, giving him CPR. I reckon he saved his life. Which has given that brother of yours a right bee in his bonnet about getting a defibrillator for the village.'

'Well, I'm glad Gerald's going to be okay, but our Jimby does have a point; we're miles away from the nearest hospital.'

'I know, I hadn't thought about it until now. Seeing how upset Big Mary was made me realise that my mum and dad aren't getting any younger. It could've been one of them lying on the ground, God forbid.' Vi shuddered at the thought.

'Don't go worrying about anything like that; they're both fit as lops.'

'True, but you never know ...'

'Are you okay, Vi?' Kitty glanced across at her friend as she set the flapjacks out on a plate, popping a stray chocolatey crumb into her mouth. 'You look like you've got the weight of the world on your shoulders. Don't let what happened to Gerald set you off worrying about your mum and dad. He doesn't exactly have the healthiest of lifestyles; he smokes like a chimney and drinks like a fish. Your parents are the complete opposite. They get loads of exercise, plenty of fresh air and have always eaten well.'

Violet sighed, 'I know, and I'm fine, it just makes you think, that's all.' Out of nowhere, her secret had pushed its way to the forefront of her mind, elbowing concern for her parents and Gerald out of the way. She tried to push it away, but it refused to budge. She was really going to have to deal with it before it completely ate her away. Could she mention something to Kitty now, while it was quiet? Her eyes flicked towards her friend who gave her a big smile in response. No, Vi didn't have the heart for it today. Or any day, if she was honest with herself. She wished it would just go away.

'Why don't you get yourself over here, chick, and get stuck into one of these little beauties.' Kitty set the plate of flapjacks down on the table in the kitchen and raised her eyebrows in expectation.

**CHAPTER 12**

Friday evening found the group of friends sitting around their usual table in the Sunne, the burble of easy-going chatter going on around them. 'I've got it,' said Jimby. He sat back in his seat and folded his arms across his chest.

'Got what?' Camm threw an apple-wood log on the fire, sending a host of sparks dancing up the chimney, the sweet scent of burning wood curling out into the room.

'Don't ask.' Vi cocked an eyebrow at Jimby as she swirled the ice-cubes round her glass of gin and tonic.

'Well, you've definitely got *something*, Jimbo. Not sure it's a good thing, though,' said Molly.

'Ha ha, very funny, you lot,' Jimby replied.

'Come on then, mate, share it.' Ollie picked up his pint and took a sip.

'I've got an idea how to raise funds for a defibrillator for the village.' He beamed round at them. 'It's a fabulous one, and it came to me this afternoon as I was making a new door knocker for Robbie and Rosie.'

'So it's all your fault, you two.' Camm nodded at the couple who'd just joined them.

'Right,' said Kitty. 'Should we be worried, Jimby?'

'I'm always worried when our Jimby gets an idea,' said Molly.

'Especially when he has a look like that on his face,' added Vi.

'Seriously, you'll love it. Honest.' Jimby rubbed his hands together and leaned forward. 'Speaking of knockers, you remember how that group of women did a calendar?'

'Oh, lord above.' Vi clapped a hand to her forehead.

'You mean the WI women who had their photos taken for a calendar they sold to raise money for charity?' asked Kitty.

'He does, Kitts. And, if my memory serves me right, weren't they all naked, too?' Vi's tone was wary.

'Oh, yes indeedy. They were all completely starkers, but their bits were all discretely covered. Anyway, I thought our version could be blokes only.' Jimby's eyes danced with mischief.

'Does this mean what I think it means?' Ollie gave his friend a look of resigned acceptance.

Jimby clapped Ollie on the shoulder. 'Yes, my friend, it does. Get that saw poised, Ollie mate.'

'Bloody hell, Jim,' he replied. 'I'm not keen on the idea of holding a saw next to my bits.'

The friends fell about laughing. 'I love it,' said Molly. She wiped tears of merriment from her eyes. 'Not the part about the saw and your bits, Oll. I mean the whole idea. Camm, you can stand beside a tractor, or the vardo, or maybe hold a sheep in front of your nethers.'

'A sheep?' Camm looked outraged. 'I think that'd send the wrong kind of message, don't you?' His response made everyone snigger.

'Just a bit,' said Robbie.

'Ollie, can have a wood planer to hide his bits.' Kitty giggled.

'Hmm. I like the sound of that more than I like the idea of a saw down there, to be honest. Not that I'm agreeing to anything at the moment.'

'Yeah, and Robbie can have a bundle of strategically placed blueprints covering his family jewels,' said Rosie.

'And it looks like I'm going to have to invest in a bigger anvil to hide the generous proportions of my manhood.' Jimby sighed.

'In your dreams,' said Vi, eliciting a sidelong dirty look from Jimby.

'Here's a likely contender.' Jimby's faced changed as he spotted Lycra Len walking by with a pint in his hand. 'You'd help us raise money, wouldn't you, Len?'

'What for?'

'A defibrillator for the village.'

Len nodded. 'After what happened to Gerald, you can count me in, mate.'

'Good man, I'll pop your name on the list.' Jimby gave him the thumbs up. 'How did the chat go with your ex-missus, by the way?'

'Hmph. Don't ask.' With a shrug, Len headed off for a game of dominoes with Hugh Heifer, Pete Welford and Bill Campion who were sipping beer, waiting for him.

'You didn't tell him what he'd have to do,' said Vi.

'Ignorance is bliss.' Molly sniggered into her glass.

'My thoughts exactly.' Jimby nodded. 'Joking aside though, folks. Gerald's collapse really brought it home to me just how much we need a defibrillator round here. There's a lot of old folks in the village and the time waiting for an ambulance could be the difference between life and death.'

Jimby's words cast a momentary sombre air over the

table. It was Molly who broke the silence. 'If you're serious about this, Jimby – which I think you are – we're going to have to look into doing it properly. Find out how much it'll cost to get a calendar professionally printed. And getting decent – and I use that word loosely! – photos taken. Suss out how to market it if we're going to make enough money to buy a defibrillator. It's going to involve a fair bit of work, I reckon.'

'Actually, leave the photography aspect to me. I've got a mate over at Middleton-le-Moors who's a photographer – Nick – I think I could twist his arm to do mate's rates,' said Robbie.

'Thanks, Rob, that'd be great,' said Jimby.

'Haven't you got enough on, what with planning a wedding?' asked Camm.

'Well, we just want the wedding to be low key, and Vi's made it perfectly clear that she's more than happy to deal with the bulk of it —'

'Too right,' Vi cut him off. 'If I left anything to Jimby it would be chaos. And, anyway, I know exactly how I want things doing.'

'We don't doubt that for a second, Vi,' Molly said behind her glass of Pino Grigio.

## CHAPTER 13

Later that evening, Vi and Jimby were in the bedroom at Sunshine Cottage, getting ready for bed. The thick, purple velvet curtains were doing a good job of muffling the sound of an owl hooting from the rowan tree in the garden to another one further down the road. Vi was sitting at the dressing table, removing her make-up with a cotton pad, her thoughts switching from Jimby's fundraising suggestion and wondering when the right moment would arise for her to broach her secret.

In the process of getting undressed, and standing in nothing but his socks and a pair of underpants that had seen better days, Jimby seemed oblivious to the turmoil in her mind. Puffing out his chest, he strutted across the room to her. 'You're one lucky woman, Violet Smith.'

'And how d'you work that out?' She stifled a giggle and arched a quizzical eyebrow at him, her worries dispersing in an instant.

'Because, this,' he gestured to himself, 'is yours. Every inch of this fine figure of a man is yours for the taking. Yes, that's right, hot man on tap, whenever you want, you lucky girl.' He slipped the fine strap of her dusky pink silk nightie off her shoulder and dropped a kiss on it.

Vi snorted. 'You reckon?'

'Oh, yes. Standing before you is a perfect specimen of raw man, primed and ready for action. I don't think you appreciate just how many women would pay big money to get their hands on this body, but they're out of luck; it's reserved just for your pleasure and delectation.' He licked his finger and pressed it against his thigh, making a sizzling sound.

'You're a nutter.' Smiling, she reached across and twanged the elastic waistband of his underpants. 'And since when have budgie-smugglers been a good look?'

'Hey, cheeky, I'll have you know there's no budgie-smuggling going on here. Down there is all me. As I've already said, you're a lucky woman.' He waggled his eyebrows at her.

Vi ignored his last comment and scrunched up her nose. 'And how come all your underpants seem to have holes in them?'

'Well, that would be my enormous manhood forcing its way out.' He flashed one of his cheeky grins, his dimples punctuating his cheeks.

Vi giggled again. 'It's something forcing its way out, not sure it's your manhood, though.'

'Come here and I'll show you.' He gave a suggestive smile.

'No thanks, I've got a throbbing headache.'

'That's a coincidence, I've got a throbbing head, too, but not where you're thinking.'

'Jimby! Are you ever serious?' Vi threw her pack of cotton wool pads at him.

'Nope, and that's exactly why you love me.'

And he was right.

~

It hadn't taken long for sleep to claim Jimby after their tender session of love-making. Snuggling under the heavy goose-down duvet, he'd pulled Violet close, wrapped his arms around her and tucked her head beneath his chin. Soon she became aware of his breathing becoming deep and regular, his heartbeat steady and strong. She lay awake listening to the familiar night-time sounds of the old cottage; the creaks and groans of the central heating pipes as they cooled down, the wind winding its way around the thick, stone walls, owls hooting to one another across the dale. Sleep seemed well out of reach for her tonight. With a sigh, Vi eased herself out of Jimby's arms; he sensed her movement and pressed a sleepy kiss to her hair. 'You okay?' he murmured.

'I'm fine,' she whispered. 'Just a bit warm, that's all.'

'Told you, I'm a hot man.' His words were heavy with sleep as he threw his arm above his head.

Vi sighed as she looked out into the darkness of the room. She'd never felt more loved, more secure, safe. How could she risk throwing all this away? How could she risk Jimby thinking differently about her? Losing respect for her? That would be unbearable; she winced at that thought. It wasn't really what she'd done that worried her ... not really, it wasn't the worst thing in the world and plenty of women had done it – it was that she'd gone all this time without telling him. And the longer she left it, the harder it was becoming to even think about starting the conversation. *Oh, by the way, there's something I've been meaning to tell you, just it keeps slipping my mind, you know how it is ...* But it wasn't the sort of thing you could skim over, dismiss like it was an irrelevant piece of information. It had influenced the person she'd become.

*What a mess!* Vi scrunched her eyes up, the worry growing as the night crept by, as worries have a nasty habit of doing.

**CHAPTER 14**

'So where are you two going to live when you're married?' Molly asked. 'Surely you can't keep switching between Sunshine Cottage and Forge Cottage, that would be too unsettling and a bit bonkers.'

The friends were enjoying their monthly Friday night pamper session at Rosie's beauty therapy rooms at The Manor House, continuing a tradition they'd started in an attempt to drag Molly out of the house when she was at a low ebb. The air was filled with the sumptuous fragrance of aromatherapy oils while soothing music tinkled away softly in the background. Kitty and Molly were sitting on the huge squishy sofa, wrapped in fluffy towelling robes, armed with glasses of Prosecco, while Vi was lying on the treatment table, having a face mask removed, soaking up the relaxing atmosphere.

'I'm not really sure,' said Vi. 'We spend most of the time at my house – for obvious reasons – but we haven't really had a proper chat about it. Jimby's so fired up about this calendar project, and I've had other stuff occupying my time, so we haven't had that conversation yet.'

'Well, don't leave it too late,' said Kitty. 'You know what our Jimby's like; he sometimes needs a nudge in the right direction about stuff like that.'

'That's because he's a man,' said Molly. 'In my experience, all men need a nudge – or bloody great shove – in the right direction. Pip was horrendous for it.'

'Neither house is ideal. Though, when I was talking to my mum the other day she was saying Dad's ready to retire, which got me to thinking how Sunshine Cottage would be perfect for them. And they wouldn't mind us still using the workshop for Romantique, which could be a problem if somebody else rented it; they'd hardly want a workshop in their garden, with me and Kitty traipsing through it whenever we wanted.' From the corner of her eye, she glanced in Kitty's direction to see her friend nodding in agreement. 'Plus, I'd get to see more of them if they were down in the village, which would be nice. Mum was saying Dad's been feeling tired recently, and what with Gerald, well, you know ... I just can't get it out of my mind that they're not getting any younger.'

Kitty squeezed her hand. 'Like I said the other day, Vi, they're in good health, but I can see the sense in them retiring and moving into a smaller house in the village.'

'Me, too,' said Molly. 'I know my dad had to retire because of Parkinson's, but he and my mum haven't looked back since we took over the farm. Mum's in her element, looking after our kids, going to all of her clubs and classes, and Dad loves pottering about in the garden and looking after his garth.'

'Hey, Vi. I've got an idea.' Kitty sat up straight. 'What about that piece of land just up from the Sunne? It's mine and Jimby's, we own it as part of the trust our parents set up for the farm and everything, but it's a lovely spot; south facing—'

'Handy for the pub,' Molly said.

'What, you mean we should build something?' said Vi.

'Yes.' Kitty nodded enthusiastically, her large brown eyes sparkling. 'You could build your dream house, Vi.'

'Ooh, that's a brilliant idea. Robbie could draw up the plans for you; mates rates,' said Rosie.

'Sounds like the perfect solution to me, if you're keen to stay in the village,' added Molly.

Vi thought for a moment. 'You know what, I really like that idea. We definitely want to stay in the village, and there's nothing on the market that would suit us at the moment – or likely to be in the near future. That could be the perfect solution.' She looked round at her friends, a smile tugging at her lips.

'Right, Vi, that's your face mask removed,' said Rosie. 'You just need to let me know which essential oil you'd like for your massage.'

'Thanks, Rosie. I think I'll go for lavender and scented geranium.'

'Good choice; nice and soothing.'

While Vi was enjoying her massage, the friends chatted away – Molly and Kitty sipping at their Prosecco and enthusing about Vi and Jimby's potential building plans.

'Oh, my goodness, Vi, you're full of knots,' said Rosie. She was kneading Vi's back, a frown furrowing her brow. 'I've never known your muscles be so tense.'

Vi knew where Rosie was coming from, she could feel the knots Rosie referred to as the beauty therapist circled her thumbs over the muscles in her shoulders. Whereas, usually the massage was soothing, tonight it could almost be described as painful.

'Don't tell me it's wedding jitters already,' said Molly.

'Come to think of it, Vi, you have seemed a bit distracted since you got back from your weekend away,' said Kitty. 'But there's no need to stress, we're happy to help with the preparations, aren't we, girls?'

'Too right,' said Molly.

'Of course, just shout up,' said Rosie.

Vi closed her eyes as her thoughts drifted off to the secret she was finding so difficult to share with Jimby. She needed to tell him soon; the worry of it was beginning to eat into her, causing a constant gnawing ache in the pit of her stomach. She'd need to tell her friends, too. What would they think of her keeping it to herself for so many years, when they'd shared everything – or, at least, she thought they did. But maybe they had secrets, too. Kitty hadn't shared how mentally abusive Dan was but, then again, Kitty herself hadn't realised herself at first, couldn't see what everyone else could see. What about Molly? She'd kept her feelings for Camm hidden for quite a long time. Though she'd even kept them hidden from herself, Vi reasoned. And Rosie? Could she be hiding anything? Vi didn't think so, from what she'd seen of her, Rosie was an open book. *Oh shit,* thought Vi, nothing was going to make this any easier.

'What do you think, Vi?' Kitty's voice pulled Violet away from her thoughts.

'She's been drifting off, haven't you, chick?' Molly grinned at her.

'Mmm. Guilty, I'm afraid. Rosie's massage is so soothing, I was almost ready to fall asleep.'

'Just as well you didn't, I don't think we could stand your snoring.' Molly giggled.

'That's rum, coming from you!' said Vi.

'We were wondering if we should have a shopping trip

to York, get some ideas for wedding bits and bobs?' Kitty said. 'I know you're wanting to keep things simple and low-key, but you don't exactly have a lot of time.'

'True,' agreed Vi. 'Any excuse for a shopping trip sounds good to me.' She hoped she sounded suitably enthusiastic. 'I wouldn't mind popping into that wedding dress shop to have a look at their shoes and accessories selection.'

'Ooh, me too. It's gorgeous in there. I'm still in love with my wedding shoes,' said Kitty.

'Right, lets arrange the date,' said Molly. 'You coming too, Rosie?'

'I'd love to.' Rosie beamed at her.

~

WHEN VI ARRIVED BACK at Jimby's, she found him stretched out on the sofa, flicking through the TV channels, a bottle of beer on the coffee table in front of him. He sat up as she walked into the room, his wide smile telling her just how pleased he was to see her.

'Hiya, beautiful. D'you have a good time with the lasses?'

Vi flopped on the sofa beside him, the soothing oils of the massage and so many nights of interrupted sleep were catching up on her. She rested her head on his shoulder and he kissed the waves of her hair. 'It was lovely, thanks. They're a great bunch of girls – don't know what I'd do without them. And it's nice that Rosie's really become part of the friendship group.'

'Yeah, Robbie's a decent bloke, he's just slotted in, too. Funny how they're so different to the Mellisons, isn't it?'

Vi harrumphed. 'Well, there's a good reason for that. The Websters are friendly and keen to blend in with village life, whereas the stuck up Mellisons arrived thinking they were better than everyone, looking down their noses. And I'll never forgive that spiteful cow, Aoife, for how she treated Kitty.' Vi could feel her blood beginning to boil at the thought of it.

'Mmm. Me, too.' Jimby frowned.

'Anyway, I don't want to talk about that poisonous family, but I do have a suggestion for you,' she said. 'And it's not what you're thinking!'

'Shame.'

'It's about where we're going to call home when we're married.'

Jimby pushed his fingers into his curls and gave his head a vigorous scratching. 'Yeah, I've been giving that a bit of thought recently, too.'

'You have?'

'Mmhm.'

'Well, it was your Kitty's idea actually. Anyway, she suggested that we should build on that plot of land you both own. You know, the one near the pub?'

'Funny she should say that, because I've been thinking the exact same thing.'

'Really? You kept that quiet.'

'Really. And you know me, I'm a quiet bloke.'

'Yeah and I'm the queen of England,' she laughed.

'Princess, more like.'

'Hey, you.' Vi whacked him with a velvet cushion. Princess was how Pip – Molly's husband – used to describe her after she'd moved to York, accusing her of becoming soft. She hadn't liked it at the time, but she didn't mind so much now, especially in light of what had happened. 'Being serious for a moment, if you're providing the land, I want to pay for the actual build.'

'I don't expect you to; it won't be cheap, you know?'

'I know that, but the land it would be sitting on is worth a hefty amount, me paying for the building work just seems fair. And I made a decent profit selling Purple Diamond.'

After university, and following a short stint abroad, Vi had completed internships at a couple of PR companies, and had left feeling sufficiently inspired to set up on her own. This she did, in the beautiful mediaeval city of York – the lure of London not at all tempting to her – naming her company after her favourite precious stone: Purple Diamond PR. Word of Vi's talents had spread like wildfire, and her business had become a roaring success, quickly allowing her to buy a luxurious riverside apartment in the city. But a couple of years earlier, she'd felt the pull of the moors – and Jimby Fairfax – and had relocated there, selling Purple Diamond, renting out her apartment and setting up Romantique with Kitty. She didn't have a moment's regret.

Jimby looked at her and Vi could almost see the cogs whirring away behind his heart-melting chocolate eyes. Unable to resist, she leaned forward and kissed him on the mouth.

'If it means I get more of those, then it's a yes.'

She replied by kissing him hard on the mouth once more.

The couple spent the rest of the evening discussing their ideas, with Vi – organised as ever – grabbing her laptop, making notes and creating a wish list, her heart feeling light and happy.

That night, Vi went to bed feeling tired but the least stressed she'd been for a long time. Her mind was thriving on this new project: the plans for her new home with Jimby. Only occasionally would the spectre of her secret loom up, vying for her attention. Now she thought about it, did she really need to tell anyone? It's not like she'd run the risk of bumping into Mike Williamson again. It was a one-off, seeing him there at the hotel. It might not have even been him, anyway. She'd kept it to herself for this long, what would be the point of telling anyone now? It would only cause hurt and unhappiness, and the thought of hurting Jimby and her friends just didn't bear thinking about. No, there really was no point in sharing it. It was in the past and that's exactly where it should stay, buried in a deep, dark place where it could be forgotten about. Momentarily, the worry of her secret drained away from her mind. With a loud sigh, Vi snuggled closer into Jimby, pulling the duvet tight up to her chin. He mumbled something indiscernible and pulled her closer to him. She ran her fingers through the dark curls of his chest hair and nuzzled into his neck, inhaling his comforting, familiar smell, and let her worries slip away.

## CHAPTER 15

'I really like the idea of building our own home.' Jimby was chomping on a slice of toast at the kitchen table of Sunshine Cottage. 'We can get it exactly how we want it, instead of buying somewhere with the intention of doing it up.'

'I agree,' said Vi. 'We've both done that – you converting Forge Cottage, and me refurbishing this place – and I really don't fancy doing that again. I like the idea of having somewhere cosy but low-maintenance; we both know how dusty old properties can be.'

'Yep.' Jimby nodded. 'And there's always something needs doing to them.'

Just then, his mobile phone pinged heralding the arrival of a text message. He made his way across to the small dresser where it was being charged, picked it up and read the message. 'Ey up, that was quick.'

'What was?'

'The reply from Robbie. I sent him a text quarter of an hour ago, asking if he could meet up with us to discuss drawing up some plans, and testing what he thought our chances of getting building consent would be.'

'Blimey, you don't mess around.' Vi felt excitement swirl around her stomach. She couldn't believe how taken Jimby was with the idea, and whilst he did usually take a while to get started on some things, if he was keen on a plan, it was full steam ahead.

'No point dithering about, we might as well get plans in ASAP and get building. It'd be nice to think we could get all done and dusted by the time I make an honest woman of you, but I'm not sure how realistic that is.'

'I think that might be pushing it a bit,' said Vi. His words momentarily knocked her off balance. *Honest woman? Oh, Lord that word: "honest".* It was the last thing she felt since she'd clapped eyes on Mike Williamson, even though she hadn't technically lied ... more like omitted a few facts. *It's as good as,* her conscience reasoned with her as she gulped down a lump of anxiety.

'Are you okay, gorgeous?' Jimby walked over to her, placing his hands on her shoulders. 'You always seem a bit distracted at the moment. If this is all too much for you, just let me know, we can put the brakes on things. I know you're busy with Romantique.'

Vi smiled up at him. 'I'm absolutely fine. I just think I had one too many gin and tonics last night. And don't even think about putting the brakes on getting plans drawn up for a house, I'm dead keen for it. I just need a breath of fresh air and I'll be right as rain.'

'Well, that's good, because Robbie wants to meet us at the plot in half an hour.' He pressed a kiss to her lips. 'I wonder how we can fill that time?' He waggled his eyebrows at her, making her giggle.

THE MEETING with Robbie went well; he thought the plot was a good size for a sympathetically built cottage. 'Look, if you've got time, why don't you come back to mine so I can show you some drawings and photographs of the sort of thing I've got in mind?'

'If that's alright with you, Rob, we're keen to get the ball rolling,' said Jimby

'Great, well, there's no time like the present. Come on.' He led the way along the trod to the Manor House.

'Because – as, of course, you know – we live in a conservation area in the National Park, we'll have to have a sympathetic design, which isn't a problem, but I think what would be quite nice is an eco-friendly, contemporary take on the cottages that are already here.' They were standing around the large white marble island in the airy kitchen, sipping tea. There was no sign of Rosie, but the air was rich with essential oils, and the sound of soothing music drifted down the hallway from her treatment rooms.

'I'm loving the sound of that,' said Vi. 'Something low-maintenance but still with lots of character.'

'Yep, me too, that's exactly what we're after,' added Jimby.

An hour later, the couple had left Robbie with a clear idea of what they wanted and his promise that he'd get things moving as soon as possible.

'Excited?' asked Jimby. He took Vi's hand as they headed back to her cottage.

'Very.' She smiled broadly. 'I'm already thinking about the décor; I've got loads of ideas swirling around my mind. I think I need a trip to Jonas Olivier.'

'Jonas who?'

'It's a shop and it's full of gorgeously tasteful things.'

'Oh, right.' It was clear to Vi that Jimby didn't have a clue what she was talking about.

'Trust me, the stuff's fabulous – the sofa and chairs at Sunshine Cottage came from there, as did the sideboard. Come to think of it so did most of the mugs and bowls I have.'

'So you obviously like this Olive Jones, then?' Jimby grinned.

'*Jonas Olivier.*' Vi corrected him. 'I so do, and talking of mugs, you needn't think that tasteless collection of rude ones you've got at your place are coming to our new home.'

'I'll have you know that collection you refer to as "tasteless" has taken years of collecting and a lot of effort from Ollie in sourcing such *individual* items. I've come to think of them as treasures. I reckon they might even be worth a small fortune one day.'

Over the years, James and Ollie had bought one another mugs for birthdays and Christmas. The gift buying had become quite competitive, with the aim of getting the rudest ones possible. Consequently, James had an assorted collection of mugs ranging from breast shaped, to those sporting offensive comments, most of which were displayed on a mug tree in his kitchen.

'Treasures?' Vi pulled a face. 'So where does Ollie keep his collection, now he lives with Kitty?'

'Not sure, but now you come to mention it, I can't remember seeing them at the house.'

'My point exactly. And we won't be seeing any at our new house. We'll have tasteful ones.'

'Jonas Olive ones?'

'Jonas *Olivier* and, actually, there's a branch in York.' Vi looked thoughtful, patting her fingers against her mouth. 'Hmm, the girls and me are planning a trip there to start hunting around for wedding stuff, so I could pop in then.' She looked up at him and smiled. 'Right, come on, Jimby, let's pop in at Oak Tree Farm, see if Kitty's around; there's a shopping trip to plan.'

'Aye, and I need to find out where Ollie keeps his mugs.'

Vi rolled her eyes and pushed Jimby in the direction of his sister's home, giving him a thwack on the backside for good measure.

∽

IN BED THAT NIGHT, Violet's mind was brimming with the plans for their new home, her imagination slipping through the sage-green painted gate and up the York stone-flagged path that led to the ochre timber-framed cottage that would be their home. Its large oak mullions would be set either side of a wide oak door, while a couple of sleepy dormers perched on the roof, would peer over at them. Slowly, she saw an image of herself pushing the door open to reveal a brightly-lit hallway. She put her hand to her chest and gasped with delight. With a flurry of excitement rippling through her, she stepped over the threshold, hearing her heels clicking on the pristine elm floorboards. *Oops!* With a sudden thought she kicked them off, *No outdoor shoes inside*. In the centre of the hallway, she could see a chunky staircase, with doors either side. The door to the right led to the living room where a wood burning stove was sitting in a huge inglenook fireplace. She rushed over to the bi-fold doors on the rear wall and opened them wide, stepping out into the patio area that was set with sumptuous all-weather garden furniture. Back in the hallway, the first door to the left of the staircase led to the state of the art kitchen, all sleek lines and understated efficiency. A generously propor-

*The Secret - Violet's Story*

tioned island unit sat proudly in the centre of the room with its built-in breakfast bar, where a breakfast of croissants and artisanal preserves was set out. The delicious aroma of freshly brewed coffee from the high-tech coffee machine was lingering in the air – the very thought of it almost made Vi's nose tingle. While a large, statement oven sat under the lintel of a mock fireplace. A highly polished tongue and groove oak door led to the utility room and downstairs toilet. Another set of bi-fold doors ran along the back wall and also opened out onto the patio, perfect for sitting and enjoying the sunrise with a cup of tea.

Her mind's eye was heading up the soft carpet of the stairs, her heart pounding with excitement as she turned into the master bedroom, the door to the walk-in wardrobe ajar, she glimpsed the neat rails of her clothes, swinging on the rails. Her joy was brought to an abrupt halt as an image of Mike Williamson pushed its way in, his arrogant smile lifting slightly higher at one side, making it almost look like a snarl. Vi's heart lurched and she rubbed her eyes, trying to erase the picture of him, eager to move her thoughts back to her new home with Jimby. But it was too late, the reappearance of her latest worry had shoved them well and truly out of reach, and try as she might, the wisps were just frustratingly out of reach, leaving her desperately trying to grasp at them and pull them back.

'Bugger!' she whispered. She turned her face to Jimby who was sleeping soundly, his breathing rhythmic and low; she could just see the outline of his face, his curls sticking up. She couldn't keep this up much longer, it had already caused a permanent feeling of nausea to sit in her gut, taken the edge off her appetite. With a bolt of courage, she sucked in a deep breath and let it out slowly. 'Jimby,' she said softly. He gave a little grunt. 'Jimby.' She gave him a nudge.

'Hmm?'

'Jimby, are you awake?'

'No,' he mumbled. He rolled onto his side and threw his arm around her. 'I'm asleep.'

In that moment, guilt at interrupting his sleep at such a silly hour to deliver something unpalatable shooed Vi's courage away. Yes, she'd have to tell him, but waking him up in the early hours of a Sunday morning wasn't the right time. It was selfish. Vi pulled the duvet up tight and snuggled into Jimby's warmth. She'd know when the time was right, and she'd put it to the back of her mind until then. Tonight, she didn't want to think about anything else, she just wanted to fall asleep in the arms of the man she adored.

**CHAPTER 16**

'Look out York, here we come!' Molly cried as they headed down the road leading out of Lytell Stangdale. She smiled across at Vi who was sitting up front beside her in the four-wheel drive. Vi grinned back, happiness flooding her chest; she loved spending time with her friends, and it had been ages since they'd had a Saturday shopping trip.

'Woohoo. Happy shopping, ladies,' said Kitty.

'Ooh, I can't wait,' said Rosie. 'The last time I went on a girls-only shopping trip was with Abbie and my mother, and didn't get to look at anything for myself.'

'Well, you will today.' Kitty beamed at her.

'I've made a list of everything I need to look at or buy today,' said Vi.

'Sounds about right,' quipped Molly.

'Vi's always really organised,' Kitty explained to Rosie. 'That's why she's such an amazing businesswoman.'

'I don't know about that anymore, Kitts.' Vi gazed out of the window, watching the moors give way to the outskirts of Middleton-le-Moors, where a building site of tasteful new builds were springing up.

'Don't be so modest, Vi. You keep everything ship-shape for Romantique, that's nothing to do with me, I just turn up and sew or sketch.'

'That's so not true, Kitts,' Vi replied.

'Do you miss living in York, or having your own PR company,' asked Rosie. She hadn't known Vi before she'd moved back to the village.

'Not a bit. It was so consuming. Don't get me wrong, I loved it at first, and thrived on making it a success, but suddenly my priorities changed and I felt the urge to do something different, and the pull of Lytell Stangdale and family and friends was getting too strong to ignore.'

'She means the pull of a certain daft-arse gentleman,' said Molly. 'Oy, tosser! Keep on your own side of the road,' she yelled at an oncoming vehicle that whizzed by, nearly taking her wing-mirror off.

'That'll be another couple of pounds for your swear-box, Moll. It must be choc-a-bloc by now.' Vi laughed.

'It's been emptied twice already this year.' Molly grinned.

'Only the twice?' Kitty giggled.

The rest of the journey to York was filled with chatter bubbling away in an air of excitement, punctuated regularly by giggles and loud snorts of laughter.

∽

'Oh, look at these, Vi, they're gorgeous.' The four women were in "Gowns", an exclusive wedding shop in the city centre. Kitty was poring over a pair of crystal embellished wedding shoes in a rich shade of clotted-cream. They were made of butter-soft leather and were absolutely exquisite.

'Mm, they are lovely, Kitts, but more like your taste than

mine. I'm looking for a pair more along the lines of fifties-inspired style.'

'Ooh, they are gorgeous,' said Rosie. 'They actually remind me of yours, Kitty.'

'Me, too,' answered Kitty, dreamily. 'That's probably why I like them so much.'

'Is this the sort of thing you're looking for?' asked Gemma, the shop owner. She unfurled tissue paper from a shoe box she was holding and lifted out a pair of ivory kitten heels.

Vi hurried over to her. 'They're perfect,' she gasped.

'Oh, you've just got to try some of these dresses on, Vi,' said Molly. She was looking through the stunning wedding gowns on the rail.

'Don't forget, Kitty and me are making mine,' Vi whispered. 'And the bridesmaid dresses.'

'So?' Molly retorted. 'Doesn't hurt to try them, does it? Might give you few ideas.'

'I don't need any ideas, I know exactly how I want my dress to look. Why don't *you* try one on?' Vi arched her eyebrows in a friendly challenge, making Molly blush.

'Don't be so daft, there's no way I'll be needing one of those any time soon.' All eyes were on her as she stepped away from the gowns and over to the doorway. 'Are we just about done in here?'

Vi picked up on the two spots of pink burning brightly on Molly's cheeks, instantly regretting what she'd said; after what Molly been through with losing Pip, she didn't want to make her friend feel uncomfortable. She went across to her and rubbed her arm. 'Yep, I'm all done, Moll.'

∽

'I DON'T KNOW about you lot, but I'm desperate for a sit down and a bite to eat.' Kitty looked shattered. They'd been shopping for hours and were laden with bags.

'Me too, my feet are killing me,' agreed Rosie. 'I wore these shoes because they're usually so comfy, but we must've walked miles today.'

'Right, how about that Italian restaurant I was telling you about? It has a great atmosphere and the food's simple but amazing,' said Vi. 'And it's not far from here, just round that corner, in fact.'

'I'm on for that,' said Kitty.

'Lead the way, Vi,' said Molly.

IN THE RESTAURANT the air was heavy with the mouth-watering aroma of garlic and fresh herbs, while Italian opera played discreetly in the background. The four friends were given a warm greeting by Pepe, the owner – a short man, with a rotund body and a pair of twinkling dark brown eyes. He led them to a table by the window, complaining in an easy-going way that they hadn't seen much of Vi since she'd left York. 'It must be the reason you are so thin, bella, you're not getting enough proper food cooked with love,' he told her.

As promised the meal was delicious; they dined on plump, juicy olives infused with garlic and herbs, garlic bread and the perfect al dente pasta in delicious sauces.

'I'll be keeping the vampires away, tonight, with this garlic breath,' said Kitty.

'Same here,' said Molly. 'If Camm has any ideas about romance, I think it'll scupper them, too.' She was finishing off a bowl of ice-cream while the others were perusing the coffee menu when an unfamiliar voice interrupted them.

'Violet Smith? It is you, isn't it?' said a man who looked to be in his early fifties. He was casually dressed in red chinos and brown loafers, reeking of cologne, with floppy hair falling into his eyes.

As Vi looked up, shock whipped her breath right out of her mouth then reached inside, pulling at her guts with a cruel twist. She felt her breathing become shallow as shock was replaced with panic, flooding her body before she had chance to process what was happening. Suddenly conscious of the weight of everyone's eyes on her, she jumped up, pulling her coat from the back of her chair, and gathering her bags around her. 'I ... er ... we—'

'I knew it was you, couldn't be anyone else really, your look has always been so distinctive. You haven't changed a bit.' His eyes roved over her. 'Well, maybe filled out in all the right places.' The leering, lupine smile that hovered at his lips made Violet want to slap him.

She pulled on her jacket, hoping her friends would pick up on her non-verbal message that she needed to leave, and quickly.

'What was your nickname at uni? Ah, yes, "Vixen", that was it.' He rolled the word around his mouth, making it sound sordid.

'Jesus, what a creep,' said Molly sotto voce while Kitty flashed him a disapproving look.

'We were just going,' said Vi, all fingers and thumbs as she picked up her bags.

'Really? Well, I've just moved back into the area, so if you fancy meeting up ...'

'Like I said, we're leaving.' Vi headed for the door.

'Yes, we need to get cracking, I've got to get back for Abbie,' said Rosie.

Kitty scooped up her bag and hurried across to pay the bill, explaining to Pepe that they'd lost track of time and were having to rush back to the car so they didn't get a parking ticket.

Outside, Vi had raced off with Molly calling after her. Rosie waited outside the restaurant for Kitty, keeping one eye on where the other two were heading.

Kitty and Rosie finally caught up with them down by the river. Molly had her arm around Vi who was fighting back tears.

'Vi, whatever's the matter?' Kitty asked, breathless.

Vi shook her head, unable to form words in her arid mouth. Her stomach was churning, she felt sick and her legs had turned to jelly.

'You look like you need to sit down, chick,' said Molly. 'Come on.' She guided her friend towards a wooden bench, while Kitty ran and grabbed a coffee from a nearby kiosk.

'So, what was all that about?' asked Molly. Vi had taken a couple of sips of the hot drink and a little colour had found its way back into her cheeks. 'I've never seen you look so pale, or scared for that matter. Has the prat done something to hurt you?'

Vi curled her hands tighter around the thick paper cup, thoughts barging blindly around her mind. *Oh shit*. Her past had well and truly caught up with her now.

'You don't have to tell us if you don't want to, Vi, but we're here to help if you need us.' Kitty was sitting beside her and wrapped her arm around her, giving her a squeeze.

'I think she should tell us, Kitty,' said Molly. 'Then we can help her.'

The moment that had been torturing Vi for weeks had

*The Secret - Violet's Story*

finally arrived, but not in the way she'd imagined. She thought it would be Jimby she'd tell first, after having time to carefully select her words, then she'd share it with the girls. Instead it had been thrown upon her. She covered her face with her free hand. 'I do need to tell you, just not here. Can we go somewhere private?' She was surprised at the mixture of relief and fear that washed over her.

'How about heading back to mine?' asked Kitty. 'Noushka's out at her dance classes in Middleton and is staying over at a friend's for the night, and Ollie's taken the younger ones over to Whitby for the day. We'll have the house to ourselves for hours.'

'Okay.' Vi nodded.

## CHAPTER 17

Sitting at the kitchen table of Oak Tree Farm, surrounded by her best friends, Vi couldn't believe she was about to lift the lid of her secret, a secret she'd kept hidden well out of sight for so many years. It was surreal. She took a fortifying breath and glanced across at Kitty who was pouring tea into mugs and handing them round. 'Help yourself to biscuits,' she was saying. 'And ignore the pair of greedy guts over there.' She nodded in the direction of her black Labrador, Ethel and lemon cocker spaniel, Mabel, who were watching closely for any stray tasty morsels.

Vi felt like it was somebody else sitting at the table occupying her body, a somebody else who'd taken charge of revealing her secret.

'So, Vi, are you ready to tell us why that creep got you so upset?' Molly was always direct and to the point.

Vi flinched and stared into her mug, taking a moment to marshal her thoughts. She cleared her throat, her eyes still glued to her tea. 'His name's Mike Williamson, he was my lecturer at uni.' She let a few beats pass. 'And I had an affair with him.'

It was several long seconds before anyone spoke, Vi's words hanging heavy in the air, with nowhere for them to go.

'Right,' said Molly. Vi could almost hear her friend processing her words.

'But why were you so upset to see him?' asked Kitty. 'Did it end badly?'

'It would be against the university's rules for a lecturer to go out with a student, wouldn't it?' asked Molly.

'Yes, and yes.' Vi nodded.

'How come you didn't tell us, Vi? We've never had secrets,' said Kitty.

'That's what I thought,' said Molly.

Vi's conscience jumped like an exposed nerve in a tooth being prodded. She rubbed her hands vigorously over her face. 'I wanted to, really I did, but it wasn't that easy, and the situation ... it was ... complicated. Last I'd heard he'd gone to live in Spain; I never expected to see him again.'

Silence hung over the table. Vi knew that her friends didn't know how to handle this new dynamic to their friendship; they were treading carefully, not knowing the right words to say.

'I was just so worried that you'd judge me, that's all,' she said.

'We've never been like that, have we?' Molly looked across at Kitty.

'I didn't think so, but if Vi thought we would, then she had her reasons.'

Tears sprang to Vi's eyes on hearing the kindness in Kitty's voice. She quickly rubbed them away, exhaling noisily. 'Here goes,' she said. 'I had an affair with him for about six, seven months when I was in my final year – God knows how I managed to concentrate on my studies. It was pretty intense; he said we should move away together after I'd finished, live abroad. It was like I was living in a dream, he was so exciting and intelligent and sophisticated. At the time he was in his mid-thirties, and really good looking, all the girls fancied him, and I was totally smitten.' Vi shook her head in disbelief as she relived those months.

'So, how did it start?' asked Kitty.

'It was at the end of one of his lectures, he'd called me back.' Vi closed her eyes, the image of that day crystal clear in her mind...

∽

'Violet, can I have a quick word, please?' Mike waved her assignment at her as she walked by his desk, on her way out of the room, his lopsided smile making her heart skip a beat.

'Sure. Is there a problem with my essay?' She hoped not; she'd spent hours working on it, researching, polishing it until it was the best version it could possibly be. Vi was nothing if not meticulous about her work.

'Anything but, it's excellent, but there are a couple of points I'd like to discuss with you.' He held her gaze. 'Not here, not now, though.'

'Oh?' Was she really flirting with her lecturer? 'When, then?'

'Well, I'll be working here late tonight – got a lot to catch up on – so you could pop round about, say, seven-ish, if that's any good? Just keep it to yourself, though. We don't want the other students thinking you're getting preferential treatment.'

'Seven-ish it is. And I won't breath a word. Cross my heart.' She demonstrated just that, and gave him what she hoped was a confident smile before leaving the room. As she headed down the corridor, her mind was all of a flutter. Did that mean what she thought it meant, she wondered? Surely not. But despite herself, she found her mind hurriedly going through her wardrobe, planning what she'd wear to meet him later that evening. She wanted to look ... what was the word ... alluring? Appealing? Either would do.

*~*

VI STOOD outside the door to Mike Williamson's room, smoothing down the plum-coloured dress that clung to her curves, her vertiginous heels pushing out her round peach of a bottom, accentuating her wiggle as she walked. She took a deep breath; should she just walk in as she did for her lectures, or should she knock? She settled on giving a quick tap, before opening the door.

'Ah, Violet, come in.' Mike was sitting at his desk, a glass of claret in his hand. She was aware of his eyes roving over her appreciatively. 'Fancy one?'

'Mmm. Sounds good.' She clicked the door shut behind her, hoping she sounded sophisticated and not like some silly school kid.

Mike poured her a glass and handed it to her before walking to the door and turning the key in the lock. 'We don't want any interruptions, do we?' He gave her a wolfish smile that made her heart quiver with delight.

'Oh.' Vi didn't know what else to say. She couldn't actually believe she was sharing a bottle of wine with her lecturer, in his room at seven o'clock in the evening. Her heart was pounding, the element of risk exciting. She pushed away the warning voice telling her she was out of her depth.

'You do know what the male lecturers' nickname for you is, don't you?' He was standing very close to her now, looking at her intently; she could feel his breath on her cheek, almost like a caress.

'Didn't know I had one.' She took a sip of her wine, peering up at him over her glass, warmth from the claret spreading across her chest. She licked the rich berry flavours from her lips. It tasted potent.

He laughed. 'Oh, you most certainly do have one. It's "Vixen".'

'Vixen?' Vi felt herself blushing.

'Mmm,' he replied. His gaze settled on her lips, lingering for a moment. He turned and set his glass down on the table. 'Look, Violet, I don't think we need to beat about the bush, do you? We're both consenting adults, and instinct tells me we both want the same thing. How good are you at keeping secrets?' He ran a finger down her cheek, triggering a bolt of electricity right through her.

'I'm very good at keeping secrets,' she whispered.

In a moment his lips were upon hers, his tongue pushing its way into her mouth as his hands roved her body, pulling up her dress.

~

THAT NIGHT, as Vi lay in her single bed, she relived the events of earlier that evening, savouring the deliciously wicked thrill of it. What was that expression her friend, Stacey, used about him? Oh yes, "He looks like he knows his way around a bed". Vi smiled to herself. He certainly did, well, desk rather than bed. His desk! Oh, Lord, she'd never be able to look at in the same way again.

Less than a week later, Vi was walking into the city

centre with Stacey when they spotted Mike. He was browsing in a shop, accompanied by an attractive woman, with large dark eyes and thick, dark hair scooped up into a ponytail.

'Wouldn't you just know his wife would be gorgeous?' Stacey nodded in their direction.

'Wife? You think he's married?' Vi's heart dropped and worry prickled it's way over her skin.

'I know he is, he referred to her in one of his lessons.'

'Yes, but did he actually use the word "wife" when he mentioned her?' Vi shifted her rucksack on her shoulder.

'Yes, he actually said – whatever her name is, I can't remember, sounded foreign, Spanish, I think, then added, "my wife" before he carried on with what he was saying. Why?'

'No reason, just he doesn't seem the marrying type.' Vi felt sick to her stomach. Going out with a married man was a big no-no as far as she was concerned. She never, ever wanted to be tagged as the other woman, or do the dirty on another woman. Anger began to unfurl inside her, as the implications of what they'd done on his desk infiltrated her conscience.

The following day, in her lecture with him, Vi was unable to hide her icy feelings. It had been difficult, nigh on impossible, to concentrate on what he was saying, his words washing straight over her head as fury ate away at her. She refused to meet his gaze and, despite his attempts, avoided getting involved in any of the discussions.

She hung back at the end, packing her things away slowly, still refusing to look at him. The sooner she got this off her chest, the better; there was no way she was going to be used by him.

'I'm sensing there's something wrong?' Mike had checked that the coast was clear before he spoke.

'How observant,' Vi replied tightly.

'Care to enlighten me?'

'Absolutely. How about, you have a wife you forgot to tell me about?'

'Ah, that. I can explain.' He ran his fingers through his floppy fringe. 'You're referring to Isabella, my ex-wife – *almost* ex-wife. We're in the process of getting divorced.'

'Really? Well, you looked pretty friendly when I saw you both in Tangerine yesterday. You looked very relaxed together, not like a couple about to get divorced.'

'Look, I'm trying to keep things amicable. We just bumped into each other there, that's all. We were mates before we started dating, been married for about three years; it's not my style to suddenly freeze someone out. Especially someone I loved, once; still do – as a friend.'

Vi mulled over his words; she desperately wanted to believe him. 'So how come you're getting a divorce, then? You sound like you still have feelings for her.'

'I do – but like I said, as a friend. We want different things. She's half-Spanish and wants to go back to Spain to live, and I don't – it's where she grew up, her parents moved back there a year ago, her father's been in bad health for a while and she wants to be close to him.' Mike shrugged, giving her a heart-melting smile.

Vi stood in front of him, searching his face. Was he telling the truth? He was bloody convincing and she desperately wanted to believe him.

'Look, I'll take you to meet her, let her tell you yourself. She'd be absolutely fine about it, she's dating, too, someone new over in Spain.'

Vi recoiled. 'No thanks! That would just be way too

weird.' She thought for a moment and sighed. Did his words imply that he thought *they* were dating? She quite liked that idea. 'Look, I'm sorry for getting annoyed and jumping to conclusions, it's just ...' She stopped short of telling him that Stacey had been the one to tell her he had a wife; she didn't want to cause any trouble for a friend. 'Never mind, I'm sorry for jumping to conclusions.'

'That's okay, you can make it up to me tonight.' His eyes darkened and he gave her one of his wolfish smiles.

She shivered with anticipation. 'I can't wait.'

～

THE PAIR HAD CONTINUED their illicit affair over the next few months. They'd almost been caught one evening when the head of department had called in on Mike in his room before Vi was due to join him. Vi had burst in, shocked to see her.

'Ooh, sorry! I didn't expect to find anyone in here,' she'd said, thinking on her feet. 'I just wanted to drop my assignment off on my way out. Get that feeling of handing something in and being free of it, you know?' As she placed her assignment on Mike's desk, she could feel the weight of the other lecturer's steely glare running over her, taking in her going-out clothes.

'Thank you, Violet. It's not like you to be so last minute,' Mike had said. 'Don't make a habit of it.'

'I won't,' she'd replied. As she'd hurried through the door, she'd heard Mike say that she was a brilliant student, but had seemed distracted recently. 'Probably something to do with a boy,' he'd laughed.

'Hmm, I'd watch that one, if I were you; she may have

the hots for you,' the head of department had replied. It had sent a prickle of annoyance through Violet.

~

THE AFFAIR HAD BEEN RUNNING for five months when a positive pregnancy test found Vi facing one of the biggest dilemmas of her life. *Oh shit, shit, shit,* she thought, as panic seeped through her veins. *What the bloody hell am I going to do?* She'd been feeling unsettled for the last few weeks anyway, sensing that Mike was losing interest, and she was convinced he was paying more attention to Dee, an American student in their class. This was hardly going to help. The timing – a couple of weeks before her final exams were due to start – wasn't exactly great either.

She hung around after her morning lecture with Mike. He seemed to be avoiding making eye contact with her. 'Can we talk?' She cursed the shake in her voice. *Oh, God, how am I going to tell him when he won't even look at me?*

He looked at his watch. 'Erm, not really, I need to be somewhere in five minutes.' He flashed one of his well-practised charming smiles that Vi was surprised to find slightly irritating.

'How about tonight, can we meet here?'

'Sorry, sweetheart, I've got plans I'm afraid – duty calls, my sister wants to chat about our mother.'

'Sounds like you're making excuses.'

'Honestly, I'm not.' There was that smile again. He paused what he was doing and thought for a moment. 'Look, be here at ten to seven; we'll have to be quick, but you quite like it that way, don't you?'

She opened her mouth to speak, when Dee breezed in through the door, oozing an easy confidence, cutting off Vi's

*The Secret - Violet's Story*

words before they had chance to leave her mouth. 'Sorry, not interrupting anything, am I?' Dee looked from one to the other. 'Just needed to pick up my file; I forgot it.' She flashed a wide smile, and flicked her tousled long blonde hair. Vi felt her hackles stand on end.

'No, it's fine, Violet was just leaving,' said Mike. It didn't escape Vi's attention that his eyes had lit up the moment Dee walked in the room.

∼

'OH MY GOD, Vi, we had no idea.' Kitty looked at her friend in disbelief, a frown troubling her brow. She reached across and squeezed Vi's hand.

'Shit, Vi, you did a bloody good job of hiding this.' Molly looked stunned.

'Did you both really have no idea?' asked Rosie.

'No,' they both replied, shaking their heads.

'How come you didn't tell us, Vi? We could've helped you,' said Kitty.

Vi sucked in a noisy breath. 'Well, if you remember, I wasn't coming home much at the time. And, anyway, you were under Dan's spell by then, and had stopped socialising with us.'

'Sorry, Vi.' Kitty hung her head as her face flushed scarlet.

'No, no, I didn't say it to make you feel bad, you've got absolutely nothing to apologise for.' It was Vi's turn to squeeze Kitty's hand. 'We didn't realise how bad things were for you at the time.'

'I don't have an excuse, though,' added Molly.

'Moll, you had your hands full dealing with married life and a set of boisterous twins; I think you had the perfect excuse. Anyway, I wasn't trying to make either of you feel guilty, I was just trying to explain part of the reason why I kept it to myself. I honestly had no idea how to start the conversation with anyone, never mind either of you.'

'So did you tell him – Mike – did you tell him that you were pregnant?' asked Rosie.

Vi nodded.

'What happened to the baby, Vi?' asked Kitty.

Vi's gaze fell to her fingers that were knotted in her lap.

## CHAPTER 18

SIXTEEN YEARS EARLIER

Vi's heart was pounding in her chest as she made her way along the corridor to Mike's room. All day, she'd been running through her mind how she'd tell him, wondering how he'd react. If she was honest with herself, she was still in shock, her brain still felt scrambled, and she hadn't managed to think much beyond giving him the news.

Standing outside his door, she took in a lungful of air, releasing it slowly. Before she had chance to change her mind, she gave a quick knock and walked in, locking the door behind her. Mike was leaning against his desk, looking out of the window, the usual glass of claret in his hand, a second – empty – glass next to a pile of papers, waiting for whom, Vi wondered? Hearing her come in, he flicked the blinds to closed, then turned and smiled.

'Hello there,' he said.

Was it just her imagination, or was his smile not quite as dazzling as it had been?

'Hi.' Her voice sounded strange in her head, detached almost.

'You don't exactly look full of the joys. I like girls who smile, not girls who look miserable.'

'I've got a lot on my mind.' Vi felt anger creep up inside her. *Arrogant sod*.

Mike appeared to ignore her words. Glancing at his watch, he took a slug of wine. 'Look, we don't have long, so why don't you come over here, let me put that smile back on your face?'

'Not tonight, Mike. I've ... I've got something I need to tell you.'

'Oh, and what would that be? I hope it's not a serious as it sounds. Serious things, at this time of day are dull, dull, dull.'

'I'm pregnant.'

'Pregnant?' Mike's smile dropped, a cold expression creeping into his eyes.

Vi nodded.

'Well, that explains why you've fattened up a bit.'

His words stung like a slap.

'Surely you're not trying to tell me it's mine?'

'You know it couldn't be anyone else's,' she cried.

'Shh! Stupid girl! Do you want everyone to hear?'

'Mike, you're the only one who could be the father.' Tears began to burn at the back of her Violet's eyes and she fought her hardest to hold them back.

'You foolish little cow. I thought you were on the pill. You've done this on purpose, haven't you? You're trying to trap me.'

'On purpose? To trap you?' *Surely he didn't mean it.* 'Of course I haven't. I was, am, on the pill, and if you think I want to be pregnant, you're greatly mistaken. I've never wanted to have children.'

'Well, that makes two of us.' He paused for a moment, his mouth setting in a hard line. A loaded tension hung in the air between them. 'So what are you going to do about it?'

'I haven't really had time to think.'

'You need to get rid of it. As quickly as possible.'

Vi couldn't believe the transformation in him. The laid-back, easy-going man who'd stolen her heart with ease bore no resemblance to the cold-eyed monster who stood before her now. She looked at him, wondering how she'd ever been so stupid as to fall for his cheesy lines. 'Is that all you've got to say, "get rid of it"?'

'What did you expect? Don't tell me you were planning on keeping it? Hoping we could play happy families.' He gave an unattractive snort.

'I've told you, I haven't had time to think. I thought it was only fair to let you know first.'

'How considerate,' he sneered. 'Just get rid of it. And not a word to anyone.' He knocked back his wine, wiping his mouth with the back of his hand, then glanced at his watch again. 'Look, you're going to have to leave, I'm running late. Let me know when it's done.' With that he steered her towards the door, his hand in the small of her back.

Out in the corridor, Vi blinked back tears. She'd never felt so alone. The urge to speak to Kitty and Molly was overwhelming; she needed to go back home this weekend, needed to be with people who cared about her. Out of the blue, an image of Jimby loomed in her mind, the thought of his strong arms around her shoulders.

On her way out of the building, she passed Dee, dressed in a pair of minuscule denim shorts, red sneakers and a flimsy blouse, tied at the waist, its buttons open as low as the knot, shouting to the world that she wasn't wearing a bra.

'Hiya, Violet.' She tucked her gum into the side of her mouth and gave a megawatt smile as she tossed her golden mane of beach-ready hair.

'Hi,' Vi replied. She knew exactly why Dee had that smile on her face – it wasn't that long since she'd worn one just like it herself. Vi didn't hang around. With anguish ripping through her, she ran to her room, burst through the door and threw herself down on her bed where she sobbed herself dry. Her relationship with Mike – she wasn't going to call in an affair – was over.

∽

SATURDAY MORNING FOUND Vi throwing things into a holdall, ready to head back to Lytell Stangdale for the weekend. She needed to get away for a few days, clear her head. Her packing was interrupted by an assertive knock at her door, pulling her out of her thoughts. Mike, she wondered? Her first instinct was to ignore it.

Another, harder knock was followed by a woman's voice with a hint of an accent she didn't recognise. 'Violet Smith, I know you're in there and I need to talk to you. It's important.'

Vi's heart froze as panic kicked in. There was an urgency in the voice, was there a problem with her parents? God, she hoped not. She opened the door to see an olive-skinned woman standing in the hallway. Vi took in the tattooed eyebrows and artfully tied headscarf. She looked vaguely familiar, and Vi was conscious of her mind trawling for a memory to match to the face; it jostled with the reason for the headwear: cancer? The two women stared at each other for several moments, the stranger breathing heavily, her eyes full of anger.

The stranger was the first to speak. 'I think you'd prefer to hear what I have to say in there, rather than out here where everyone else can hear it.'

'Why? Who are you?'

'I'm Isabella, Isabella Williamson. *Mrs* Isabella Williamson, wife of Mike Williamson. Ring any bells?'

A beat passed. 'Oh.' Vi felt her knees turn to jelly as her stomach churned wildly. That would explain the slight Spanish accent.

'As I've already said, I think you'd prefer it if I came in, rather than letting the rest of the corridor hear what I have to say to you. It's your call, I really don't care.'

Violet opened the door wider and Isabella stepped inn, her hands balled tightly into fists.

'You've been having an affair with my husband.' Vi could hear the wobble in Isabella's voice. 'Don't insult me by denying it, I know you have.'

'I'm not ... I mean, I won't ... I didn't think he was ... he said you were getting a divorce.'

'Ha! And you expect me to believe that?'

'Yes!' said Vi. 'I thought he was single, until a friend told me he had a wife ... we saw you together in a shop ... I confronted him about it and he told me you were getting a divorce, he said it was because you wanted to move to Spain and he didn't ... he said your divorce was amicable and that he was even cool about you seeing someone else. Honestly, I'm telling you the truth.' The hurt in Isabella's eyes was almost too much for Vi to bear.

'Is that what he told you?' she whispered, a tear tracing its way down her cheek.

'Yes.' Vi nodded. 'I'm so sorry, if I'd known he was married, I'd have run a mile. Please don't cry.' She reached out and touched the other woman's shoulder.

'Don't pity me!' Isabella shrugged Vi's hand off and snatched the tear away. 'It's not the first time he's done it and it won't be the last. But he always comes back to me. And don't dare feel sorry for me because of this.' She pointed to the scarf. 'I may have breast cancer, but it doesn't mean that I can't fight for my marriage.

'I ... I ... I just feel ... I had no idea.' Tears began dripping down Vi's cheeks, falling of her chin; she had no idea how to answer the woman.

'He tells me it's over,' said Isabella. 'That he finished it.'

Vi nodded. 'Yes.'

'It had better be.' With that, Isabella turned on her heel and left, her words swirling around Violet's head.

*But he's replaced me with somebody else.*

∼

'Shit a brick,' said Molly.

'Oh, Vi, that sounds awful; for you and for her.' Kitty hurried over to Vi and threw her arms around her friend.

Vi sniffed and wiped her tears away. 'It was pretty crap, you're right.'

'Shall I put the kettle on for more tea, Kitty?' asked Rosie.

'Good plan,' she replied. She turned back to Vi. 'Is that why you went travelling on your own?'

Vi nodded.

'So what happened to the baby?' asked Molly.

This was the part she'd been dreading the most, fearful that it would make them hate her. Vi rubbed her temples and looked up at her friends. Three faces, etched with concern for her, blinked back.

## The Secret - Violet's Story

∽

THAT SATURDAY, Violet had gone home to Lytell Stangdale to find Kitty reluctant to meet up; she was still too consumed with Dan. As for Molly, she was too loved-up with Pip – the pair of them blissfully happy with their twin boys and Molly trying to fit a part-time nursing course into what little time she had spare.

As far as Vi could see, the dynamics in the village had changed, and there was no longer a space for her to slot back into. Admittedly, she hadn't been back much over the last six months, but there'd seemed little point, no one had any time for her, everyone had moved on and were busy living their own lives in this quiet little backwater where life moved at a slow pace. And, in truth, she'd been distracted by her own things in York.

Feeling the walls closing in on her at home, and sensing the warning signals that it wouldn't take much for her to fly off the handle at her mum's incessant fussing, Vi had taken herself off for a walk into the village. Jimby had called over to her as she walked along the trod by the pond on the green; he was heading out of the forge where he was working as a blacksmith with his dad. She stopped and he crossed the road to speak to her, his habitual broad smile lighting up his face, his dimples adding a cheeky air. 'Now then, Violet, haven't seen you for a while. Still looking as gorgeous as ever, I see.' His rich brown eyes twinkled, triggering a feeling of warmth deep inside her; a connection that went back her whole life.

Before she knew it, he'd pulled her into a hug, squeezing her tight, just as he'd done many times before. *Oh, that feeling!* She'd never had it with anyone else. It made her feel safe and protected, like in his arms was where she was meant to be. She gasped as she felt herself melt into him, unable to speak until he released her.

'Hi, Jimby. Well, I don't know about that, but I thought it was time I sneaked in a quick visit to my parents. It's my final year so it's been a bit full-on and I've hardly had any free time.' She knew it sounded like a pathetic excuse.

'Yep, well, as I'm sure you've already found out, nothing much changes round here, except we don't see much of our Kitty – even less than we do of you, come to think of it. But that's another story.' His face clouded over, taking his smile with it.

'Oh.' Vi didn't know how to answer that.

'Look, if you've got time, why don't you pop in at Oak Tree Farm? My mum and dad would be chuffed to bits to see you.'

'Oh ... I, er, I might do that, if I've got time. I'm not here for long, got to get back to my studying...'

'Fair enough, but no excuses next time; come back for longer so we can catch up properly.' He grinned down at her. 'But, I'm afraid I'm going to have to dash, my dad's gagging for a cuppa and if I don't get back with a pint of milk there'll be hell to pay.'

Vi laughed. 'You'd better get moving then.'

'Aye, I had. Been good to see you, Vi.' He squeezed her arm.

'You, too, Jimby.' Tears threatened and she swallowed down a thick lump of sadness. Before he had chance to notice, she turned quickly and headed home, conscious of the weight of Jimby's gaze upon her. What she'd give to feel his big, strong arms around her again. Jimby always made everything feel alright.

Back at Rowan Slack Farm, she found herself even more irritated by everything her parents did. Her mum's old-fashioned comments that Vi used to find sweet, her fussing about how much weight Vi had lost (*yeah, right*), and how "peaky" she was looking, were driving her mad. And don't get her started on how loud her dad was when he ate his meal, and that plate scraping, making sure he didn't miss a tiny morsel – ughh! Instead of feeling happy and safe at being back home, she felt stifled. Her stress levels seemed to amplify with all of the daily noise at the farm, making it impossible to have any headspace to think about what to do with this thing that was growing inside her.

One thing had stood out to her since bumping into Jimby, her time with Mike had seriously knocked her self-esteem. She thought back to his little jibes about her curves, his references to her being plump. They'd been slowly chipping away at her confidence, making her feel self-conscious, but seeing Jimby today, and him saying she was gorgeous, made her realise how stupid she'd been at wanting to continue in their pathetic excuse of a relationship. What had happened to the young woman who'd always embraced her curves? Vi wanted her back in place of this woman who'd become reluctant to look in the mirror.

Her head was all over the place and before she knew it, the urge to leave found her packing her bag and heading back to York a day early.

∽

ONCE IN THE quiet of her student accommodation, Vi weighed up her options. One thing was glaringly obvious to her, she didn't want to be a mother. Never had, never would. She didn't have a maternal bone in her body and having children had never been part of her future as a dynamic, ball-breaking businesswoman. Having a child would also irrevocably link her to Mike Williamson for the rest of her life, and that was out of the question. Yet, perversely, she couldn't imagine having this baby and handing it over to someone else. The mere thought of it tore at her heart. Much as she hated herself, she knew that there was only one option left open to her. First thing Monday morning she'd ring the doctors and make an appointment. Violet didn't want to think too deeply about the implications; the sooner she got it over with, the sooner she could concentrate on her final exams.

VI HAD BEEN GIVEN a hospital appointment a week and half hence. Still trying not to dwell on what she was about to do, she'd woken up two days before her appointment, feeling off-colour, a nagging ache low in her abdomen, it reminded her of period pain. As the morning progressed, the pain had intensified sufficiently for her to skip lectures and head back to her room for a lie down. As she was preparing a hot-water bottle, the pain became more stabbing, making her bend in two. She rushed to the small bathroom where bright, angry spots of blood in her knickers glared back at her accusingly.

Relief merged with sadness as Vi realised that the final decision, the final act, had been taken out of her hands. Her difficult situation had resolved itself, but somehow, it didn't make her feel any better.

There was no way she could face going back to Lytell Stangdale; she'd worry her secret would be plain for all to see. Instead, she decided to go travelling, like she'd planned to do with Molly and Kitty. Stacey had mentioned something about going to work for her aunt and uncle at their hotel in Sorrento. She said that Vi would be welcome to tag along, too; there was always plenty of work over the summer. The idea had suddenly become very appealing to Violet. It would give her the opportunity to put some space between herself and her home while her body and her mind recovered from the last six months. She needed to move on from the person she'd become. She needed to heal.

# CHAPTER 19

PRESENT DAY

'Oh, Vi,' Kitty whispered. 'You went through all that alone?'

Vi nodded and swiped her tears away. 'I didn't know what else to do, my mind was all over the place.'

'Hormones won't have helped that,' said Molly. 'But you should've come to me, Vi. I would've had time to listen to you, to support you.'

Kitty remained quiet, at the time, she would've struggled to talk to anyone other than Dan or his parents.

'Jimby's going to hate me for it, and for keeping it secret for so long.'

'He won't hate you at all, Vi,' said Kitty. She pulled another tissue from the box on the table and handed it to her friend.

'Thanks. I think he will, and I wouldn't blame him.' Vi blew her nose.

'You know Jimby as well as we all do, and I bet there isn't anyone here who thinks he could hate you for this,' said Molly.

'Even I can see how much Jimby loves you, and I haven't known him as long as all of you,' said Rosie.

'There, you see, Rosie agrees,' said Molly. 'Jimby doesn't have a bad bone in his body. True, he might find it hard to understand why you've waited so long to tell him, but he definitely won't hate you.'

'You're going to have to tell him, Vi, and the sooner the better. He's going to wonder what's the matter with you when you get back home today. He'll be expecting you to be all happy and excited and you look about as far removed from that as I can imagine.'

'Kitty's right, and the sooner you share it with him, the sooner you'll feel better. It must've felt awful bottling that up inside you all these years without sharing it with anyone.' Rosie's words made Vi wince.

'Can I ask, how come a university lecturer had wine in his room?' Kitty looked puzzled. 'Do they all have it, do you think?'

'He always kept a bottle and a couple of glasses in a locked part of his desk for when he was "working late". And he was the only lecturer I knew who did that.'

'It was probably all part of his schmoozing process.' Molly pushed herself up and took the teapot over to the Aga. 'The effing creep.'

'Very probably,' Vi agreed.

'Right, Vi, one more cup of tea, then I think you should get yourself back home to that lovely man of yours and tell him just what you've told us,' said Molly as she filled the kettle.

'Okay.' Violet swallowed the lump of nerves that had gathered in her throat. She'd absorbed their words; everything they'd said about Jimby being wonderful and kind was true, but there was just one tiny detail she'd held back. A detail that could be a deal-breaker for Jimby, and that terrified her.

**CHAPTER 20**

Vi paused at the gate of Sunshine Cottage, anxiety clawing its way up inside her, her heart thudding like the clappers in her chest, her pulse thrumming in her ears. She walked down the path like some kind of automaton, the moment looming ever closer. Before she knew it, the door flew open to reveal Jimby, beaming and wearing her purple and lilac gingham pinny. The aroma of food wafted out into the garden, curling round her nose. It made her stomach churn.

'Now then, gorgeous. I spotted you getting out of Molly's car with all those bags. I'm secretly hoping there's some naughty underwear in there.' He waggled his eyebrows at her as he took the bags of shopping from her. 'Have you had a good day with the lasses? I bet none of you came up for air with all that chatting you do once you get together.'

Vi did her best to muster a smile as she followed him into the house. 'Yes, thanks. How about you?'

'My day's been great. Wait till you hear the news about our plans.' He made his way into the kitchen, depositing Vi's bags in the hall en-route. 'Tea?'

'Please.' She nodded, peeling off her jacket and hanging it on the back of a dining chair.

'Right, well, Robbie called round not long after you'd gone out. Said he'd had a word – "off the record" – with a mate of his who works in the planning department and ran our ideas past him. He didn't want to do anything dodgy, just get an idea of what's likely to get passed and what's likely to be rejected. And the good news is that he loved our plans – apparently it's exactly the sort of thing they're looking for with new builds on the moors, so Robbie's going to submit them on Monday; he just wants us to have a last check over them before he does.' Jimby beamed at her, his eyes dancing with happiness.

'Well, that is good news.' Vi dug deep to find a smile, hoping the one she returned was bright enough.

'It's great news,' he said. 'It means that our plans are likely to sail through without any problems.'

'So now we just need to find a builder who can get cracking as soon as possible.' She really hoped her voice didn't sound as flat to Jimby as it did to her.

'And that's where the news goes from being great to being bloody fantastic. Robbie has a friend who has a traditional timber-framed building company and he's just had a cancellation – apparently the clients have split-up and don't want to go ahead with the project. Anyway, the slot that's free is the week after the decision for our plans is due, which means he'd be ready to go with ours pretty much straight away.' Jimby pulled her into a hug and planted a noisy kiss on her cheek. 'It's as if it was meant to be, isn't it?'

Vi nodded as a loud sob escaped her lips.

'Vi, sweetheart, what's wrong? I thought you'd be pleased.' Jimby's smile was whipped away, replaced with concern and confusion. 'Don't cry, angel.' He wiped her tears away with his thumbs. 'If it all feels like things are going too fast, like I said before, we can put the brakes on. I know there's a lot to think about, and you've got the wedding to plan and your dress to make but—'

'Jimby, I need to tell you something. Can we sit down?' The knot of anxiety twisted tighter in her stomach.

'Are you ill, is it serious? Is it your parents? What can I do to help?'

Vi shook her head. 'No, it's nothing like that.' She could feel him looking at her, desperately trying to work out what to do or what to say. She sat down in the chair he'd pulled out for her, waiting as he sat in the one opposite.

'Before you go any further, can I just ask, are we okay?'

'I hope so, Jimby, I really do.'

∽

JIMBY SAT in silence as Violet relayed her story, his head bowed, eyes fixed intently on the table.

'That's not all,' Vi said. She took a minute before she delivered the words she most dreaded. 'After the miscarriage, I developed an infection and had to have a procedure – I won't go into details, but I was in hospital for a couple of days. I didn't tell anyone, I didn't want anyone to know, especially not my parents. The thing is, Jimby, the complications caused scar tissue that mean … that mean I might not be able to have children.'

Violet's revelation had thrown an icy cold bowl of water over Jimby's enthusiasm, and only when she'd finished sharing it could she look up at him to see his face crumpled. Her heart twisted as she saw tears trickling down his cheeks. She sniffed and wiped her own tears away. 'I'm so sorry, Jimby.'

He lifted his gaze and wiped his eyes with the backs of his hands. 'You were alone, Vi. You went through that alone. But what I don't understand is why, after all these years, you've never told me? Or why you've never shared it with Kitty and Molly. I thought you lot told each other everything. I'm not a monster, Vi. I love you, I would've listened, I would've understood.'

'I know, and I'm sorry. I've been stupid. I kept trying to tell you but the words just wouldn't come out. And the longer I left it, the harder it became. I just didn't want you to stop loving me.'

'I'm sad to hear you thought that.'

They sat in silence for a moment, uncertainty hanging between them. After what seemed to Violet like an age, Jimby pushed back his chair, the resultant scrape making her wince. 'I need to get my head around this. Need time to think,' he said. He gathered up his phone and his keys, then whistled for Jarvis and Jerry who bounded through the open kitchen door after him.

Vi sat alone, her heart heavy and feeling as if every last ounce of energy had been sapped out of her. The white noise in the kitchen was suddenly deafening. She'd never seen Jimby look so upset before and it made her heart ache for him. He was such a good man and she'd hurt him. 'What a mess I've made of things,' she said under her breath. The bags in the hallway caught her eye. There was no way she could face going through her shopping; the excitement of what she'd bought had faded. Instead, she heaved herself up from her seat and dragged herself upstairs to the bedroom. The anxiety of the last few weeks, topped off with what had happened that day was emotionally draining. She wanted to sleep the rest of the day away.

~

VI WOKE with a crick in her neck. She squinted at the alarm clock on the bedside table; it told her she'd been asleep for the best part of three hours. Flopping back on the pillow, she groaned as memories of her conversation with Jimby poured into her head, reminding her why there was such a feeling of doom in the pit of her stomach and her eyes felt so puffy. She lay quiet for a moment, trying to hear if there were any sounds from downstairs to indicate that he'd returned, but the only sounds were from outside, a dog barking out on the moor, Hugh Heifer calling a hello to Lycra Len as Daisy gave a low bellow, a tractor trundling along the road, and the birds twittering in the tree by the bedroom window. Village life was continuing as it usually did on a sunny Saturday afternoon. Except, it wasn't at Sunshine Cottage.

Pulling herself out of bed, Vi slipped on her dressing gown and padded downstairs, hating the feeling of emptiness Jimby had left behind. In the kitchen she reached inside her handbag and rummaged around for her mobile phone, hoping he'd been in touch, but the only messages were from her three friends, all wishing her well and asking how her conversation with Jimby had gone. With a heavy sigh, she threw the phone down onto the table; she didn't have the heart to reply to them just yet.

~

BY NINE O'CLOCK THAT EVENING, Vi had accepted that Jimby wasn't going to spend the night at her house. They'd never had a night apart since she'd moved back to the village full-time – other than Ollie's stag night in York – and the house felt empty without him. Had he gone to Kitty and Ollie's, or Molly and Camm's she wondered? A nagging ache in Vi's gut told her what had made him most upset; that if he stayed with her, he might not get the chance to be a dad. She should really share it with Kitty and Molly, in case he turned up on the doorstep. 'Oh, shit. What a mess,' she said to herself as she picked up her phone.

Ten minutes later, she was still struggling to find the words. 'Bloody hell, how difficult can it be?' She flung the phone down on the sofa and took a deep breath, releasing it slowly. 'Right, just stop farting about and tell them straight,' she told herself. It seemed to do the trick; she snatched up her phone, tapped out a brief message, and with her heart pounding, she pressed send.

Within minutes, replies from both women pinged on Vi's phone causing nausea to swirl around her stomach. Her emotions surged from mild relief straight back to anxiety as she read their messages. Neither of them had seen nor heard from him, but both assured her that Jimby loved her too much to end their relationship.

Violet wasn't so sure.

With frustration and sadness torturing her, she decided to cut the day short and go to bed. But that didn't make her feel any better. Instead the vast empty space beside her, where Jimby usually lay, just emphasised her problem. Feeling tears prickle her eyes, Vi reached for his pillow and hugged it tight, the scent of Jimby, soothing her; the scent of home. It triggered an image of his smiling face, his cheeky dimples and his twinkly eyes. Before she knew it, tears were once more pouring down her cheeks.

Sorrow soon turned to anger, as she tried to justify keeping her secret to herself. What right had Jimby to walk out on her for something like this? She hadn't committed a crime. She'd been manipulated by a lecherous older man – and, yes, she'd been flattered, been stupid, but she hadn't been dating Jimby at the time, so how dare he judge her like this? She snatched her tears away and set her mouth in a firm line. She wasn't going to cry any more tears over a man. And this was exactly the reason she'd never wanted to get close to one. She'd had a brief romance with an accountant when she was living in York, but when he'd suggested moving in together, she'd run a mile. He'd already started to pass little comments, judging her, criticising her work ethic, hinting that she should stop burlesque dancing. The annoying little niggles had started to add up, setting alarm bells ringing. Vi knew that moving in with him would only lead to her resenting him. She'd been happy living on her own, didn't need the drama of living with someone, then having to ask them to leave, so before he'd had time to argue, she ended the relationship. As the memories and feelings of frustration flooded back, Violet sensed the low grind of her barriers rising.

*Ah, but you know Jimby better than that, and you know, deep down, he's not judging you, not wanting to control you. He loves you for you*, the voice of reason piped up. *And you know exactly why he's upset.*

The barriers came to a halt, slowly sliding back down; she wasn't ready to shut Jimby out. Not unless that was what he wanted.

**CHAPTER 21**

Vi reached for the alarm clock. 'Nearly half past ten,' she said to herself. Jimby would probably still be awake, too. No matter how hard she'd tried, sleep was still out of reach. Her mind had been too busy, turning things over, always coming back to the same place; a place where she and Jimby were together. She couldn't imagine her life without him in it; didn't want to. She closed her eyes and his handsome face, smiling, appeared. It triggered an overwhelming surge of love for him that tingled in every fibre of her body; there was no way she was going to give up on their relationship without a bloody good fight.

She hadn't turned her back on her life in York with a successful career and exciting social life, for nothing. After years of being so driven and focused, it had taken something powerful to make her move back home to Lytell Stangdale. And that something was Jimby. Vi could remember the very day it had dawned on her; seeing him in the street, the usual broad smile on his face, his shoulders strong and broad. Yes, they'd always enjoyed a bit of gentle flirting; they'd even shared the odd snog when they were younger. But this new feeling had tugged at something deep inside her, catching her unawares. As did the sudden yearning to become a mother, after being so dead set against it. *That was a complete bolt out of the blue,* she thought.

Before she'd had chance to think about it, Vi had pulled her dressing gown on and slipped downstairs.

In the kitchen, she found her mobile phone and called Jimby's number. She couldn't leave things any longer; she wanted to speak to him, to put things right between them. 'Bugger!' His mobile went straight to answerphone. She scrolled through her contacts for his landline. It was picked up after a couple of rings.

'Hello.'

Vi's heart started at the sound of his voice; warm and familiar. She took a fortifying breath. 'Jimby, it's me, Vi.' She could hear her heart thudding in the long pause that followed.

'Oh, right. Violet.' The warm tone had been replaced by one that was stony and cold.

Undeterred, she continued. 'Jimby, can we talk? I really want to get this sorted out so we can move on and put it behind us.'

Silence hung in the air.

'Jimby?'

He sighed. 'Look, Vi, my mind's all over the place at the moment. I need some time to think.'

'What's there to think about? What happened was a long time ago; I'm a different person now.'

'Maybe, but it still doesn't alter the fact that you lied to me.'

'I did not lie to you, Jimby! I've never lied to you.'

'As good as; you lied by omission.' There was that cold voice again. 'What about everything else that you've told me

– or haven't told me, for that matter? What else is going to come crawling out of the woodwork?'

'That is so unfair.' Sadness leached away as anger began to boil in her stomach. 'That's the only thing I've kept to myself. You know that and you know why. I've never had you down as a judgemental tosser, Jimby, but clearly I was wrong.' She cut the call before he had chance to throw any more hurtful words at her.

Staring out into the shadows of the garden, Vi could feel her relationship with Jimby slip further out of reach and it broke her heart.

**CHAPTER 22**

Vi had lain awake through the early hours of Monday morning, listening to the rain lashing relentlessly against the windows. The wind had gathered strength, and she was thankful that her refurbishment of the cottage – including triple-glazed windows – had put paid to any draughts that used to sneak in and shoo the warmth away. But it didn't stop her from wishing Jimby was in her bed to snuggle up to; she hated the wind, found it unsettling, always had.

Vi hadn't heard from him since their ill-fated phone call on Saturday night and it was tearing her apart. She'd toyed with the idea of going round to Forge Cottage, but the fact that he was acting out of character held her back; she was fearful he would turn her away. She wouldn't be able to bear it if he did that.

She made her way down the path to the Romantique studio, glad that the wind and rain had moved on, wondering how she was going to rustle-up any enthusiasm to work on the wedding dress for Becky Ventress who was marrying local vet, Chris Crabtree.

It wasn't long before Kitty came bustling in, bringing

with her the fresh scent of early summer and a paper bag of their favourite chocolate-dipped flapjacks. She wrapped her free arm around Vi and kissed her cheek. 'It'll all work itself out, chick, I promise.'

As Kitty headed to the kitchen area, Vi struggled to fight back her tears. 'I don't know if it will, Kitty, I've never seen Jimby look so hurt, and he's said some horrible things.'

'It was just a lot for him to take on board, that's all. He'll be fine once he gets his head around it. Anyway, you know what men are like, they enjoy a bit of a self-indulgent brood every now and then.'

'I hope you're right. I just wish I'd told him when things first started to get serious between us, it wouldn't have been so bad then. I think I just got so used to keeping it at the back of my mind, that's where it stayed.'

Kitty nodded. 'I totally get it, Vi, and I know he's my big brother, so I'm biased, but he's a good bloke. He's not being hard-hearted or cruel; I think because he's so uncomplicated himself, he'll be struggling to understand why you never told anyone, that's all. The phrase "what you see is what you get" could've been coined for our Jimby, and I think he tends to assume everyone's that way but, for their own reasons, not everyone can be. Honestly, everything'll be okay, I can feel it in my bones. And, you know, it's things like this that can actually make relationships stronger. Look at Ollie and me.' She set a tray with tea and flapjack on the small table and motioned for Vi to join her. 'Anyway, get yourself over here and get your chops around a piece of this. Lucy's flapjacks are famous for fixing everything.'

'Well, let's hope they can work miracles,' said Vi. She pushed herself up from her seat and joined Kitty. 'I know I sound like a right miserable moo, but can you take over Becky Ventress's wedding dress for me? I haven't got the heart to do it today and she's coming in for a fitting tomorrow. I think if I sewed another stitch on it, I'll risk sewing my misery into it.'

Kitty's eyebrows shot up. 'Oh, heavens, we don't want that!'

'Exactly,' said Vi.

~

Wednesday arrived and Vi still hadn't heard from Jimby, nor clapped eyes on him. *He's doing a good job of keeping out of my way, he must really hate me.* The ache in her heart was growing, and sadness sat like a lump of lead in her stomach. She felt utterly deflated; what if he couldn't bring himself to speak to her ever again? Several times, she'd tentatively picked up her phone, pushing their last conversation out of her mind, her fingers itching to text him, but her all the words she wanted to say upped and ran away, taking her courage with them. *Oh, Lord, how I wish I could turn the clock back.*

She was sipping tea, still in her silk pyjamas, gazing out of the kitchen window, watching a couple of pheasants strut in and out of the borders, when the ping of a text message landing on her phone made her heart leap. *Please let it be Jimby.* She quickly set down her mug on the worktop and picked up her phone, hardly daring to look at the screen. In an instant, disappointment washed over her, making her spirits sink; it was Molly, sending a group text, inviting her, Kitty and Rosie up to Withrin Hill farm for a cup of tea after they'd finished work. With a sigh, Violet flopped into a chair. Though her mood was low, she couldn't help but think how lucky she was to have such a wonderful group of friends who genuinely cared about her. And, yes, the text may not have been from who she'd hoped, but now she came to think about it, the idea of a chat with the girls was appealing; she'd had enough of stewing on her own, and Molly's house with little Emmie and Ben and Kristy was always a lively place, full of laughter and chatter – a place that could take your mind off your worries. She dashed off a quick reply, saying she'd be there.

As she sat alone with her thoughts, a feeling of guilt flashed through her; she hadn't seen her parents for a week. If she was honest with herself, she'd been avoiding them. They'd know something was the matter straight away – especially her mum – and she just couldn't bring herself to tell them what she'd shared with Jimby, what had made him walk away from her. The thought of their disappointment in her didn't bear thinking about.

∽

LATER AT THE ROMANTIQUE STUDIO, Vi had kept her mind focused on her work and was relieved to find that the day passed quickly, even though it was Kitty's day off and she was alone. She'd made sure she kept her eyes away from Beckie Ventress's wedding dress on the tailor's dummy in the corner. She didn't want to think about weddings, especially when it was highly likely her own would be called off.

At four o'clock, she decided to call it a day. Though her heart hadn't been in it, she'd managed to come up with a few designs for a new underwear range, which was more than she'd hoped for the way her inspiration was on a go-slow.

She'd almost finished tidying away when she was pleased to hear the beep of Kitty's car outside, waiting to whisk her and Rosie up to Molly's. She hurried down the path, her heels clickety-clacking as she went. Her heart lifted a little when she saw the smiles on the faces of the two women.

'Hiya, Vi. Jump aboard,' said Kitty.

'Hi, Vi. Have you had a good day?' asked Rosie.

'Hi, ladies. I've had worse. How about you? Where are the kids?'

'Noushka was meeting up with friends in York after her lecture at uni, and Lucas and Lily are with Ollie,' said Kitty.

'And Ollie, very kindly, said that Abbie could go and play at theirs. Last I saw they were having great fun in the tree house,' said Rosie.

'Ah, he's a good man is Ollie,' replied Vi.

Five minutes later, Kitty's four-wheel drive nosed its way into the neat yard of Withrin Hill Farm, scattering a handful of hens that were pecking about in the gaps between the old flagstones. They squawked in annoyance which piqued resident cockerel Bernard's interest and he strutted over to investigate what had cause the disharmony amongst his ladies, glaring at the vehicle with his beady eyes.

As the women climbed out, the door to the farmhouse flew open and black Labrador, Phoebe, shot out. She charged over to them, her tail wagging so hard it made her whole body wiggle.

'Kettle's on, lasses.' Molly's voice boomed around the yard.

'Hi, Molly. Hello, Phoebes. It's good to see you, too.' Kitty laughed. 'Are you going to take us to your mum?'

'Sounds good, Moll,' said Vi. She gave her a watery smile.

Emmie peered round her mum's legs and shouted, 'Hi dere!' Her chocolate brown curls were a fuzzy mass framing her pretty face.

'Hi there, Emmie.' Rosie waved at her.

'Look at dis!' Emmie held up a toy tractor for them to see.

'Oh, that's smart, Em,' said Kitty.

'Wow! I wish I had a tractor like that,' said Vi. The comments seemed to please Emmie, who ran off into the house, smiling and chattering away to herself.

The three women followed Molly down the hall into the light, airy kitchen, the warmth of the early summer sun filling the room and highlighting the ochre yellow walls. The kettle was whistling away on the Aga hotplate and Molly dashed over to scoop it off. 'Bloody awful noise, that,' she said.

The friends made small talk while Molly made the tea and set biscuits out on a plate and directed them to sit at the table.

Vi released a noisy sigh, there was no time like the present to broach the elephant in the room. 'So, have any of you seen Jimby?'

'Not to speak to,' said Rosie. 'But I saw him driving by in his Landie the other day.'

'Nope, 'fraid not, hun,' said Molly. 'But I'm furious with him for treating you like this, and if I do see him, I'll kick his bloody arse. I didn't think he was the sort of bloke that would flounce off and go all sulky for days on end.'

'Blimey! He'd better watch out if Molly's on the warpath,' said Rosie.

'Cuggle, Auntie Kitty.' Emmie was struggling to clamber onto her aunt's knee.

'And I haven't seen him; I can't seem to get hold of him.' Kitty bent to help her up. 'I'd love a cuddle from you, Em.' She kissed the top of Emmie's chocolate brown curls before smoothing them so she could see over the little girl's head. 'But Ollie said they had a bit of a chat this morning.'

Vi's heart leapt. 'Oh? Did he say anything? About us, I mean.'

Kitty nodded. 'He didn't go into detail – and I haven't had a proper chance to have a chat with him as the kids were around – but he said Jimby's feeling low and guilty. Oll said he's never seen him like this. He told him that he should speak to you, but Jimby said he thought you wouldn't want to see him after he walked out the way he did and what he said to you on the phone.'

'He thought *I* wouldn't want to see *him*? I've been absolutely desperate to see him, but I thought *he* wouldn't want to see *me*.' Vi grabbed the tiny glimmer of hope and held on tight. 'Do you think I should go and see him? You don't think he'd turn me away?'

Kitty nodded. 'Yes, I think you should go and see him if all that's keeping him away is his daft male pride and, no, Jimby adores you; he won't turn you away, chick.'

Molly's mobile phone pinged. 'There's no bloomin' peace up here.' She huffed and reached for her phone, an expression of disbelief spreading over her face as she read the text. 'The old bugger!' She clapped a hand to her forehead.

'Granny Aggie I presume?' Kitty asked.

'Yep, Granny, flaming, Aggie,' Molly replied.

'Oh, dear,' said Vi. 'What's she done now?' She glanced across at Kitty who had started to giggle.

'She's only gone and sent Maneater a text saying that Rev Nev's got the hots for her.' Molly shook her head.

'What?' said Kitty.

'Why?' asked Vi.

'No idea. You know Granny Aggie, she never needs a

reason. Oh, no.' Molly couldn't help but laugh. 'Oh, lord, it gets worse. She's going to have to explain this one herself. I won't be able to keep a straight face if I have to do it.'

'Come on, you can't keep us hanging like this, what's she said?' asked Kitty.

Molly took a deep breath. 'She says she's told Maneater that the vicar likes to do it doggy fashion.'

'What?' Kitty's eyes were like saucers as the three women collapsed into fits of laughter.

'That poor man,' spluttered Vi. 'I'm surprised he hasn't asked for a transfer.'

'Bloody hell, I've got a flippin' horrible mental image going on in my mind. One of you, say something to make it go away,' said Molly.

'Oh, my face is aching with laughing so much,' said Kitty. 'What do you think she really means?'

'God knows, but she's going to get herself into hot water if she's not careful.' Molly rolled her eyes. 'Pip's got a bloody lot to answer for leaving me with the troublesome old bugger. How many women do you know would put up with their husband's octogenarian grandmother who thinks there's absolutely nothing wrong with pestering the vicar with mucky texts, and leaving you to sort it out?'

Kitty did her best to stop laughing and pulled a sympathetic face.

Emmie reached her arms out to Vi. 'Cuggle, Auntie Wiolet.'

'Ooh, is it my turn now, Em?'

Emmy nodded and Vi pulled her onto her knee, wrapping her arms around the toddler's chubby body. It sent a wave of warmth right through her.

Vi turned her attention back to Molly. 'So, does Granny Aggie still blame it on predictive texts and arthritic fingers?'

'Every time. Though I think it's a load of old bollocks; the old sod knows exactly what she's doing.' Molly blew a stray curl off her face. 'Uhh! After that, I think we need more tea.'

'Where's that swear-box, Moll?' Kitty giggled.

Once the laughter had subsided, Vi's mind wandered back to her situation with Jimby. 'What worries me the most is what if I really can't have children, especially when Jimby's already said he can't wait to be a dad?'

Kitty rubbed her friend's arm. 'Don't worry about that just now, there's lots of help out there and lots of different ways of making a family. Just concentrate on getting you and Jimby back on track.'

'Vi's right. And the more you worry about it, the more it doesn't happen. Abbie took ages to come along thanks to me having endometriosis. Robbie and me had just about given up and were getting ready to consider other options when suddenly, "boom", I was pregnant.'

'Really?' Vi felt the warmth of hope bloom inside her.

'Yes, just like that. The doctor said it was probably because I'd stopped fixating on it, so my body relaxed and it just happened.'

'There you are, listen to Rosie, Vi, and stop fretting over something that you don't know can't happen yet.' Kitty smiled at her friend.

Vi mustered a small smile back, Rosie's words working their way around her mind.

The rumble of a Landie pulling into the yard drew the women's attention away from their conversation. Phoebe jumped up, her tail wagging fast enough to beat eggs. She shot down the hall, whining to be out.

'Camm's back,' said Molly. She stood up and peered out of the wide Georgian window. 'He's been over to Middleton, picking up some stuff. Looks like he's brought Ben and Kristy back with him.'

They heard the rattle of the back door as it opened. 'Hiya, Mum, I'm starving, what's for tea?' Ben's voice reached the kitchen before he did.

'Hello, son. Have you had a good day? Hi, Kristy, lovie,' Molly replied.

'Hi, Molly,' called Kristy.

'Yep, today's been good, thanks. Hiya, ladies, I thought that was your car out there, Aunty Kitty.' Ben walked into the room, beaming at them, Kristy following closed behind.

'Yep, we've been having a natter with your mum.'

'Bet there weren't many quiet moments.' Ben grinned, earning himself a whack on the arm from Kristy.

'Hey, you, don't be so cheeky,' she said. She flicked her glossy dark ponytail over her shoulder.

'Only joking.'

'How's uni?' asked Vi.

'I'm loving it.' Enthusiasm shone in Ben's brown eyes. He looked the vision of health with his clear skin already lightly tanned from working outside.

'Mmm, me too.' Kristy nodded. 'There's a lot more work than you'd expect, but it's so interesting, and with it being our final year, it's noses to the grindstone.'

'Too right,' said Ben. 'Anyway, we're just going to grab a couple of cokes and a snack to have while we do our revision.'

'Okay, lovie, but don't eat too much, I've done a big pot of goulash for dinner.'

'We won't,' he called as they disappeared upstairs.

'Revision, is that what they're calling it now?' Vi raised her eyebrows.

'Don't,' said Molly. 'I don't want to think about that.'

'Camm!' Emmie climbed down from Violet's knee and ran over to him, her chubby arms outstretched.

Looking relaxed in a pair of faded jeans and a dark blue checked shirt, he scooped her up and kissed her plump cheek. 'Hello, little miss, isn't that a lovely welcome?' He smiled as she flung her arms around his neck, resting her head on his chest.

'Ahh.' Kitty smiled.

'Hello, ladies.' He squeezed Vi's shoulder as he walked by. 'You okay, Vi?'

'I'm fine thanks, Camm, but I think it's probably time we were off, and let you good folks get your dinner.'

'Don't rush off on my account.'

'Nope, Vi's right, it's time we got back to our own homes,' said Kitty.

Molly walked her friends to the yard. 'Don't forget what we said about talking to that daft-arse cousin of mine, Vi.'

'I hope you're not talking about me!' Kitty giggled.

'Definitely not you, hun.' Molly gave her a friendly nudge with her shoulder.

'Good luck with Granny Aggie,' Vi called through the car window as they were leaving the yard.

'I'm going to need more than luck.' She rolled her eyes as she waved them off.

**CHAPTER 23**

'Can you drop me at Jimby's forge please, Kitty?' They were driving along Church Street and Vi felt a sudden surge of courage.

'Course I can, chick.'

'No time like the present, eh, Vi?' said Rosie.

'Exactly. If I go home and start stewing on what I should say, I'll still be in the same position in a week's time.' Vi's stomach was churning; it would be so easy just to go straight home but the thought of the current situation dragging on and becoming more difficult to sort out held no appeal. After all, that's what had got her into this mess in the first place.

Kitty pulled over and Vi jumped out of the car. 'Thanks for listening and for the advice, girls. Wish me luck.'

'You're welcome and good luck – though I know you'll be fine. But you know where I am if you need me,' said Kitty.

'Same here, Vi. I hope it goes well for you,' added Rosie.

Vi watched the car disappear down the road, then turned and made her way to the door of the forge. The somersaults in her stomach were getting so strong, she was beginning to feel like she could throw up. What if Ollie had got it wrong? What if Jimby didn't want to speak to her?

Though there were lights on in the building, when Vi went to open the door it was locked firm and wouldn't budge, and the usual sounds she associated with the forge sat silent. Her heart plummeted as the adrenalin that was pushing her forward suddenly leached away. She felt the threat of tears as she turned and walked across the yard.

'Now then, Vi. If you're looking for Jimby, I saw him heading up on to the moor with the dogs about five or ten minutes ago. If you're quick, you might be able to catch up with him.' It was Lycra Len, heading back from the village shop with his evening paper.

'Thanks, Len. I'll see if I can do that.'

'Aye, it's a grand afternoon for a walk. Enjoy, lass.'

'Will do.'

Realising her current outfit of fifties style sundress and kitten heels was hardly appropriate for traipsing across the moors, Vi hurried home. She'd get changed and see if she could catch Jimby up.

Back at Sunshine Cottage, she raced up the stairs and pulled out her only pair of jeans – designer figure-hugging ankle-grazers that cost a small fortune – and had a rummage for a pair of socks. At a loss for what top to wear, she grabbed a checked shirt of Jimby's and threw it on. It was way too big, but she didn't care. She whizzed downstairs and dragged out her leather country boots, pushing her feet into them.

Before she knew it, she was slamming the door of Sunshine Cottage behind her, and marching along the road to the track that led the way up to the looming rigg of Great Stangdale.

Vi had forgotten just what a pull it was to climb up the

bank side and was thankful that her dedication to Pilates classes had left her with the knack of being able to control her breathing. But it didn't mean that she didn't get out of breath.

'Phew!' she stopped and turned to look at the view, shielding her eyes with her hand. She'd built up a sweat, and the cool air was deliciously refreshing as it swept over her skin. It must be years since she'd been up here, a good decade, even. How shameful was that, she thought as her gaze followed the undulations of the dale set out below her. It was breath-taking in its sumptuous shades of green with hints of purple where the heather was just coming into flower. She craned her neck to catch a better glimpse of Danskelfe Castle, it's looming east-wing just visible from here as it jutted out near the crag on the right. The seat of the Hammondely family – local landed gentry and proprietors of the sprawling Danskelfe Estate – it was a stunning building, not without its scars, that had stood the test of time and all that the harsh moorland winters had thrown at it over the centuries. The latest rumour from the castle slipped into Vi's mind. Lady Carolyn – daughter of Lord Hammondely – and her husband, Sim, were supposedly expecting their first child. But that's all it was, a rumour, and there had been plenty of those flying around the moors about Caro over the years. Sim had definitely been a calming influence on her, Vi mused.

Putting her hands on her hips, Vi sighed. Why had she been so scornful of the moors when she was in her teens and twenties? What had made her in such a hurry to get away from them? They had the opposite effect now, pulling her back with a longing that was rooted deep inside her. She looked across at the thatched rooftops of the ancient cottages of Lytell Stangdale, huddled together against the capricious moods of the moorland weather. It was achingly beautiful; a classic example of the perfect rural idyll. How could there ever have been a time when she didn't appreciate it, or this rugged beauty before her, softened today, by the springy mounds of heather and tall fronds of bracken, brightened by the vibrant yellow flowers of the randomly dotted gorse bushes? It was stunning whatever the time of year, its changes dramatic and, at times, harsh, but always beautiful. Vi felt ashamed of her younger self, ashamed of how she'd mocked her parents' lifestyle to her city friends. But there *had* been a time when she'd loved it here, in her youth. A carefree time when she'd scrambled all over the moors with Kitty, Molly, Jimby and Ollie, having so much fun she didn't want to go home for tea, and was back out again straight after when daylight allowed in the warm summer months. She'd go to bed at night feeling happy and tired in the way that only days of fresh air can make you feel. What finer playground for children to explore and have fun? It was exactly what she'd want for her own children. God willing...

The inimitable "peewit" cry of a lapwing in the field below pulled Vi from her thoughts. The sun was glinting off the white of the underside of its wings that flapped noisily as it swooped down to the ground, warning off a crow that was showing an unwelcome interest in its nest.

Vi's gaze moved further along the dale, stopping at her parents' dairy cows who were munching on grass. If she wasn't mistaken, they were sitting down which could only mean one thing: rain. She shivered, the temperature had suddenly nose-dived and the sun had disappeared behind a surly-looking cloud that was beginning to sprawl across the sky, swamping the blue. Vi turned back to the path and was startled by a brightly coloured pheasant that scurried in front of her. It showed its annoyance by cackling irritably before taking flight, skimming over the tops of the heather.

She continued up the track, if her memory served her correctly, there was a seat a couple of minutes' climb from here. Jimby mentioned that he often stopped there to catch his breath when he was walking the dogs and to admire the view. Just then, a large, cold spot of rain landed on the end of her nose. 'Typical,' she said aloud. But it wasn't going to put her off, she was determined to plough on. If Jimby was up on this moor, she was going to catch up with him.

Soon, the single drop of rain turned into several and was getting heavier by the minute, but Vi ploughed on, her steps kicking up the scent of damp earth – so evocative of her childhood – she'd got this far, she wasn't turning back now. She'd already decided not to rehearse what she was going to say to him; she'd let him take the lead. But whatever she did say, she was going to leave him in no doubt that she loved him with all her heart and wanted to be with him.

As Violet continued up the track, she heard the bark of a dog in the near distance, followed by a long whistle and a man's voice calling. Jimby! Her already thudding heart surged and a host of butterflies took flight in her stomach. Suddenly Jarvis and Jerry came tearing down the path towards her, their tails wagging furiously. 'Hello, you two.' She bent to ruffle their heads. 'Come on, let's go and find your dad, he'll be in trouble if the gamekeepers see you off your leads.' The pair belted along the track and whipped around the corner, never veering from the designated path.

Before she knew it, Jimby was standing in front of her. His appearance startled her. He looked so different without his smile and without the twinkle in his eyes; it made him look older. He clearly hadn't shaved for days, his face was wan and dark circles sat like bruises beneath his eyes. Vi's heart ached for him, she'd never seen him look so sad. And she hated that she was the reason for it.

'Jimby.'

'Violet?' He looked surprised to see her.

'I came looking for you.'

'You did?'

She nodded.

'But you don't like walking on the moors.'

'I do if it's to find you, Jimby.'

He swallowed and dragged a hand down his face.

'Can we talk, get this sorted out?' she said. 'Please, Jimby.'

'I've been a bloody idiot, Vi, and I'm so sorry.'

She stepped towards him, reaching out and touching his arm. 'We've both been stupid, we're both at fault, Jimby – me more than you – but I'd like to think we can fix things and move on.'

He nodded. 'Me, too.'

'Why don't we sit down for a bit?' Vi headed over to the bench. Uncharacteristically, she didn't care that it was a bit grubby and that wet was creeping into her expensive designer jeans.

'Where do we start?' he asked. He rested his elbows on his knees, putting his head in his hands.

'Well, first of all, I just want to tell you how sorry I am that I didn't tell you about what had happened long before now. I wanted to, really I did, but whenever I thought the moment was right, the words just wouldn't come out, and I'd see your face, so happy, and I knew what I had to tell you would make that smile disappear, make you feel differently about me, and I didn't want that to happen.'

'I knew something wasn't right ever since we came back from Kirkbythwaite. It was obvious you had something on your mind. I just thought it was because you were getting focused on organising the wedding, then we had the house plans, and on top of that, you were busy with Romantique. It did cross my mind that you weren't coping with it as well as you normally do; you usually seem to thrive on having loads to do.'

'You're right, I do get a buzz out of having loads to do, and all our plans for everything, I just love them, but it was something that happened at the hotel that set me off worrying.' She paused for a moment, sensing Jimby's gaze turn to her.

'Oh?'

'He was there.'

'Who? Not the bloke you had an affair with?'

Vi's heart twisted at Jimby's words. She nodded. 'Yes. I didn't see him to speak to, he was in the restaurant, having a meal with a young woman, not his wife – no surprises there.'

'Right.' Jimby shifted his eyes back to the ground as silence hung between them.

'And, in case you're wondering, when I saw him again, the only thing I felt for him was repulsion. He clearly hasn't changed, and I can't think what I ever saw in him to start with.'

'You were only young, you had your head turned by the charms of an older man.' He shrugged.

The rain was getting heavier and the view of the dale was slowly disappearing behind a thick veil of mist that was floating down. Vi pushed her hair out of her face, surprised at how saturated it was. 'Which part of what I told you made you leave the cottage?' She squeezed her eyes shut, praying that it wasn't the fact about her not being able to get pregnant.

'I can tell you exactly what it was: you hadn't told me. Any of it. It made me feel like you couldn't trust me or something. I thought we were so close, but that made it feel like there was a kind of void between us that had never been there before and I couldn't imagine it ever disappearing.'

His words stabbed like a knife in Violet's heart. 'Oh, Jimby, please don't think that. We are close and that void will disappear, I promise. And of course I trust you. I wouldn't be with you if I didn't. You know how I used to feel about marriage and motherhood; being with you has changed all that.'

'That's not how it felt. It made me feel that you thought so little of me, that I'd leave you for what had happened to you.' He turned to her. 'Vi, all I want to do is protect you, take care of you – and by the way, if I ever get my hands on the bastard that did that to you, I won't be responsible for my actions.'

Vi felt a tiny glimmer of hope squeeze its way in; she grabbed it, not wanting to let it go. She rested her hand on his and he wrapped his fingers around it.

'Your hands are freezing,' he said.

'I don't care,' she replied. 'I felt so ashamed of what I'd done: have an affair with a married man – and a married man whose wife was seriously ill – get pregnant, book an abortion, then miscarry so badly it looks as though I've ruined the chances of ever having a family with a man I adore with all my heart. On top of all of that, I keep it secret, knowing that I shouldn't. Knowing it would only make things worse; which it did.' Tears were stinging her eyes but she was determined to fight them back.

'It was a lot to take on board when I thought we knew everything about each other, Vi. But when I sat down and thought about it, I realised it's to be expected when you'd

*The Secret - Violet's Story*

lived away from here for years and the rest of our crowd haven't. You know how it is, you can't fart in this village without it making headline news, and living here, you get used to that – just about, anyway.' The small smile that tugged at his lips gave Vi another sliver of hope.

'I know. And I can promise you, Jimby, that's the only thing you don't know about me. I couldn't cope with any more secrets like that.'

'I believe you.' He wrapped his arm around her and pulled her close.

Vi felt the first layers of anxiety peel away, but it still didn't stop her heart from pounding as she asked the question she most feared the answer to. 'So, can I ask, the fact that I might not be able to get pregnant, is that a deal-breaker for us?' Her voice wavered; she was finding it more difficult to keep the tears at bay.

'Vi, do you honestly think I'd leave you because of that? Do you really think I'm that shallow?'

'No, of course not, but you said before that you couldn't wait to be a dad.'

'I won't deny it, I'd love to be a dad, but if that's not meant to be, then I'm more than content to be a doting uncle.'

Her heart soared and she finally released her grip on the tears that had been ready to brim over, but this time, instead of sadness, they were tears of happiness. She swiped them away with her fingertips and swallowed. 'Are you sure?'

He turned to her and smiled, his dimples reappearing, lighting up his face like sunshine after a rainstorm. 'As long as I'm with you, Vi, I'm absolutely positive.'

'Oh, Jimby, you've no idea what it means to hear you say that. I've missed you. I love you so much I can't put it into words. My happy place is being wrapped in your arms, feeling your heart beating against mine. I never thought I'd experience anything like this, I'd convinced myself I didn't believe in it, but you make me feel that everything in the world is alright. I'm nothing without you, Jimby.'

He stood before her, taking in her words, the rain getting heavier. 'That's exactly how I feel about you, Vi. We're meant to be together.'

Before she had chance to reply, he pulled her into his arms and she felt herself melt into the warmth of his embrace, enjoying the way only being there could make her feel. Oh, how she'd missed him, how she'd missed this. There was no feeling like it, there never had been; it was overwhelming and wonderful. They were the perfect fit, as if they were made for each other, and this was exactly where she was meant to be, here in his arms.

As he took her face in his hands and kissed her gently on the mouth, the heavens opened with a vengeance and rain pelted down. 'You're getting soaked,' he said, his lips still touching hers.

'I don't care.'

'Me neither.' He kissed her once more.

When they eventually pulled apart, Jimby started to laugh.

'What?' said Vi. Rivulets of rain were pouring down her face and her hair was plastered to her head.

'I've never seen you look like that.'

'Like what?'

'I think the word's "deconstructed". And, if I'm not mistaken, isn't that my shirt you're wearing?'

'Might be.'

'Well, can I just say how very sexy you look in it?'

'Funny man.'

'I'm being serious. Come on let's get you back home,

Miss Smith, I need to get you out of those wet clothes; we've got some serious making up to do.'

'Lead the way.' She arched a suggestive eyebrow at him and giggled.

As they headed down the path, one behind the other, hand-in-hand, Vi felt the weight of weeks of anxiety drift away. Happiness bloomed once more, filling her heart. She didn't think she would ever stop smiling.

∽

'You know what?' Vi lay in Jimby's arms, stroking the dark hairs on his chest. They were back at Sunshine Cottage, having showered together before tumbling into bed.

'What?' he asked. He was stroking her arm with his fingertips and it felt delicious.

'I quite liked that walk on the moors.'

'That's because you were looking for me, I was the end result.' Jimby grinned, giving her a squeeze. 'I was the prize.'

'Big head.' She prodded a finger in the firm muscles of his stomach. 'No, I actually mean it felt good to be getting some fresh moorland air in my lungs. I'd forgotten how it felt, and being up there reminded me of when we were kids, tearing about all over the place, playing hide-and-seek in the grouse butts.'

'Yeah, we had an amazing childhood, didn't we? Actually, I remember thinking about trying to steal a kiss from you in one of those grouse butts, but it was the week after I'd pinched one in the school playground and got a kick in the nads for my trouble.'

Vi laughed. 'Yep, well-deserved it was, too, taking liberties like that. Anyway, what I'm trying to say, is that it would be nice to do it more often.'

'What, kick me in the nads?'

'No, you nutter, go for more walks on the moor.'

'Mmm, you could take the dogs.'

'I would, but they're a bit frantic for me. I'd end up getting dragged all over the heather.'

'That would be something to see.' He laughed, earning himself another prod in the stomach.

'Anyway, Miss Smith, I've got something else I'd like to discuss with you that is far more important.' He rolled on top of her, pinning her hands above her head.

'Really?'

'Why don't you come off the pill and leave fate to take her chance? Just a thought, no pressure. I won't mention it anymore, I'll leave it up to you.' His eyes searched hers.

She pulled her hands free and wrapped them around his neck. 'I already have,' she whispered.

He flashed a heart-melting smile, then bent his head towards her, dropping a meaningful kiss on her lips before tracing a trail down her neck. Violet pushed her fingers into his thick curls and released a groan of ecstasy.

˷

AN HOUR LATER, they were sitting in the kitchen sharing a pot of tea, wearing only their bath robes. The weight that had sat on Vi's shoulders like a heavy, solid mass had lifted. Happiness had erased her earlier feelings of hopelessness and she couldn't stop smiling. She was relieved Jimby had suggested coming off the pill – they were on the same wavelength there – but she'd promised herself she'd try not to obsess over what the consequences could mean.

She was flicking through the texts that had come in quickly after she'd told her three friends that she'd made up

# The Secret - Violet's Story

with Jimby. 'Everyone's chuffed to bits we've got sorted out,' she said. 'And your Kitty says Ollie wants you to know he's glad you've seen sense.'

Jimby laughed. 'He's a right one to talk; do you remember what he was like over that barrister bloke he caught holding Kitty's hand that time? He had a right flounce.'

'Oh, yeah, I'd forgotten about that. Honestly, you men and your fragile egos.' Vi gave him a meaningful look before breaking into a giggle. 'Anyway, the girls and me are meeting up for lunch at the teashop tomorrow.'

Jimby looked hopeful. 'It's girls only,' she said. 'If you want to join us you'll have to put on a skirt, and I don't mean to be blunt, but you don't have the legs.'

'I don't know what you mean, I think these are rather shapely.' He pulled his dressing gown aside revealing two muscular, hairy, and extremely manly legs.

'Jimby, TMI!'

'What?' he asked before looking down at his dressing gown. 'Ah, the problems of having such a huge manhood means it's always trying to escape.' He pulled his robe closed.

She shook her head. 'In your dreams.'

**CHAPTER 24**

'I'm absolutely starving,' said Vi. She watched Lucy disappear into the deli's kitchen with their order.

'Same here,' said Molly. 'Running around after a three-year-old, a campsite and a farm definitely works up a fearsome appetite.'

'I can imagine.' Kitty smiled, looking around the teashop. 'And Lucy and Freddie have done a lovely job of this place; it's hard to imagine what the décor was like before.'

'Bloody awful,' said Molly.

'That's an understatement,' said Vi.

'Anyway, I'm so pleased things worked out for you, chick.' Kitty gave Violet's hand a squeeze.

'Yep, hear, hear,' agreed Molly. 'You and Jimby were always destined to be together. If it wasn't for him, you wouldn't have moved back to the village and we were missing you like crazy when you lived in York, weren't we, Kitts?'

'Yes ... oh, er ...' Kitty glanced out of the window and gasped. Aoife Mellison was walking by dressed in her usual vivid walking gear, glaring at her with unbridled hatred in her eyes.

'What the bloody hell's she staring at?' said Molly. 'That look's enough to sour milk.'

'She doesn't look very happy, does she?' said Vi.

'Stuck-up cow needs to get over herself.' Molly was practically snarling.

'Don't worry, I'm used to it, she always looks at me like that.' Kitty sighed.

'I think it might be something to do with school,' said Lucy. 'Apparently, Lily got top marks in a test the other day and Evie didn't do very well. According to Abbie, Aoife wasn't very happy about it and went into school to ask why.'

'Oh, right,' said Kitty. She took a sip of her tea.

'I don't know why she has to be so competitive. All Robbie and me ask of Abbie is that she tries her best.'

'That's all you can ask It's a recipe for disaster otherwise,' said Kitty. She averted her eyes from Aoife.

'Piss off,' Molly mouthed through the glass.

'Molly!' gasped Kitty, while the other two struggled to stifle their giggles. 'I know you won't agree with me, but I can't help but feel sorry for her. I think she must have some sort of personality issue she can't help.'

'Kitty, will you stop being so bloody nice. The woman made yours and Lily's lives a misery, never mind the fact she thinks she's superior to everyone. She puts a ridiculous amount of pressure on her kids, wanting them to be better than everyone else, which just results in them being obnoxious little twa—'

'Okay, I get the picture.' Kitty giggled, cutting her cousin off.

'Yep, and I'm with Moll,' said Vi.

Rosie nodded in agreement. 'Same here.'

They were interrupted by Lucy bringing out two plates of food. 'Right then, who's having the brie and redcurrant jelly open sandwich?'

'That's for me, thanks, Luce,' said Vi.

'Me, too,' said Rosie.

Lucy set the plates down and Sophie, the waitress, followed with Molly's maple roasted ham salad and Kitty's goats cheese, beetroot and walnut on wholemeal bread.

'Wow, this looks amazing,' said Vi.

'That's good to hear.' Lucy watched Sophie disappear back into the kitchen. 'By the way, did any of you hear that screaming this morning, first thing?'

'Oh, yes. Ollie and I did, we looked out to see where it was coming from but couldn't see anything.' Kitty nodded.

'Now you come to mention it, Jimby and me thought we heard something, too. Just one long, hysterical scream, wasn't it?' added Vi. 'We thought it must be some wild animal or something.'

'I think I know where this is going.' Molly reached across and pinched a beetroot crisp from Violet's plate which earned her a tap on the wrist from her friend.

'According to my sources, it was Aoife. Apparently, she'd been out at her sister's the night before and had left Dave with instructions to help Evie revise for a spelling test. Anyway, he forgot, so when she came to test her this morning before school, Evie only got a couple right, which made Aoife go into the garden and scream her head off in frustration.'

'Blimey,' said Vi. 'That's a bit over the top just because of a spelling test, isn't it? How old is Evie, ten, eleven?'

Kitty nodded. 'Same age as Lily.'

Lucy raised her eyebrows and leaned in. 'And from what I can gather, she's putting more and more pressure on the kids, and blaming Dave if they don't do well at school – he was in here the other day, telling Fred how she'd told him it's his fault they're not top of the class because his genes aren't as academic as hers.'

'Oh, my God, that woman is seriously deluded.' Molly's top lip curled in disgust.

'Well I wish they'd just move away; the atmosphere in the village was a whole lot nicer before they arrived here,' said Kitty.

Just then, Sophie appeared with a bowl of extra coleslaw. 'Right,' said Lucy. 'I'd best get back to the shop before Fred starts to think I've got lost. Enjoy your lunch, ladies.'

They tucked into their food, making appreciative sounds and offering each other tastes from their plates. 'We should do this more often,' said Rosie.

'Too right.' Molly nodded. 'I could get a zip-line direct from Withrin Hill straight into here.'

'You would, too,' giggled Vi.

'So, does this mean,' Kitty waved her fork around, 'now that you and Jimby are back on track, he'll be turning his attentions to the fundraiser calendar again?'

Vi swallowed her mouthful of food. 'I'm afraid it does, he was rabbiting on about it last night. You'll have to tell Ollie he hasn't managed to wriggle his way out of it, Kitts.'

Kitty laughed. 'Oh, he'll be gutted when he hears.'

'Not sure you should be using words like "wriggle" when we're talking about blokes' bits,' said Molly. 'Makes me think of worms.' She popped a crisp into her mouth and gave it a vigorous chomping.

'Must you, Moll?' Vi rolled her eyes.

'Yeah, I thought you'd finally managed to get all of that kind of chat out of your system since you'd given up nursing,' said Kitty.

'I'm nearly there, but not quite,' Molly replied.
'Well, we'd appreciate it if you'd keep trying,' said Vi.

∽

As Molly was driving out of the village on her way back home, she was flagged down by another driver, heading in the opposite direction. She wound down her window to see a face that looked vaguely familiar. It only took her a couple of seconds to realise where she knew him from.

'Hello, there, are you a local?' He flashed a smarmy smile.

'I am.'

'Ah, good, then you might be able to help me. I'm looking for someone I used to know a long time ago. Last I heard, she lived here.'

'Oh, really?' Molly made no attempt to hide the frostiness in her voice.

'Yes,' he replied. He looked uncertain. 'Er, she's called Violet Smith – that was her maiden name, at least. Actually, I think we've met before, haven't we? I'm Mi—'

'I know exactly who you are,' Molly snarled. 'And let me tell you this, Violet doesn't want to see you. She doesn't want anything to do with you. And, after what you did to her, the cold-hearted self-absorbed way you treated her, I can't blame her. In fact, after bumping into you the other day, she says she can't understand what she ever saw in you, and she's not the only one. She's happy now, madly in love with a wonderful, decent man who she's getting married to in September. So you can see, she's moved on and left you well and truly in the past, which is exactly where you belong.'

'I don't know who you think you are but—'

'You lost the right to pass comment on anything to do

with Violet sixteen years ago. So I suggest you turn your car round and sod right off out of this village and leave my friend alone, or you'll have me to answer to and, trust me, I can make your life hell.'

'That sounds like a threat.'

'Oh, it's not a threat, it's a promise. And I always keep my promises.'

Mike paused for a moment, before reversing his car, performing a quick three-point-turn in the road and roaring off out of the village with Molly in hot pursuit, sending a plume of dust after her, making sure he didn't change his mind. She would never mention to Violet that she'd seen that tosser.

**CHAPTER 25**

Vi was making the most of having a couple of hours to herself in Sunshine Cottage. After collecting a basket full of washing, she began sorting through her clothes, wondering why she'd ever thought she needed so many. After a brief deliberation, she put the ones she hadn't worn for at least a year in a pile on the bed, remembering what Kitty had said about Noushka being keen to have any of her cast offs. Seizing the moment, she dashed off a text to Kitty asking if the young girl had been serious. A reply pinged back almost instantly telling Vi that Noushka was very excited at the prospect.

After folding the clothes neatly and placing them in a couple of bin bags, Vi turned her attention to her wedding things. From the bottom of her built-in wardrobe, she pulled out her prized designer suitcase she'd allocated especially for things related to her and Jimby's special day. She undid the leather belts and flicked open the locks, carefully lifting out her exquisite handmade underwear, made of the lightest of silks, adorned with tiny bows and beads and fine gossamer lace. A shiver of excitement fizzed through her as

## The Secret - Violet's Story

she took out all of the other items she'd tucked away; amongst them, silk stockings and the frilly garter she'd made herself, embroidering an amethyst spider into the lace as a symbol of good luck. The wedding was inching ever closer, and they still had a lot to do, not necessarily for the wedding itself, but for all the other things they seemed to have taken on. Still, she didn't mind. She was just relieved to have got the whole Mike Williamson situation out of the way and was now free to look forward to marrying Jimby. It still took her by surprise how she'd gone from being a hard-nosed businesswoman with no desire whatsoever to get married and have children, to a woman whose insides turned to marshmallow every time she was in Jimby's arms, and how she couldn't wait to become his wife and – she hardly dared wish – start a family. Feeling broody was the biggest surprise of all to her. She'd given up trying to get her head around that one because it, quite simply, made sense; there was nothing to get her head around.

As Vi was packing the suitcase away she heard the door go and Jimby's voice float up the stairs. 'Hiya, gorgeous, I'm back.' Her heart lifted and she smiled; she always looked forward to seeing him.

She picked up the washing basket and made her way downstairs to the kitchen where Jimby was looking out of the window. Hearing her walk into the room, he turned, his face lighting up with a heart-melting smile. Vi's insides turned to mush.

'Hi, had a good day?' she asked.

'The best, but seeing you just made it even better.' He strode over to her and cupped her face in his hands, kissing her full on the lips. 'Sit yourself down and I'll make us a cup of tea and then tell you all about it.'

Vi was still reeling from the intensity of Jimby's lips on

hers. She'd been expecting him to grab her by the hand and lead her up to the bedroom, which was usually what followed a kiss like that, rather than offering her a cup of tea. She needed a moment to steady herself, for her passion to dissipate.

'You alright?'

'Mmm. Fine thanks.' She nodded. 'Just feeling a bit lightheaded, I must've stood up too quickly before I came downstairs.'

'More like you were knocked sideways by the power in these bad boys.' He puckered his lips to demonstrate what he was talking about. 'I'll show you what else they can do after I've told you my news.'

Vi couldn't help but giggle. She watched as he threw a handful of teabags into the pot before covering them with hot water.

'Right, I'll just leave them to mash a bit. Come on, park your backside over here.' He set the teapot down on the table and pulled out a chair. 'So, I've priced up defibrillators, and we're looking at anything from just under a grand to fifteen hundred quid. I've got the details right here.' He pulled out a scrappy piece of paper covered in a variety of illegible jottings.

'I thought they'd be more expensive than that; I shouldn't think it would take you too long to raise enough money.' Vi put the basket down by her seat and sat down.

'Too right, I reckon we'll make all the money we need within the first week of our calendar sales. What with all those hot-blooded women hoping to get a glimpse of my secret weapon.' He gave her a cheeky grin and waggled his eyebrows.

Vi shook her head. 'Have a chuckle, more like.' She reached into the washing, pulled out what appeared to be a pair of his underpants and threw them at him. He ducked and they slipped onto the chair beside him.

'Your problem is you're spoilt, having me at your fingertips whenever you want. You just take my generous proportions for granted.'

'Oh, please.' Violet giggled. 'Anyway, I've heard Maneater's ordered every copy.'

Jimby frowned. 'Ughh, don't. Mind you, part of me wouldn't be surprised if she did.'

'Me neither.'

Jimby visibly shuddered at the thought. 'Right, I'd best get my scruffy notes written up. I'm having a committee meeting with Ollie and Robbie in the Sunne at half seven to discuss our next steps.'

'A "committee meeting"? Is that what you're calling it these days?'

'Hey, don't mock it, we've had to set one up, it's a legal requirement when you're dealing with fund-raising money, and we want to do this properly. I've been appointed chairman and am a very important person. I'd be grateful if you wouldn't forget that.'

'Okay, Very Important Person, I'll do my best.'

## CHAPTER 26

'I've just seen Robbie.' It was Monday afternoon and Vi had arrived back at Romantique's studio after popping to the shop for more milk. 'He was looking for Jimby. Said things are all set for the photography session on Saturday.'

'This Saturday? Really?' Kitty put her sewing down. 'Ollie will be past himself when he finds out.'

'To be honest, I thought Jimby was just joking when he first mentioned it, but it looks like it's definitely going ahead.'

'Well, you know what Jimby's like when he sets his mind to something. Did he tell you that Dave Mellison was in the pub the other night when they were having their "committee meeting"?' She put finger quotes around the words.

Vi laughed. 'He did. Said something about him trying to take over, oust Jimby and appoint himself as chairman.'

Kitty rolled her eyes. 'Ollie said he muttered something about needing to find a reason to get out of the house and away from Aoife.'

'Really?'

'Mmhm.'

'That's interesting.'

'That's what I thought.'

'Time for a brew, so we can discuss this further,' said Vi. She headed to the kitchen and filled the kettle.

∽

Later that afternoon, the pair had finished work and were tidying away. 'Have you got time to pick up those bags of clothes for Noushka?' asked Vi.

'Oh, yes. She's so excited about them. Keeps saying how she loves your style.'

'That's really sweet. And is she still pleased she took the dance course at York uni, rather than moving away?'

'No regrets. She says after it being just her and Ollie for so long, she loves being part of a bigger family and wants to be at home for as long as possible so she can enjoy it.'

'Ah, bless her, she's such a lovely girl.' Vi picked up the keys. 'Please don't tell me she's still thinking about cutting all that gorgeous long blonde hair off?'

'No, she's changed her mind about that, thank goodness! Ollie and me managed to convince her she'd regret it.'

'I'm sure she would. Most women would kill to have hair like that – me included.' Vi went to flick the light switch. 'Ready?' she asked Kitty.

'Ready.' Kitty flung her bag over her shoulder. 'I know it's not far, but I might as well drive us along to your house then I can just chuck the bin bags into the boot.'

'Good thinking.'

As the friends stepped into the hallway of Sunshine Cottage they were greeted by the sound of growling coming from the kitchen. They exchanged a puzzled look before Vi tentatively pushed the door open revealing Jarvis and Jerry fighting over a piece of fabric that almost stretched from one end of the room to the other. Neither dog looked up nor stopped what they were doing. Jerry's growl deepened and he shook his head vigorously, teeth still firmly clamped down on the fabric. Jarvis did the same, undeterred by the loud ripping sound that followed.

'What on earth are they fighting over?' asked Kitty. Her elfin features creased by a frown.

'I don't kno ... oh, I do know. It's Jimby's underpants!' Vi threw her head back and laughed. 'I chucked them at him this morning and they slipped onto the chair. I'd forgotten about it but the dogs must've found them.'

'I won't ask.' Kitty giggled and shook her head. 'But they've got an awful lot of fabric in them to stretch so far. My brother must wear enormous knickers.'

'He doesn't actually, he wears budgie-smugglers, but they've clearly got a lot of give in them.'

'TMI, Vi,' said Kitty, pulling a face.

'Sorry,' Vi giggled. 'But this could explain why so many pairs have holes in them.

∼

As Vi and Kitty were loading the bags into Kitty's car, Jimby bowled along the trod. His hands were thrust deep into the pocket of his jeans and he was whistling loudly. His face broke into a broad smile on seeing the women.

'Now then, ladies.'

'Hiya, Jimby,' replied Kitty. 'I'm just collecting these for Noushka.'

'Ah, yep, Vi's been freeing up some wardrobe space just so she can fill it up again. He laughed and went to give Vi a kiss on the cheek.

'Exactly,' Vi shot back. She noticed that Jimby was looking particularly pleased with himself.

'I have news.' He rubbed his hands together, his eyes twinkling.

'Why does that make me nervous?' said Vi.

He laughed. 'I've just been speaking to Robbie and the photo session's all organised for Saturday.'

'So I hear, I saw him earlier and he mentioned it then,' Vi replied. 'It's all happening very quickly.'

'No point in hanging around. The sooner we raise the money, the sooner we get the defibrillator fitted. Anyway, his mate Nick's coming over here and we're hoping to have some of the photos taken in our workplaces and some outside – weather permitting. I don't think any of us will fancy getting goose-bumps on our nethers.'

'God forbid,' said Vi.

'I think the forecast's good right through to next week,' said Kitty. 'Oll will be gutted when I tell him.'

'Oh, don't worry about that, I've already broken the news to him so he's got plenty of time to prime his plane.'

'Not sure I like the sound of that.' Kitty giggled as she threw the last of the bags into the boot of her car and closed the door.

'Any road, we're having a committee meeting at the pub tonight, to finalise who's doing which month etc.'

'That's what they're calling it these days, Kitts; going for a pint is now disguised as a "committee meeting", isn't that right, Jimby?'

'Might be.' He grinned. 'Anyway, why don't you ladies

join us? It's been a while since we've all been to the pub together.'

'I'd love to, Jimby, but I'm feeling shattered. I just fancy having a soak in the bath and getting into some lounge-wear. You don't mind, do you, Kitts?'

'Lounge-wear? That's pyjamas, to you and me,' Jimby said to Kitty, earning himself a prod from Vi.

Kitty smiled, ignoring her brother's comment. 'Course not. Anyway, we don't have a babysitter, Noushka's sleeping over at her friend's tonight. Friday night would be good, though, if you can manage that?'

'Hmm. I'm going to need my beauty sleep for the photos the following day. Saturday night would be better,' said Jimby.

'Good point,' agreed Vi.

'Saturday it is then, I'll mention it to Ollie.' Kitty climbed into her car. 'Right, I'll be off. Thanks for the clothes, Vi. See you tomorrow. Try to behave yourself for one night, Jimby.'

'I'll do my best, sis' he said, grinning.

Vi and Jimby stood on the trod, waving as Kitty's car disappeared up the road. 'Are you okay? You look a bit pale.' Jimby threw his arm around her.

'I'm fine, just feeling a bit tired, that's all. I think the last couple of weeks has caught up with me.' She looked up at him and smiled. For the last few days she'd woken up feeling absolutely drained, and hadn't felt any better as the day progressed. In fact, if she closed her eyes where she was standing, she was convinced she'd be able to nod off right there on the spot, which wasn't like her at all.

Jimby kissed the top of her head. 'Right, gorgeous, I think what you need is a cup of tea and to put your feet up. Come on, let's get you inside and I'll put the kettle on.'

'Sounds good.' Vi rested her head on his shoulder,

enjoying the closeness. *Jimby Fairfax, you are such a gorgeous, thoughtful man!* Their misunderstanding was still close enough to feel raw when her thoughts ventured onto it. She couldn't bear to think how she'd nearly lost him. Vi hadn't thought it possible, but she was convinced her love for Jimby had grown stronger since that day.

**CHAPTER 27**

Saturday morning arrived in a blaze of sunshine. Jimby leapt out of bed bright and early, pulling back the thick curtains and letting in the day. 'Perfect!'

'Jimby,' Vi grumbled. She turned away from the gleaming rays of the sun and pulled the duvet over her head. She felt so tired, it was as if she hadn't been to bed at all.

'Look at that, Vi. Just look at that glorious sunshine, that clear blue sky. It's absolutely spot on for the photo shoot. I need to ring Ollie.' He pulled on his pyjama bottoms and headed towards the door. 'You stay put, I'll bring you a cup of tea up in half an hour.'

But Vi didn't hear him, she was fast asleep.

∽

An hour later, Vi was sitting in the garden, enjoying a cup of tea in the early morning sunshine. She was watching a butterfly and a bumble-bee move from flower to flower as if they were performing a carefully choreographed dance. She sighed and closed her eyes, enjoying the sun's warmth on her face. It was so tranquil here, what on earth had ever made her want to leave it, she wondered?

'Can I get you any breakfast?' asked Jimby, interrupting her thoughts. 'There's some nice croissants; I could warm one through for you?'

She looked up at him, shielding her eyes from the sun with her hand and smiled. 'No thanks, I'm not hungry, I'm just going to grab an apple or something later.'

'You sure?' He bent down to kiss her. He was still just wearing his pyjama bottoms and Vi reached up to touch the hairs on his chest, her fingertips delighting in the warmth.

'Yep.' She sighed happily. It was good to have the old Jimby back, with his usual smile fixed to his face once more.

A knock at the door set Jarvis and Jerry off barking and racing down the hall. Jimby checked his watch. 'It's only ten past eight.'

'Who on earth would call this early on a Saturday morning?' asked Vi.

'No idea,' he replied, making his way into the house. 'And there's no need for all that noise, you two,' he called as he followed the dogs down the hall.

He reappeared in a moment wearing a look of disbelief, while Maneater followed close behind. Vi was surprised to see that, even at this early hour, she was wearing one of her trademark too short, too clingy, too much cleavage dresses in a scratchy, stretchy fabric, and the woman could barely take her eyes off Jimby's bare chest.

'Morning, Anita, this is an early call,' said Vi.

'Morning. Her voice sounded even raspier than usual. She ran her eyes greedily over Jimby's body and Vi found herself having to stifle a laugh. 'I've just come to volunteer my services. I'm very good with make-up, you see. Used to work on a cosmetics counter a few years ago.'

*I think it's more than a few years ago,* Vi thought. She took in the thick, too-orange foundation and the heavy-handed eye-shadow.

'Make-up?' Jimby looked outraged.

'Yes,' she continued, 'and I was wondering if you would need to have any skilfully applied for the photo shoot I've been hearing so much about. You know, to keep everything looking professional. Like the proper models do.' Her eyes had become glued like a couple of magnets on Jimby's crotch. He was obviously aware of it as he went and stood behind Violet.

Vi pressed her lips together; it was getting harder and harder not to laugh.

'Thanks for the offer, but we're going to keep it au naturel,' said Jimby. Vi could have sworn he sounded nervous.

'Au naturel, eh?' Anita arched a suggestive eyebrow at him and ran her tongue along her thin top lip.

Vi heard Jimby gulp. Unable to hold on to her giggles any longer, she snorted but did her best to pass it off as a sneeze. 'Ooh, sorry about that. Hay fever. Took me by surprise,' she said. Maneater flicked her eyes quickly over Violet before returning them to Jimby.

'Well, thanks very much for the offer, Man … I mean Anita, but we need to crack on, so if you don't mind …' Jimby gestured for her to leave.

'Oh, yes, there'll be lots of masculine bodies to prepare to make sure they look in prime condition.' She moved towards the kitchen door. 'And don't forget, if any of you need touching-up, you know where I am. I'll see myself out.'

With that she disappeared into the house leaving Vi and Jimby looking after her open-mouthed.

'Jesus, what d'you think she meant by that?' asked Jimby.

'I'm not sure, but I think it was meant to be a double entendre,' replied Vi.

'Well, she can keep her bloody hands off my double entendres. Women like that absolutely bloody terrify me.'

Vi looked at him and burst into a fit of giggles.

∽

First up to be photographed was Ollie, who was champing at the bit to get it over and done with. He was being photographed in his workshop, poised as if working at his bench, planning a length of wood, the floor covered in curls of wood-shavings. He'd banned everyone except Kitty and Jimby from being present, and breathed a sigh of relief when Nick said he was done.

'Phew! I'm glad that's out of the way,' he said. He pulled his t-shirt over his head, smoothing down his dark blond hair.

'Ha! You did well, me aud mucker.' Jimby clapped him on the back, laughing.

Ollie shook his head. 'I still can't believe I actually let you talk me into it.'

Jimby threw his head back and laughed even louder. 'I knew you wouldn't be able to refuse when you knew it was for such a good cause.'

'So who's next?' asked Nick.

'That would be me,' said Jimby. We just need to bob across the yard to my forge.' He made his way out of Ollie's workshop with Vi and the photographer in tow.

Jimby had stripped down to his underpants when Kitty called through the door, covering her eyes with her hand. 'Jimby, you need to come and stop Reg, he's taken a dislike to the vicar cycling by on his bike and he's chasing him down the road. Rev Nev looks terrified.'

'Of all the times, the little sod, I'm going to wring his bloody neck. Sorry, Nick, I'm going to have to deal with this'. Jimby hurriedly pulled on a pair of old wellies that were near to hand, then shot out of the forge.

'Jimby, you can't go—'

'It won't take long,' he cut Vi off.

'But don't you think you should put some—'

'It'll be fine,' he called over his shoulder. He ran out of the yard and into the street.

'Do you think he's realised he's just wearing his underpants?' asked Nick.

'I haven't a clue,' Vi replied.

'Which way?' Jimby called to Kitty. He didn't notice her shocked expression.

She pointed towards the village green. 'Don't you think you should put—'

'No time,' he said. She watched as her brother pelted along the road as fast as his wellies would allow.

Jimby followed the sound of squawking and pleas for help, and in a matter of moments he was met by the sight of Rev Nev and Reg, who were mid-tousle just by the duck pond.

'Reg,' Jimby bellowed, but the cockerel ignored him. He raced towards the pair, his wellies pounding on the ground as he went. As he reached the conflict, he went to grab the bird but Reg had seen him and made a break for it. Jimby lunged once more but judged it badly and ended up face-planting the ground. Sensing victory, Reg strutted over to investigate but Jimby seized the opportunity and grabbed him by his scrawny legs amid an ear-splitting diatribe of squawks. 'Gotcha, you little shit.'

Taking a moment to get his breath back, Jimby pulled himself to his feet to the sound of peals of laughter around him. Half of the village looked on in hysterics at his exploits. Vi was amongst the sea of faces, tears of laughter pouring down her cheeks. 'Oh, Jimby, you should see yourself.'

'Uncle Jimby, that was ace!' Lucas's eyes danced with mischief. 'I've filmed it all on my phone and I'm gonna put it on YouTube!'

'You little bugger, don't you dare,' said Jimby.

Ollie wiped tears of mirth from beneath his eyes. 'Mate, are you alright? You should see the state of your knees.'

'And your chin. I think we might need Maneater's help after all,' said Vi.

Jimby held an objecting Reg at arms-length. 'Well, all I can say is, thanks for the sympathy, you lot. And, now you mention it, my bloody chin doesn't half sting.'

'I'm not surprised.' Kitty was doing her best to calm her giggles.

'Right, I need to stick this little sod somewhere.' He nodded to Reg. 'Then I can get on with the photoshoot.'

'I'll have to clean your grazes up first,' said Vi. 'Bloody knees aren't exactly photogenic.'

Jimby harrumphed and looked at Reg. 'As for you, you little shit, you're for the bloody chop.'

Vi walked along beside the pair, giggling so hard, her body shook.

'It's not funny,' said Jimby.

'Oh, Jimby, it is,' she replied.

Back at the forge, and with Reg fastened safely out of harm's way, Vi dug out the First Aid kit and turned to the photographer. 'I think you might need to go and shoot Mr February while I clean this mess up. Actually, maybe do a few more, give this scrape time to dry up.'

Nick looked at Jimby. 'Sounds like a good idea.'

'Thanks,' said Jimby. 'I'm a mess, now, am I?'

'Well, I don't think you can say too much when you're sitting there in nothing but a pair of wellies and your budgie-smugglers, with a dirty great scrape on your chin and a matching pair on your knees,' said Vi.

Jimby sighed. 'I'm never going to live this down, am I?'

'Nope,' said Vi. 'Especially if Lucas puts it on YouTube.'

'Ouch!' Jimby winced as she dabbed his chin with some liquid wound cleaner. 'That bloody bird's going to have to go. He's caused one problem too many.'

'And exactly how many times have you said that?' Vi dabbed his chin some more.

∽

BY LUNCH TIME Nick was halfway through taking photos and had headed back to Jimby's forge to pick up where they'd left off. Vi had done her best to disguise the injury on his chin, but his knees were still a bit raw.

'I think we'll have you behind your anvil and keep your knees well out of shot,' he said. 'And if you tilt your chin down, that should hide the scrape on it.'

Jimby did as he was instructed. He sneaked a quick glance over at Violet who was having a quiet chuckle to herself in the corner. 'What's so funny?' he asked, doing his best to keep a straight face.

'Nothing.' Vi shook her head, not daring to look at him.

Once they were done, and the photographer was happy with the shots, Jimby said, 'Right, I'm off to the pub for a pint. After the morning I've had, I think I've earned it.' He slipped his shirt on then inched his jeans carefully over his sore knees.

'I like the sound of that,' said Nick. 'I think that's where the others were heading.'

'I'll just pop back to the house, then I'll join you,' said Vi. She needed to pop to the loo and have a quick spritz of perfume.

'Okay, gorgeous, I'll have a cheeky little gin and tonic waiting for you. Don't be long.' He went over to her and pressed a quick kiss to her lips which triggered a wave of butterflies in her stomach. She hoped his kisses would always affect her in that way, right up until they were old and grey.

~

THE PUB WAS HEAVING when Vi arrived, and the photography session seemed to have generated an upbeat mood. Loud laughter filled her ears and the delicious aroma of roast dinner hung in the air as she made her way over to their usual table.

'Hello, darling.' Bea gave her a warm smile as she squeezed by. 'You should've been here earlier when Jonty was having his photo taken, it was hilarious. Managed to spill a full pint over himself – if you get what I mean. Made him jump sky high. Though, I can't tell you how absolutely thrilled he is at being Mr February.'

Vi laughed. 'Honestly, Bea, there must be something in the air today. Did you hear what happened to Jimby?'

Bea nodded, covering her mouth to hide her chuckle. 'I did. Doesn't seem to have dampened his spirits though, does it?'

Vi looked across to where he was sitting, laughing and chatting animatedly in his usual place as life and soul of the party. 'No, it doesn't, Bea.' She smiled as a feeling of warmth spread across her chest.

Just then, he spotted her and waved her over, patting the empty seat beside him. 'I'll catch up with you later, Bea,' she said before weaving her way across the bar.

'Hi, Vi,' said Molly. 'It's been quite a morning from what I can gather.'

'You could say. Hi, everyone.' Vi was happy to see the whole group of friends at the table. She sat down next to Jimby who wrapped his arm around her.

'I see bugger-lugs has been up to his usual.' Molly nodded towards Jimby. 'I don't think we've got a single photo of him at some function without him having some sort of injury.'

'I am here, you know?' He grinned at her, before taking a long slug of his beer.

'I'll tell you what,' said Camm. 'You lot don't know how lucky you are getting your photo over and done with. I should've thought about it when I agreed to be Mr December; I didn't realise you'd pretty much be doing it in order of months. My guts have done nothing but churn all morning, worrying about it.'

They were interrupted by Jonty who was wearing a worried expression. 'I don't know if any of you have heard, but Dave Mellison has just been in and said he won't be taking part in the photographs.'

'What?' Jimby looked exasperated. 'Did he say why?'

'It's because he's a knob,' said Molly. 'No other reason.'

'I knew we shouldn't have agreed to let him take part. It went against all our better judgements. There's always a bloody problem with that family,' said Jimby.

'I'll bet it's something to do with Aoife,' said Kitty.

'You're absolutely right, my dear. Apparently, she told him that such photos are demeaning and beneath him,' said Jonty.

'What? It's just a laugh, to raise money for something in the village. Something that could benefit them one day.' Ollie shook his head in disbelief.

'I know, that's what I told him. But Aoife has said that if he takes part, then she'll leave him.'

'I know what I'd do if I was him,' said Jimby.

'She's unbelievable,' Vi said. 'And who can we get to take his place at such short notice?'

At that Hugh Heifer walked through the door. The friends looked at each other and burst out laughing.

'Don't even think about it,' said Vi. 'It'd take forever to clean him up.'

'Even if you could, I think it would have the opposite effect of what we're hoping to achieve,' added Molly. 'He's not exactly hunk material, is he? We'd end up with people demanding a refund.'

'Don't be so mean, Moll.' But, despite herself, Kitty giggled.

'Hasn't stopped you from laughing about it, though, has it?' Molly fired back.

Jimby was scratching his head as he wracked his brain for a substitute.

'Excuse me, Jimby.' It was young Beth Gillespie, the GP from Danskelfe surgery. She was sitting at the table next to them with her boyfriend Liam and an out-of-the-way attractive man with dark wavy hair and a dimple in his chin. 'I hope you don't think I'm being nosy, but I may have a solution to your problem.'

'Oh?' Jimby's expression switched to one of hope.

'My cousin Zander is visiting for the weekend. He could step in, couldn't you, Zandie?'

Vi scrutinised Dr Beth. Was she mistaken, or was there an air of mischief about her?

'Could I?' said Zander. 'Stand in for what?'

Liam had obviously cottoned on to what Beth was up to and pulled a face of disbelief, but his girlfriend's cousin didn't seem to notice.

'No need to worry about the finer details now, but you'll be absolutely perfect. All you need to do is say yes.' Jimby beamed at him.

'Well, that's a slight fib,' said Molly under her breath. 'But I wouldn't mind taking a peek at those rugby-player muscles he's got hidden under his shirt.'

Vi giggled. 'Get your tongue back in Moll. Wait till he finds out he has to take his kit off.'

'By the way, did anyone ever tell you, you look like that actor from the series that's on the telly on Sundays? The good-looking one with dark hair.' Molly's question made Zander blush and shift uncomfortably in his seat.

'Er, maybe once or twice.'

'Mm. Thought they might.'

'Just ignore my cousin,' said Jimby. 'And let's get back to the matter in hand.'

Together with Dr Beth, the friends quickly outlined how they were trying to raise funds for a defibrillator, all conveniently excluding the part about being photographed naked.

'Well then, how could I refuse,' said Zander, smiling. 'I love the way you all pull together in this village.'

'Fanbloodytastic. Let me get you another pint.' Jimby clapped him on the back

**CHAPTER 28**

With the photo shoot back on track, Vi headed home; she'd been feeling tired and in need of a sit down. She was making her way along the trod when she sensed a car slowing down beside her. She didn't think too much of it initially, assuming it was just someone making a meal out of parking up, But instinct caused the hairs on the back of her neck to bristle when she heard the front passenger window being lowered and the last voice she wanted to hear say her name.

'Vi.'

She walked on, quickening her pace.

'Vi, please. Can you stop for a minute?'

Still she ignored him, hurrying as fast as her three-inch heels would allow on the uneven trod.

Before she had chance to think, the car stopped and in a moment Mike Williamson was falling into step beside her. 'Just give me a minute of your time, Vi, that's all I ask.'

'I've got nothing to say to you.'

He jumped in front of her and before she knew it, his hands were on the tops of her arms. 'Vi, when I saw you at

Kirkbythwaite Hall it triggered something in me. Made me remember how good we were together.' He squeezed her arms as if for emphasis. 'Please, Vi, for old time's sake, just listen to me, will you?'

She wriggled free of his grip. 'What, like you listened to me all those years ago?' She went to move round him but he blocked her path. 'And what about your wife? Does she know you're here?'

Mike flinched. 'Look, I just want to know what happened to our child? If we have a girl or a boy? I want to know what their name is? They'll be around fifteen now, won't they?'

'What? "We" don't have a child.'

'What do you mean? You got rid of it?'

Vi couldn't believe the audacity of the man. 'Don't dare stand there and judge me. "Get rid of it" is exactly what you told me to do, or does your memory fail you?'

'I can't believe you actually took such drastic measures.'

His self-pitying expression made her see red. She wasn't prepared to go into the details of her miscarriage and its consequences with him; that would only offer him an opportunity for further conversation. No, she wanted to get away from him as quickly as possible.

'How dare you judge me? You're the man who was cheating on his wife. A wife who was having treatment for breast cancer. So don't dare think you've got the moral high-ground here.' Adrenalin was coursing round her veins, forming a red-hot ball of anger in the pit of her stomach.

'Vi!' A voice called from behind her. She turned to see Molly racing down the trod. 'What the bloody hell are you doing here? I thought I'd told you to sod off.' Molly prodded Mike in the chest.

'Hey! Don't do that,' he said.

'You've already seen him?' Vi asked.

'After we'd had lunch at the tea shop. He stopped me as I was driving home. I recognised him straight away. Gave him a piece of my mind, and a piece of advice. Looks like he ignored it, though.' Molly glared at Mike.

'What's going on?' Jimby appeared beside Vi. 'Is this man bothering you?'

Vi's heart began pounding louder in her chest as a wave of nausea washed over her. 'Jimby! He's, er …'

'Yes, he sodding-well is bothering her,' said Molly. 'She's told him to leave her alone but he's not listening.'

'You keep out of this,' Mike hissed. 'I'm only trying to find out what hap—'

'Jimby,' she paused, steadying her nerves. 'This is Mike Williamson, my old lecturer from university.'

'Letch, more like,' added Molly.

Vi watched Jimby's handsome features change as a black cloud descended over them. His eyes darkened and he pulled himself up to his full six-foot-two, towering over Mike. 'I've been hearing about you,' he said.

'Right, well, I'm sure Vi's given you *her* version of events.' Mike pushed his floppy fringe off his face; he suddenly didn't sound quite so confident.

'And that's the only version I need to hear. So I think it's time you stopped troubling my fiancée and got back in your car.' Jimby glared at him and placed a proprietary arm around Violet.

Mike had flinched at Jimby's used of "fiancée". He paused for a moment. 'I will when Vi tells me that's what she wants me to do.' He looked at Vi, his smarmy smile of old spreading across his face. The young, impressionable girl she used to be may have found it attractive, but the confident woman she'd become could see right through the sleaze, and it made her skin crawl.

'I have absolutely no feelings for you. I can't believe I ever had. I want you to go away, leave this village and I never, ever want to see you again. Is that clear enough for you?'

Anger flashed across his face. 'Crystal.' He stood for a moment, holding eye contact with her. When she didn't waver, he turned and walked back to his car, driving off at speed. The three of them watched in silence as his car disappeared along the road to Danskelfe.

'You okay?' Jimby turned to Vi.

Vi nodded, but tears were pouring down her cheeks. He pulled her close, smoothing her hair. She rested her head against the warmth of his chest, soothed by the strong, steady pounding of his heart.

'Don't cry, Vi. Don't give him the power to spoil another day.' Jimby pressed his lips to her head.

Molly squeezed Vi's arm. 'Honestly, chick, you can treat that as closure. You've exorcised the prat and you're now totally free of him.'

Vi gave a soggy laugh. 'You know what, Moll, you're absolutely right. It does feel like I've finally got closure. I can move on and shove him firmly in the past.'

'Which is where the creep belongs,' added Jimby. He fished a tissue out of his pocket and handed it to her.

'Thanks.' She took it and blew her nose. 'I feel absolutely jiggered. I might go and have a lie down, if you don't mind?' In truth, she felt like she could sleep for a week.

'A little power-nap'll do you good, hun. All of the emotions you've been going through recently will've worn you out,' said Molly. 'I'm going to grab Camm and head to

Mum and Dad's – we're keeping away from home while Ben's being photographed as Mr whatever month he is.'

'He's Mr October.' Jimby grinned, his dimples returning. 'Yep, the last thing he'll need is his mother hanging around, Moll.'

Francis Jessop, the head gardener from Danskelfe Castle, drove by, waving. 'Ah, and there goes Mr April.' Jimby waved back.

'Trust me, it's mutual. We'll steer well clear until it's time for Camm to be snapped as Mr December.' She turned to walk away. 'You still coming to the pub tonight, Vi?'

'Definitely.'

'That's my girl,' said Jimby. 'Now get yourself home for that nap so your batteries are re-charged for it.'

'Yes, boss.' Vi smiled up at his handsome face, relieved that the sudden appearance of Mike Williamson hadn't put the dampers on things.

**CHAPTER 29**

Once back at Sunshine Cottage, Vi gave in to her yearning for an apple and grabbed one from the fridge. She bit into it, savouring its crisp tanginess that set her taste-buds zinging. As she sat in the chair, she could feel her eyes getting heavy; the urge to have a nap was becoming harder to resist, so she finished her apple and made her way upstairs.

Too tired to fold her clothes, Vi lay them on the chair, quickly slipped into a pair of silk pyjamas and climbed into bed, pulling on her silk eye mask. Within seconds of her head hitting the pillow, she was fast asleep.

∼

'Time to wake up, gorgeous.' Jimby set a mug of tea down on the bedside table before bending to kiss her cheek.

'Uhh? What time is it?'

'Half five, you've been asleep for a good few hours – you were flat out when I called in just after three.'

'Thank you, Jimby.' Vi yawned, the bed felt so warm and

cosy; she still felt like she had a couple of hours more sleep in her yet.

'We're meeting the others at the pub at seven thirty-ish. Jonty's given us the okay for a sing-song, so don't let me forget my guitar. Thought you might like to take your tambourine, too.'

'Sounds good.' She pushed the duvet back and smiled at him sleepily.

'If you didn't look so knackered, I'd climb in there with you, and let you have a private viewing of the contents of my underpants. I can tell you, this bad boy's drawn gasps today.' He waggled his eyebrows at her as he patted his crotch.

Vi giggled and threw her eye-mask at him. 'Yes, but how do you know what the gasps meant? They could've been gasps of horror.'

'I'll have you know, I have it on very good authority that they were gasps of the "he's hung like a horse" variety.'

'And whose authority was this exactly? Maneater's?'

Jimby shuddered. 'On those words, I'll leave you to wake up in your own time, there's plenty of tea in the pot for when you're ready for a fresh cup.' With that he disappeared downstairs leaving Vi chuckling to herself.

~

VI AND JIMBY were the first of their group to arrive at The Sunne. The evening had turned chilly and Vi claimed the seat next to the fire. Jimby propped his guitar against the wall, out of the way. As they were getting settled, they were joined by Kitty and Ollie.

'Ooh, it's nippy out there,' said Kitty.

'I know, that's why I'm hugging the fire,' Vi replied.

'You okay, chick? You look a bit peaky.' Kitty slipped off her jacket and hung it on the back of the chair.

'Just tired. Though I shouldn't be; I slept for a few hours this afternoon. Don't feel any better for it.'

'You've had a lot going on recently, it'll have taken it out of you,' said Kitty.

'Now then, Vi.' Ollie smiled across at her. 'I'll just go and give Jim a hand at the bar. Prosecco, Kitts?'

'Mm, please.' She sat down and turned to Vi. 'Moll told me about what happened with Mike Williamson, that'll have knocked the stuffing out of you.'

Vi sighed. 'Just a bit. But the funny thing is – and Molly called this "closure" – I actually feel so much better for it all happening. Like I do, finally, have closure on the situation.'

'Well, I'm pleased for you, hun. And it's good that it's all out of the way before the wedding.'

Vi nodded, Kitty was right. It was time to look forward.

〜

Before long, the pub was teeming with locals, the air filled with the hum of jovial conversation, with everyone sharing their stories of the calendar photo shoot. Molly and Camm arrived shortly before Robbie and Rosie and joined the others round the table. They were mid conversation when Zander Gillespie pulled up a chair beside them.

'Still talking to us then, Mr August?' Jimby gave him a knowing wink.

'Yes, though I'm not so sure I should be after what you roped me into.' He picked up his beer and took a sip, licking the froth from his top lip.

'Hah! I heard about that,' said Ollie. 'Traumatic, wasn't

it? I was glad to get mine out of the way first thing, otherwise I'd have spent the whole day fretting about it.'

'Well, I would've been grateful of the chance to fret about it, actually. I hadn't got a clue what I was letting myself in for. I just rocked up at the field where the photographer was shooting his photos, and was told to get my kit off. No explanation, or anything.'

Jimby, who had just taken a sip of his beer, snorted. He turned, spraying it all over the fire which hissed and sizzled in annoyance. He wiped his mouth with the back of his hand. 'Sorry about that, mate.'

'No worries. Luckily Robbie was there and explained everything to me which, I have to say, was a huge relief.'

'Well, we really appreciate you stepping in for us like that.' Jimby gave him a friendly pat on the back.

'Thanks to that cousin of mine, I wouldn't exactly call it "stepping in", but it's for a fantastic cause, and being a GP, I could hardly turn you down, could I?'

'A GP? Jimby could've done with your help this morning, couldn't you, Jimbo?'

'I'd rather not talk about that.' Jimby feigned an offended expression.

'This doesn't have anything to do with the story of a cockerel, a vicar and a man running down the road in nothing but wellies and his underpants, does it?'

Kitty sniggered and pointed to the graze on Jimby's chin.

'Ahh.' Zander nodded, trying not to laugh.

The sound of Jonty ringing the bell at the end of the bar silenced everyone. 'Can I have your attention, folks. To round off this wonderful and eventful day, Bea and I are happy to announce that there'll be an impromptu session of Songs at the Sunne this evening. Jimby, as it was your idea in the first place, I wonder if you'd start proceedings.'

Everyone started clapping and cheering. Molly stuck her fingers between her teeth and gave a shrill whistle. 'Ever so ladylike, Moll,' said Vi.'

Jimby leaned across and picked up his guitar. 'Come on, Vi, grab your tambourine. Let's go and make some music.'

'Way-hay!' said Molly.

The pair made themselves comfortable on the tall stools, with Jimby strumming a few chords, checking the tuning of his guitar. 'Right then, I think we should start with a song dedicated to those of us who were brave enough to get our kit off for a good cause earlier today, wouldn't you agree?' His suggestion was met with cheers and whoops as he launched into a rousing, feel-good song. It went down a storm and when it came to an end, everyone called for an encore.

'Okay,' said Jimby. As you seem to be enjoying it, I think we should stick with the old school style for the next one.' He turned to Vi and whispered the name of the song; she nodded with a smile. 'Okay, you'll all know this one, so feel free to join in.' In no time, the whole pub was singing and clapping along.

Between them, Jimby and Vi sang five more songs before the audience allowed them to take a break. 'We need to give someone else a chance, and I'm gagging for a pint.' Jimby grinned as he unhooked the guitar strap from his shoulder.

'That was amazing,' said Zander. 'You just about brought the house down.'

'Thanks.' Vi smiled as Jimby took a long glug of his beer.' 'There's usually a sing-along session once a month on a Thursday, today's a one-off.'

'Ahh.' Zander nodded.

'So, whereabouts did you say you were from?' asked Molly.

'He didn't, Moll, you're just being nosy,' said Camm, which earned him a nudge from her.

'S'okay,' Zander replied. 'I've got the cottage out in the dale, appropriately named Dale View Cottage. I bought it a couple of years ago and have been slowly doing it up. I live over in Leeds but I'm going to start renting Dale View out as a holiday cottage and just wanted to come over and give the place a final checking over before I do.'

'Ooh, Dale View Cottage, it looks gorgeous now, you've done a really good job of it.'

'Thanks,' said Zander. 'I love the location, it's so peaceful. The cottage needed a lot doing to it, but I've enjoyed it.'

'So does that mean we won't be seeing much of you?' asked Ollie.

'Well, I intend to pop over in my time off when the property's empty, so I'll be calling in to the Sunne whenever I get the chance.'

'Good stuff,' said Robbie.

'Oh, fabulous.' Molly rubbed her hands together as Dave Mellison, armed with his saxophone, made his way to the stool Jimby had just vacated. 'You're in for a treat, Zander.'

'Oh?'

'I can guarantee, you'll never have heard anything like this before,' she said with a wicked smile.

'Actually, he's the bloke you've got to thank for you having to get your photo taken in the buff, Zander,' said Jimby.

'I don't think "thank" is the word I'd use,' Zander replied.

'I think he's got a bloody nerve, turning up here when he let you down the way he did,' said Rosie.

'I think he did everyone's eyeballs a favour,' added Molly.

'If it wasn't for him doing that, we'd have to look at his scrawny little body for the whole of bloody August. Instead we get to have a perv over Zander's pecs.'

'Apologies, my cousin's not always this much of a letch, honest,' said Jimby.

Kitty giggled. 'I think I would've drawn some clothes on him – Dave, I mean.'

'I think I would've had to rip the whole month out,' said Vi. She picked up her gin and tonic, had second thoughts about taking a sip, and set it back on the table.

'Ooh, I knew I had something to tell you.' Rosie sat up straight. 'It's a bit gossipy, but well ... when you consider the family, they deserve it.'

'Ooh, I'm intrigued,' said Vi.

Rosie shuffled forward on her chair and leaned in. 'Earlier today, a client told me something very, erm, interesting about Dave Mellison – don't ask who, they made me promise not to name them. Anyway, they told me that on several occasions, they've seen him climbing over the back fence of Maneater Matheson's cottage – sometimes going into the garden, and sometimes coming out.'

For several long seconds, Rosie was faced with a row of bemused expressions as the friends processed the information she'd just shared.

Molly was the first to speak. 'What? You mean, they think he was going to see her for a bit of hanky-panky?'

Rosie nodded.

'No?' Molly looked horrified. 'Urghh! No, you've got to be kidding! I really wish I could unhear that. Now I've got a hideous mental image I won't ever be able to get rid of.'

'Well, I, for one, would never have put them together,' said Ollie.

'Desperate men take desperate measures, mate,' added

Jimby. 'But that would explain why we haven't seen much of him cycling back from the Fox at Danskelfe, three sheets to the wind.'

'Good point.' Ollie nodded in agreement.

Kitty scrunched up her nose. 'I must admit, they make an odd pair. Is the person who told you sure he wasn't just going to do her garden?'

Jimby snorted. 'Is that a euphemism, sis? He's just going to "do her garden".'

The friends burst out laughing. 'Oh, Kitts, I do love the way you always try to see the good in people.' Vi wrapped an arm around her friend, giving her a squeeze.

'That's one of the things I love about her.' Ollie smiled.

'Me, too,' said Vi.

'Well, I didn't want to be unkind, and was trying to think of a logical reason for him going there.' Two spots of pink coloured Kitty's cheeks.

'Yep, landscape gardeners regularly hurl themselves over peoples fences rather than use the gate.' Molly laughed. 'Stop being so bloody nice, Kitts. He's clearly having it off with the old tart because he's not getting it from his frosty cow of a wife at home.'

'Succinctly put, Molly.' Robbie raised his glass to her, and she chinked hers against it.

Vi picked up her gin and tonic and went to take a sip, but her stomach lurched as the sweet juniper fragrance hit her nostrils. She quickly put the glass down.

Jimby turned to her. 'Is that poison? You've hardly touched it.'

'I'm just not in the mood for it tonight. I'm still feeling shattered. I could murder an apple juice, though.' She could feel the weight of Kitty's gaze settling on her.

Attention was suddenly diverted to Dave Mellison as a

screeching note sliced its way across conversation. 'Shit!' Zander started, spilling his beer over his jeans.

'Speak of the devil ...' giggled Molly. 'We did warn you, Zander.'

'Not nearly enough,' he replied, wiping the excess beer away.

The friends looked on in disbelief as Dave dragged out a tuneless rendition of slow-tempo tune, with notes regularly crashing off key. Zander's face was a picture when it was finished.

'What a crock of shite,' said Molly.

'Bet you're glad you were here for that, mate,' said Jimby to Zander.

'Er, yeah, you could say,' he replied. 'So was that him playing seriously?'

'Yup,' said Molly. 'You should hear him play his favourite. Don't ask me what it's called, but it's hilarious.'

'Ah.' Zander nodded.

'His obnoxious wife keeps telling people he was in a band who nearly made it big,' said Molly.

'Big as what, though?' There was a mischievous twinkle in Zander's eye.

'Hah! Good point.' Jimby threw his head back and laughed.

'Where do we start?' Molly gave a dirty laugh that turned a few heads.

'Something tells me you're going to fit in really well here.' Ollie raised his pint glass. 'Cheers.'

'Cheers,' the friends chorused.

**CHAPTER 30**

'So that's another thing ticked off my wedding to-do list.' Vi had been checking her emails on the laptop.

'Oh, what's that?' Kitty looked up from the burlesque costume she was working on.

'The tiara I've chosen has arrived. Gemma at "Gowns" – you know, the wedding shop – had been having trouble sourcing it as her usual supplier had sold out. Anyway, she's sent me an email to say she's managed to get her hands on one and it's just arrived at her shop.' Vi flipped down the lid of the laptop and headed over to the kitchen where she reached into the fridge. 'Apple?'

'Not for me thanks. I think I might nip over to the village shop and grab a couple of pieces of chocolate flapjack. We need some more milk, too,' Kitty replied.

'Okay. Will you grab half a dozen apples while you're there? There's only one left.'

'What is it with you and apples at the moment?'

'What d'you mean? I haven't eaten them all.'

'Well, I think I've only had one.'

'The kids must've had them, then.'

'Hmm. While I remember, I wouldn't mind if we had a quick fitting of your wedding dress when I get back. Time's cracking on, and we want to make sure you're happy with it, save us having to make any last minute alterations.' Kitty grabbed her purse. 'Won't be long.'

When she returned Vi was standing in her gown. Close fitting, with its sweetheart neckline, three-quarter length sleeves and full skirt, it flattered Vi's figure. And, though the fabric was still plain since the embellishments had yet to be added, the gown looked stunning.

'Oh, Vi, it takes my breath away every time I see you in it. You look so elegant.'

'Thanks, Kitts. It's going to be perfect when it's finished. When you've got a free hand, will you fasten me up?'

'Course.' Kitty dumped the shopping in the kitchen and washed her hands. She went over to Vi and tried to pull up the zip which was concealed by tiny fabric covered buttons. She frowned, it didn't seem as easy as last time.

'What do you think's wrong?' Vi peered back over her shoulder. 'Something doesn't feel right. It was a struggle to get it over my hips, and my boobs feel like they're being crushed to death. I reckon I've been eating too much of Lucy's flapjacks.'

'Mm,' said Kitty. 'Two ticks.' Before Vi could quiz her, Kitty had nipped out of the studio leaving her nonplussed.

When she returned, Kitty thrust a small paper bag at her friend. 'There, get yourself to the loo and take that with you.'

'What? What d'you mean?'

Kitty gently guided Vi in the direction of the washroom. 'Just do as I say. I'll be waiting here for you when you're done.'

Violet peeked into the bag and gasped. 'Oh my God. You

don't seriously think I could be do you?' Her heart took off in a gallop.

'It might explain the tiredness, the going off gin and tonics, the serious craving for apples and the fact your dress feels different.' Kitty's large brown eyes shone as she smile at her friend.

Vi swallowed. 'I can't do it on my own.'

'Well, I'm not coming in with you. There's not enough room for starters, it'd end in disaster,' Kitty laughed.

'Fair enough. But I don't think I need a wee.'

'You will once you're in there. Go on, Vi. I have a good feeling about this.'

Vi's throat tightened as tears started brimming. She hugged Kitty before she disappeared into the loo. 'Ahh! I'm scared.'

'You'll be fine. Go.'

Two minutes later Vi reappeared. 'I can't do it,' she said.

'What? Of course you can. Get yourself back in there.'

'Not that bit, I've weed on it, but I'm too scared to look at the result. Will you do it for me, Kitts?' Vi's stomach was doing somersaults, making her feel sick. She felt the colour drain away from her face.

'Course I will. Come on, let's go and sit down while we wait.'

After the allotted time, Kitty peeked at the test then glanced up at Vi.

'Well?' Vi scrunched up her face, hardly daring to hear the result. 'Actually, just give me a minute while I brace myself.' She took a couple of deep breaths and released them slowly. 'Okay, now you can tell me.'

'Congratulations, chick. It's positive. Look.' Kitty rushed over to hug her friend, pushing the stick into her hand.

Vi was too stunned to speak and sat staring at the test as

tears trickled down her face. Thoughts raced through her mind, colliding and bouncing off one another and she could feel the colour return to her cheeks in a wave of warmth.

'Wait till Jimby finds out.' Kitty's voice brought her back into the room.

'Oh, Kitts, I can't believe it. How accurate are they?' She'd hate for it to be wrong, to have her wonderful news snatched away before it even got chance to sink in.

'They're pretty accurate,' said Kitty. 'But I've got another one at home if you want me to go and get it.'

'Would you mind?'

'Course not. I'll go now.' Kitty jumped up and left the studio.

Vi was like a cat on hot bricks while she was away; it felt like an eternity before she returned.

'Can I ask, how come you have so many of these?' Vi took the second test from Kitty.

'I had a false alarm about six months ago and bought a handful just to have handy.'

'As you do,' replied Vi. Kitty giggled.

Vi did the second test and this time both friends watched the result develop. Vi's heart beating faster and faster as the second blue line grew stronger and stronger.

'I think we can safely say you're going to be a mummy, Vi.'

'I think we can,' Vi murmured. She felt her heart surge with happiness.

**CHAPTER 31**

Vi couldn't wait for Jimby to get home that evening. He'd gone over to Middleton-le-Moors to fit some gates he'd made, and Vi had expected him back a good forty-five minutes earlier.

She was sitting on the sofa, sipping an icy cold glass of apple juice when she heard the familiar sound of Jimby's whistling, then the creak of the gate as he turned into the path. Vi set her drink down and jumped up.

'Honey, I'm home,' he called. He bowled through the front door carrying a paper shopping bag. 'And I bring gifts.'

'Jimby!' said Vi. She rushed along the hall to greet him, butterflies running riot around her insides.

'Hello, gorgeous.' With his free hand he pulled her to him and kissed her full on the mouth. 'Delicious!' he declared. 'Have you had a good day?'

'The best.' She beamed at him.

'Well, it's just about to get better – and still on the subject of delicious – I took a slight detour to Arnthorpe before I headed home, just so I could pop into the Cosy Corner teashop and pick up some of their delicious cakes for you – Lee and Jools say hi, by the way. There's a slice of their apple and custard tart in there – seeing as though you're into apples at the minute. Freshly made it is, too, might still be warm.'

The thought of Cosy Corner cakes made Vi's stomach rumble, she'd only eaten apples all day. She peered inside the bag, lifting out the box containing the cake, just the smell was enough to set her drooling. She'd enjoy that with a cup of tea, after she'd shared her news with Jimby.

'Jimby,' she said. She was surprised at how nervous she felt about sharing her news. Excitement joined the mix as she pulled out a chair. 'Come and sit down. I've got something to tell you.'

'Oh? Is everything alright? Come to think of it, you do look a bit flushed.'

'I'm fine, Jimby. In fact, I'm more than fine, I'm so happy I could burst.'

'Well, that's Cosy Corner cakes for you, they are bloody awesome.'

'Yes, they're awesome, but that's not why I'm so happy.' She paused for a moment and looked into his dark brown eyes that twinkled back at her. 'Jimby, I'm going to have a baby.'

His jaw dropped and he stared at her. 'You're …? Say that again, I think all the noise at the forge is finally starting to affect my lug 'oles.' He waggled a finger in his ear.

Vi took hold of his hands. 'Jimby, you're going to be a dad, and here's the proof. Look.' She handed him the pregnancy tests. 'I did two tests and they're very accurate.'

Jimby stared at the sticks before raising his eyes to hers. He ran his fingers through his hair, momentarily dumbstruck, which made Vi laugh.

'Am I dreaming, or something? Did you just tell me you're pregnant?'

'Yes.' She nodded.

A beaming smile spread across his face. 'Woah,' he yelled. He scooped Vi up and twirled her round. 'You clever girl.'

She squealed and Jimby set her down gently. 'Oops, sorry. I probably shouldn't have done that.' He looked at her, his eyes shining, oozing happiness. 'I'm over the moon, Vi. I'm going to be a dad!'

'Yes,' she giggled.

'Woohoo.' His voice filled the room. Before she had chance to say anything else, he tore out of the kitchen and out into the garden where he ran around waving his arms in the air. Vi looked on laughing, until he tackled a cartwheel and ended up tangled in the washing line, pulling the whole thing down and falling in an ungainly heap in a bed of flowers. Jarvis and Jerry shot across to him, jumping on top of him, eager to join in on the fun.

'Are you okay, Jimby.' Vi could barely speak for laughing as she ran out into the garden to help him.

'I will be when I get these daft bloody dogs off me,' he said, wrestling with the pair. Vi was laughing so hard, she couldn't get the words out to call the dogs off.

When Jimby had managed to pull himself to his feet, they made their way back into the house, Jimby dusting himself down as he went. 'Flaming hounds,' he muttered.

'Jimby, I think that was all of your own doing.'

He grinned back at her then cupped her face in his hands, kissing her tenderly. 'I can't tell you how happy you've made me, gorgeous.' He pressed his head against hers.

'I still can't quite believe it,' she replied. 'But I've made an appointment with Dr Beth, just to make sure everything's okay. I want to do all the right things. I don't want to take any chances.'

Jimby nodded, his face serious. 'Of course, we don't want you to have to go through what you did before. Come on, you need to sit down, then you can tell me how long you've known and what made you think you might be pregnant. I want all the details, every single one, nothing missed out.'

Vi tucked a purple lock behind her ears. 'It was your sister who first had an inkling – something to do with all the apples I've been munching my way through, all the really cold apple juice I've been drinking, the tiredness and going off gin and tonics,' she explained. 'She got me to try on my wedding dress, which was a bit of a squeeze since my boobs have grown.'

'An added bonus.' Jimby gave her a cheeky waggle of his eyebrows. She nudged him playfully.

'Anyway, she had some spare pregnancy tests at home.'

'Really?'

'Yep, false alarm a few months ago – don't say anything to Oll in case he doesn't know.'

'My lips are sealed.' Jimby made a zipping motion across his mouth. 'Though, he probably does, they tell each other everything.'

Vi's heart sank at hearing those words. Jimby clocked her expression. 'I didn't mean anything by that, I just meant, well, you know?' He took her hand, giving it a squeeze.

'I know, it's just going to take a while for the guilt to go.' She smiled at him. 'Anyway, back to Kitty, she grabbed a test and brought it to the studio, and the rest you know.'

'Wow, all in the space of ten minutes.'

'Pretty much.' Vi nodded.

She watched Jimby as he sat and processed her news, his

eyes shining with happiness. She never expected to be in this situation, and the love she felt for this wonderful man had taken her completely by surprise.

'And to think you hadn't been off the pill five minutes.'

'I know.'

'I always knew these bad boys were potent.' He pointed in the direction of his crotch.

Vi responded with a roll of her eyes.

**CHAPTER 32**

A week had passed since Violet had found out she was pregnant. She and Jimby were slowly getting used to the idea, allowing themselves to really believe it was true. Vi's appointment with Dr Beth had gone a considerable way to assuaging her concerns about the risks of her losing the baby after her earlier experience.

Jimby had left for work early that morning after preparing her a breakfast of stewed apples and a glass of crisp apple juice. Vi was enjoying the delicious tartness on her tongue, sitting at the table in the garden, basking in the morning sun.

The sound of the letter box rattling caught her attention and she slipped into the house, scooped the letters from the doormat and flicked through them. One was from Middleton Hospital, one looked like it was from the planning department, both of those set her stomach churning. Her monthly copy of Yorkshire Portions magazine had arrived, and the rest were a mix of bumf– the usual circulars – she put those straight into the recycling bin once she was back in the kitchen. She peeled open the one from the hospital, it was a scan date in a week's time, with a leaflet explaining what she could expect to happen. She felt the thrill of excitement ripple through her; it was really happening. Jimby would want to be there, she thought.

Moving on to the official-looking letter, she eased it out of the envelope, her stomach flipped, they were expecting their planning decision any day. With one eye closed she steeled herself as she looked at the piece of paper. One word leapt out: Approved! 'Oh, wow!' She pressed her hand to her mouth, could things get any better? She couldn't wait to tell Jimby. She picked up her phone and called his number.

'All of that's bloody fantastic,' said Jimby. 'Best of all is the appointment, I can't wait to see an image of our little Fairfax. Only then will I believe you're having an actual baby and not an apple, which is what I'm beginning to think the way you've been getting through them. And I'm going to call round to see Robbie straight away, get the ball rolling on the build as quick as we can.'

'Good idea, I'm going to get back to my breakfast.'

~

'Thanks.' Jimby took the mug of coffee Robbie handed to him. 'We need to get moving with the build as soon as possible. Can you get on to your builder friend and let him know?' he asked.

Robbie nodded. 'Yep, not a problem, he's raring to go. Actually, I'm glad you've called round, you've saved me a journey.'

'Oh, how's that?'

'These have arrived. I haven't looked at them yet. Seeing as though you organised the whole thing, I thought you'd like to be the first to see them.' He handed a puzzled-looking Jimby a large envelope. 'Photos.'

'That was quick,' Jimby replied. 'I think we should have a committee meeting to choose which ones we like best. Not at the pub, though, or everyone will want a look. I'll save opening them until then – we can all have a laugh together. I'll get in touch with Ollie and Camm and see when's good for them, then let you know.'

'Righto, and I'll let you know what Mart has to say about a building schedule.'

'Good stuff. Bloody hell, it's all happening, isn't it?' Jimby flashed him a smile before heading off.

∼

'Right, brace yourself, fellas. The moment of truth has arrived.' Jimby was sitting at the table at Withrin Hill farmhouse. Four pairs of eyes were looking at him, each with a hint of mirth combined with nervousness. Vi had been banished to the living room along with Kitty, Molly and Rosie.

'Hurry up, Uncle Jimby, this is killing me,' said Ben.

'I'm not sure I want to see them, actually,' said Ollie. He clamped a hand to his forehead. 'What the hell was I thinking, letting you rope me into this madness?'

'After what happened to poor old Gerald, your conscience got the better of you and wouldn't let you say no,' said Robbie.

'I don't ever remember saying yes,' said Ollie.

Jimby eased the first photo out of the envelope. 'Bloody hell!' He threw his head back and let rip with a hearty laugh.

'What? Let's have a look,' said Ben. Jimby put the photo on the table and the men peered in at the image of Ollie.

'Jesus!' Ollie groaned, hanging his head in his hand.

'Hey, there's nothing wrong with it, Oll,' said Robbie.

Jimby set out a few more pictures of Ollie, all slightly different. Ollie could barely bring himself to look. 'Nick says we can pick the ones we like the best then let him know and he'll organise the printing for us,' Jimby stopped laughing long enough to explain.

The next one out was of Jonty, which generated even louder guffaws from the men.

In the living room, the women couldn't stand the suspense any longer and piled into the kitchen. 'Come on then, let's have a look,' said Molly. 'I could do with a laugh.'

'Oh, my God, look at the state of Jonty,' giggled Rosie. 'He's like a pasty stick insect.'

'Yep, but he looks chuffed to bits about it,' added Ollie.

'He's a good sport.' Kitty smiled.

'Wow, look at the muscles on Zander.' Molly's eyes were practically popping out of her head.

'Should I be worried?' Camm gave her an amused look.

'I doubt that very much, Camm, this one's all talk. She's only got eyes for her Romany heart throb,' said Vi.

'I'm just admiring the male human form, that's all,' said Molly. 'And what have I told you about calling Camm my Romany heart throb?'

'Sorry,' said Vi.

'I don't mind,' said Camm.

Vi gave him an apologetic smile. The name wasn't intended to hurt, it was just a harmless nod to his gipsy heritage.

'Blimey! Look at the size of Jimby's anvil. I didn't know you could get them so big.' Rosie sounded genuinely incredulous.

'That's what they all say.' Jimby feigned a swagger.

'I reckon you've paid Nick to photoshop it so it looks bigger,' said Molly.

'I think we all know why I need to have such a big anvil, don't we?' He waggled his eyebrows.

'Get over yourself, Jimbo.' Vi rolled her eyes.

'Poor Nick.' Molly frowned as she flicked through the photos.

'Why poor Nick?' asked Camm.

'Having to look at this lot in the flesh.'

'What do you mean?' asked Jimby. 'We're fine specimens.'

'He'll have seen worse,' said Camm.

'You reckon?' Molly held up the photo of Jonty. 'I'm not so sure.' It made them all fall about laughing.

'Right, back in the real world.' Ollie sat back. 'Shall we get stuck into choosing which photos are most suitable for the calendar?'

'I think we need beer and wine to help the decision making process.' Molly headed over to the fridge, closely followed by Violet.

Vi leaned in to her. 'Just apple juice for me, Moll.'

Molly nodded. 'I wasn't sure if you'd told everyone just yet, so I thought I could pour some apple juice in a glass and pass it of as wine, if you like?'

Vi smiled at how thoughtful her friend was. 'Only Kitty and you know – and Ollie and Camm, of course – but I'd rather keep it quiet until the three month mark, just in case.'

'Yep, I understand, chick.' Molly squeezed her arm. 'But it's bloody exciting, all the same.'

∼

THAT NIGHT in the cosiness of their bed, Vi lay in Jimby's

arms, his hand laying protectively on her stomach. The bedside lights cast a soothing glow around the room and Vi felt swathed in contentment. She snuggled closer into Jimby, he responded by bending forward and kissing her nose.

'So is the little pippin still making you feel as tired?' he asked.

'Little pippin?'

'Mmm. The little apple you're incubating in here.' He gave her tummy a gentle rub.

Vi giggled. 'Pippin, I like that, it sounds sweet. But, yes, I'm still feeling jiggered, though Dr Beth said that should pass soon.'

'It's been quite a day, hasn't it? What with getting a date for your scan, hearing about the plans and then the photos arriving. No one could ever say life's dull round here.'

'You can say that again.'

'No one could ever say life's dull around here.'

Vi groaned, she could hear the smile in his voice. 'Your jokes don't get any better, Jimby.'

'You're probably right.'

They lay in silence for a moment, each lost in their own thoughts.

Jimby was the first to speak. 'It's going to get pretty full-on with when the building work starts and I really don't want you to stress about any of it. You've got enough on your plate planning the wedding on top of running your business.'

'You're busy, too, Jimby. I can't just leave everything to you, especially now you've got the calendar to sort out.' She looked up at him.

'Well, we're both busy. So I wondered what you think about having Robbie project manage it for us? He's offered and I said I'd run it by you first, then let him know. He's worked with Mart on loads of projects before and he says they get on really well. It just means if there are any problems, he can deal with them for us.'

'Sounds like it's a no brainer, then.'

'That's what I thought.'

'Well, I'm happy to do that if you are?'

'Great. I'll let him know first thing.'

Vi yawned. 'It's making me feel even more tired just thinking about it. I don't think my eyes can stay open any longer.' She closed her eyes and let herself drift off into blissful sleep.

**CHAPTER 33**

Jimby awoke bright and early. He made Vi's usual breakfast of stewed apples accompanied by an icy cold glass of apple juice and set it on a tray with a small vase of flowers.

'There you go, gorgeous, breakfast in bed for you and the pippin.' He grinned broadly.

Vi smiled. 'Thanks, Jimby.'

'How are you diddlin' this morning? Looking forward to seeing the scan of our little Fairfax?'

She swallowed her mouthful of tart apple. 'Mmm, definitely. I'm a mix of excited but nervous. I just want everything to be okay.'

'Everything will be fine. Don't worry about it.'

'I keep thinking about Romantique, too. Worrying about how Kitty and I are going to keep it going, us both having a young family.' A feeling of warmth washed over her; it felt lovely to put herself in the same category as Kitty in that way.

He sat on the edge of the bed. 'Well, worrying isn't going to help anything. You'll just have to take someone on. You were saying that yourself, before you found out about

Pippin, how business was growing quicker than you expected so you might have to have an extra pair of hands.'

'True. I think I'm just feeling this way because there's a lot going on at the moment. It all feels a bit overwhelming, though Kitty says my hormones won't be helping and that they should settle down soon. She did say that Noushka has offered to help out at Romantique in her spare time, which is good.'

Jimby took Vi's face in his hands. 'Honestly, stop worrying. Things have a habit of taking care of themselves. You don't have the house build to worry about, things are going smoothly with that, so if that's what's niggling you, just get it out of your mind.' He kissed her gently.

She smiled up at him. 'You're right. I need to get out of the habit.'

'You do, and as I've said before, I'll help in any way I can.'

'Thank you, Jimby. Mind you, I can't see you sewing lacy underwear.'

He scratched his chin. 'Hm. You're probably right. Anyway, I'd best crack on, Cinders here has the dishwasher to stack.' He jumped up and started walking gingerly across the room.

A frown knitted across Vi's brow. 'Jimby, why are you suddenly walking like you've filled your pants?'

'I'll have you know, I'm just practising my catwalk strut for when I've been headhunted to be the next big-name underpants model. Which, mark my words, will happen once these calendars hit the shops.' His reply made her giggle; she knew he was trying to take her mind off worrying.

∼

## The Secret - Violet's Story

IN THE WAITING room of the ante-natal department at Middleton Hospital, Vi's feet were dancing on the ground. 'I'm so desperate for a wee. If I hang on any longer, I'm going to wet myself.'

'Oh.' Jimby's face was a picture. He looked at his watch. 'Forty-five minutes late,' he said.

'And my bladder's feeling every single one of those extra minutes,' said Vi. 'They shouldn't tell you to arrive for your appointment with it full, then keep you waiting this long. It's torture.'

'Do you want me to say something?' he asked.

'God, no. That won't make any difference, they're overstretched, that's what it is. I'll just have to hang on for as long as I can.' Her feet jigged up and down on the spot. 'Just take a look at some of the other women, they're doing exactly the same as me.'

Jimby glanced around the waiting room; he had to agree.

Someone filled a paper cup from the water-cooler, the trickling sound just about sent Vi over the edge. She pulled a face, and caught the eye of a heavily pregnant woman opposite who was wearing an equally pained expression. 'Oh, my God,' the woman mouthed. Vi smiled back sympathetically.

Fifteen minutes later, Vi's heart leapt into her chest when her name was called out by a smiling midwife. 'That's us,' she said, then under her breath, 'I almost wet myself when I heard my name.'

Jimby laughed and took her hand as they made their way to the sonographer's room.

Vi lay on the bed, a ball of nerves, watching the sonographer's facial expressions as she ran the transducer across her abdomen. Her heart suddenly pounded faster as the woman's forehead creased into a tiny frown. 'Actually,' she said, 'your bladder looks like it's a bit too full for me to get a decent image, would you mind going and emptying it a bit?'

'Really?' Relief mingled with disbelief. 'I'll try, but I think once I start, I might never be able to stop.'

'Just hang on to what you can, I'm sure you'll do fine.' The sonographer smiled kindly.

'Do you want me to come with you?' asked Jimby.

Vi giggled. 'No thanks, I think I can manage.'

In a couple of moments Vi returned to the room and they picked up where they left off. It felt like an eternity to her, while the sonographer started the procedure again, quietly scrutinising the screen. Eventually, the woman turned and smiled, manoeuvring the monitor round so Vi and Jimby could see.

'It's all looking good in there, Violet. I'd say you're eleven weeks pregnant – I'll be able to give you your due date when I've finished this. You can see the baby's spine along here, we have a pair of hands just here and a nice strong heart beating away right here.'

'And everything looks okay?' Vi asked.

'Everything looks perfect, exactly as it should.'

Happiness bubbled up inside Vi and she looked across at Jimby. His eyes were glued to the monitor screen. 'Everything's fine, Jimby.'

He turned to her, his eyes glistening with tears. 'That's our baby right there. It's amazing Vi, it's just amazing. Hello, little Pippin, I'm your dad.'

Vi glanced across at the sonographer – she must have seen this thousands of times – but the woman gave her a kind smile, no doubt taken by the gentle giant gazing at the screen.

## The Secret - Violet's Story

'So we can expect little Pippin around the ninth of February, eh?' Jimby was holding Vi's hand as they walked across the hospital carpark back to his car. He looked at her, his smile wider than ever. 'That should give us plenty of time to get little Pippin's room ready in the new house.'

Vi glanced up at him, her heart fit to burst. 'Yes, it should.' At last she could let go of the bubble of anxiety that had hovered at the back of her mind, never really letting her dare be fully excited about their baby. She released her grip and felt the bubble rise up and slowly float away. She closed her eyes and breathed a sigh of relief.

'Right, I think we should mark this occasion,' said Jimby.

'Oh, how?'

'I want to buy you a piece of jewellery, then in years to come, whenever you look at it, you'll never forget this day.'

'Jimby, I'll never forget this day, whether I've got a piece of jewellery to remind me or not.'

He stopped walking and turned to her, cupping her face in his hands, smoothing his thumbs over her cheekbones. 'Vi, I'm not articulate enough to put into words exactly how I'm feeling, but a piece of jewellery can do that for me. Just let me get you something.' He bent his face to hers and pressed a kiss to her lips that turned her legs to jelly.

'Oy, you two, get a room,' a voice called across the car park.

The couple pulled apart. 'Sounds like a plan.' Jimby grinned.

∽

'Oh, they're gorgeous, Vi.' Kitty was admiring the delicate purple diamond earrings that Jimby had bought for her at the jewellers in Middleton-le-Moors – the same one he'd bought her engagement ring from. 'I've never had my brother down as an old romantic, but it just goes to show how wrong you can be.'

'Less of the old, if you don't mind, sis.'

Jimby and Vi had taken the rest of the day off and, after choosing a piece of jewellery, had gone for lunch and a mooch around the shops in Middleton, before heading over to York so Vi could take a look at baby things in the shops – she hadn't dared even think about getting anything until after she'd had the scan. On returning to Lytell Stangdale, they'd decided to call in on Kitty and Ollie to share their news.

'Look at this, Kitts.' Vi picked up a bag, lifting out a tiny pair of white bootees with rabbit faces and pricked-up ears.

'Oh, my goodness.' Kitty pressed a hand to her chest. 'I know it's not that long since I had Lottie, but you really do forget how tiny they are.'

'And how about this?' Vi produced a feather soft sleep-suit in white with grey dots. 'And these ...' She pulled out a set of three tiny white vests.

'I always thought Jimby's smile couldn't get any wider, but look at the state of him, it's almost touching his ears.' Ollie reached into the fridge and pulled out two bottles of beer, flicked the tops off and handed one to his friend.

'Cheers, mate.' Jimby took the beer and obliged by making his smile even wider.

Vi laughed. 'He's been like it ever since I had the scan.'

'So, are you making it public knowledge now?' asked Kitty.

'Not yet, I still want to get the full three month mark out of the way. I know we've only got a week, but I just don't want to tempt fate.'

**CHAPTER 34**

Vi was making her way to the village shop, smiling to herself and enjoying the soothing warmth of the sun as it kissed the back of her neck, slipping down to the skin of her bare arms. The summery boat-neck sundress she was wearing in the colour of sugared-almond lilac, was beginning to feel just a smidge too tight; it wouldn't be able to fit over her growing curves for much longer. Vi's smile tugged a little wider at that reason.

Jonty drove by, waving enthusiastically. Vi waved back, watching him disappear round a bend in the road. When she turned back, she started; Aoife Mellison's face was scowling down at her. 'Lord, you made me jump,' Vi said.

Despite the heat, the woman was dressed in her usual layers of fluorescent running gear, topped off by a Hi-Vis tabard. At the end of a matching fluorescent yellow lead was lurcher, Rufus. He, too, was wrapped in a Hi-Vis coat. *Talk about overkill, no wonder the poor animal's panting heavily* thought Vi.

'I'd like a word, if you don't mind.' Aoife's awkward fake Queen's English set Vi's teeth on edge.

'Oh, really? What about, Aoife?' Vi felt like commenting on how unusual it was for Aoife to stoop so low as to speak to her, but for the sake of peace and harmony, she thought better of it.

Aoife laughed scornfully. 'I'm surprised I need to tell you, actually.'

'Well, I'm afraid you're going to have to, since I don't have the foggiest idea what you're going on about.' The woman had the sort of face that just begged for a slap, thought Vi, wondering if it was pregnancy hormones that was making her feel that way.

'It's the view.'

'The view?'

'Yes, the view that you'll be blocking from the village by building that house of yours.' Aoife jutted her chin.

'And it bothers you because …?'

'It bothers me – and no doubt many other residents in the village – because it will block the view we all enjoy of the dale when we walk by.'

Vi looked at her in disbelief. 'Are you being serious?'

'Extremely. When, I'm walking along the road, it's one of the pleasures I get; I look forward to it, and now you and your *boyfriend* are going to spoilt it.'

Vi looked at her in disbelief, momentarily at a loss for how to answer her. 'Aoife, you're the only one who has come up with something like that, everyone else has been very positive. As you know, housing in villages like this is in short supply so by Jimby and me building a new one, it's freed up two more.' Vi could feel her blood boil. 'And if you're so keen to take a look at the view, there's plenty of gaps between the other houses, or you could walk a little further to the edge of the village and it's right there in front of you. Miles of it.'

'That's not the point, and I don't think the village needs any new builds, they spoil the look of the place.'

'This is beginning to sound an awful lot like sour grapes from the woman whose building plans were rejected,' said Vi.

'I don't know what you mean. I don't have the sort of personality to suffer from such things.' Vi enjoyed the fact that she'd made Aoife squirm. She knew the woman didn't like having her personality considered anything other than perfect.

Aoife and Dave had submitted plans to have a large, contemporary extension on their house, but they were refused on the grounds that it wasn't in keeping with the village. To make matters worse, their plans had attracted the attention of the National Parks who'd noticed that the couple had installed uPVC windows and rooflights without obtaining the necessary consents. As a result, they were served with an enforcement notice to replace the windows with timber ones and apply for retrospective planning permission for the rooflights. It hadn't gone down well with Aoife who couldn't cope with criticism or with being wrong.

Vi couldn't help herself, and snorted. 'Not much. Anyway, it's good to see you've got that dog of yours on a lead for a change.' It wasn't so long ago that there'd been a spate of sheep worrying and, though they'd denied it, everyone knew it was the Mellison's dog that was responsible.

Aoife's eyes bulged and she tugged at the lead. 'Come on, Rufie. I can see I'm not going to get anywhere talking to this woman.'

Vi pulled a face and let out a noisy breath as she watched Aoife stomp off down the trod.

'Just as well it's not windy, pet,' said Gerald as he made

his way across the road to her. He was carrying a large, flat object which was wrapped in paper.

'Oh, hi there, Gerald?' Vi wondered where this was going. 'What was that you were saying about it not being windy?'

'Well, if it was, and it changed direction, you'd be in real danger of your face staying like that,' he chuckled.

Vi smiled as the penny dropped. 'Oh, it's just that flaming woman and her ridiculous comments.'

'Well, don't let her bother you, we all think the same of her as you do. What she's doing living in a community like this, I don't know. She can't seem to stop looking down her nose at everyone.'

'True,' said Vi. 'Hopefully her and her obnoxious family will move away.' She looked at Gerald, taking in his cheesecloth shirt in garish stripes that was hanging loose on him. He'd clearly lost a lot of weight since his heart attack. 'You look well.'

'Thank you, pet-lamb. Mary's had me on a strict, healthy diet since I had my bad turn. I feel like a different man. No more beef-dripping sandwiches.' He gave her a wide, toothless smile.

Vi's stomach lurched; she hoped he didn't see her gag at the thought of beef-dripping sandwiches. *Who on earth eats stuff like that?* 'Good for her,' she said.

'Anyway, it was you and Jimby I was coming to see. I've got a little something for him to say thank you. If it wasn't for that lad, I honestly don't think I'd be stood here talking to you, I'd be pushing up daisies.'

Vi eyed the parcel under his arm, it could only be one thing. *Oh, bloody hell*, she thought. 'There's really no need, Gerald, and I know Jimby would feel the same,' she said. *Especially if it's what I think it is!* 'As long as you're alright, that's all that matters, and I know Jimby wouldn't expect anything.' A painting of Big Mary, naked, was the last thing they needed.

'Well, it matters to Mary and me. She'd be a widow if it wasn't for him.' His voice wavered and Vi reached out and touched his arm.

'It's very thoughtful of you both.'

Gerald nodded, composing himself.

'Jimby's just at his forge if you'd like to pop over to see him, or would you like me to take it for you?'

'Thanks, pet, but if it's all the same with you, I'd like to see his face when he unwraps it. It's one of my favourite pieces. It'd be nice if you'd come along, too.'

*Oh. My. Days. How will I ever keep a straight face?* 'Of course, that would be lovely, Gerald. Come on, let's go and see him.'

He swallowed and brushed a tear away from his cheek. 'Right you are, chick.'

The forge was ringing out with the sound of metal hitting metal, the acrid smell of coal dust hanging in the air. Jimby paused and looked up, smiling when he saw Vi. He set his tools down, pushed his goggles to the back of his head and removed his earplugs. 'Now then, Gerald.' He winked at Vi. 'How are you diddlin? You look well, I have to say.'

Vi couldn't make eye contact with Jimby while Gerald explained the purpose of his visit. 'So here you, go, a token of mine and Mary's gratitude.' He handed the parcel over to Jimby.

Jimby removed his gloves. 'My hands are a bit mucky, would you do the honours Vi?'

Violet shot him a dirty look. 'Me?'

'Yep, you.' Jimby nodded, a mischievous glint in his eye.

Doing her best not to send him a death stare, she slowly peeled back the paper, hardly daring to look at what lay beneath.

'Oh, Gerald, that's absolutely bloody fantastic.' The smile on Jimby's face was broad and genuine.

Vi looked at the painting to see the most beautiful water colour of the dale in all its summer glory. It was stunning and about as far removed from Gerald's usual style as possible. 'Gerald ... I'm lost for words ... it's just beautiful,' she said.

Gerald beamed. 'Thank you, pet. I thought you'd like it, especially with all the purple of the heather. Thought you could hang it in your new house.'

Jimby went across and pulled Gerald into a hug. 'Means the world that, mate, especially with you being alright and all. And it'll look absolutely perfect in our new home, won't it, Vi?'

Vi nodded. 'It will.'

'Whenever we look at it, we'll think of you and Mary.' Jimby smiled.

When Gerald had left, Vi relayed the conversation she'd had with Aoife to Jimby. He shook his head. 'I'm beginning to think that woman searches for ways to make people feel uncomfortable or to dislike her – even her own husband, if what people are saying is true. Don't let her bother you, you've got enough to think about without her stupid comments getting under your skin.' He went over to Violet and kissed her full on the lips. 'And did I tell you, you're looking absolutely bloody gorgeous?' He treated her to a full-on beam, making her stomach flip.

'Well, I was just going to pop home, take Gerald's painting out of harm's way, if you fancy joining me ...' She arched a suggestive eyebrow.

*The Secret - Violet's Story*

'Don't tempt me,' he groaned. 'Much as I'd loved to, I can't leave this.' He nodded to the project he was working on. 'But hold that thought, and I'll knock off early, see if you can do the same.'

'And what makes you think it wasn't a once in a lifetime offer?'

'I'll show you when I get home, then you'll be glad it wasn't.' He waggled his eyebrows at her, making her giggle.

'Sounds good,' she said. 'Well, since you've turned me down for now, I'd best get back to the studio. Kitty will be wondering where I've got to.'

'See you later, gorgeous.' Jimby winked at her.

Vi walked back out into the sunshine and the cacophony of birdsong carried on the soft, summer breeze. Happiness suffused her body and she pressed a gentle hand against her stomach, a secret smile playing at her lips.

~

Jimby finished work early, as promised, and Vi was surprised to see him back before her.

'You're home early.' Smiling, she set her bag down on the table.

'That's what happens when a bloke's on a promise.' He walked over to Violet and took her in his arms. 'God, you're beautiful, I could devour you right here on the spot.'

Vi groaned as she melted into the blistering heat of his kiss.

'Come on, let's get you upstairs,' Jimby said huskily. He took her hand and led the way to their bedroom.

~

'Wow!' Vi gasped.

'That's what all the girls say,' replied Jimby. It earned him a nudge from Violet's elbow.

He chuckled and hugged her closer. 'Your pregnancy hormones seem to be making you extra delicious,' Jimby said. 'I can barely keep my hands off you.' He was stroking her arm with the tips of his fingers, making her shiver with delight.

'You won't find any complaints from me.' Vi snuggled into him. She was in her favourite place, with her head resting on his chest, savouring the intimacy. She breathed in deeply, inhaling the inimitable scent of Jimby: his cologne mingled with a hint of muskiness and the slight bitter tang of his forge. It was undeniably masculine and it reached deep down inside of her, setting her emotions stirring in some primaeval way. She ran her fingers through the dark curls of his chest hair, still damp with sweat from their lovemaking. Moments like these were precious, the two of them spending uninterrupted quality time together. She was so relieved they'd managed to move on from the awkwardness her secret had caused.

'I was panicking a bit when old Gerald walked in with a picture under his arm.' Jimby broke into her thoughts.

'Oh, me too. I thought it was going to be of the usual stuff – you know, bits of Big Mary – I could already picture it hanging on the wall at your forge, keeping your collection of tasteless mugs company when we move into our new house. And when he said he wanted to see your face when you unwrapped it, I hardly dared look at you as I was peeling the paper back.'

'Same here. But the painting he gave us is stunning; he should do more in that style, he'd sell loads.'

'He would, more than paintings of naked bits of Big Mary in garish colours. I can't think who they'd appeal to.'

'Quite, and just talking about it has made me conjure up a rather scary image and I'd like it to go away.'

Vi giggled. 'Why do you think he started to paint stuff like that when he's so talented at painting scenery?'

'No idea. Maybe he just likes to be controversial.'

'Well, he and Big Mary are that alright,' said Vi. 'And speaking of controversial, have you heard about Dan?'

Jimby's face darkened at the mention of Kitty's first husband. 'What about him? He's not coming back to the village is he?'

'I think he'd be chased out if he did,' she said. 'Kitty was telling me she'd bumped into that barrister who used to be in the same chambers as Dan – Henry, I think he's called. Apparently Dan's been working as a sort of legal adviser to some big London firm and had fallen head over heels for this woman who worked there. Sounds like it was serious because he proposed to her with a very expensive, very ostentatious diamond engagement ring.'

'Hmm. Sounds about right, him being a flash git.'

'That's what I thought. Anyway, according to this Henry bloke, Dan was absolutely besotted with her, they'd been living together and everything. He'd even bought her a fancy car and showered her with gifts – so different to how he was with Kitty.'

Jimby gave an angry sigh.

'But here's where karma makes an appearance: one night, when he went home after work, she'd gone, taken everything. She'd even found the password to his bank account and helped herself to a load of money out of it.'

'Hah! Just goes to show, what goes around, comes around.'

'Exactly. Henry said Dan's absolutely devastated, especially when he thought he'd treated her like a queen.'

'Well, I don't have an ounce of sympathy for the prat, after what he did to our Kitty. He deserves everything he gets, and some.' Jimby flung an arm behind his head.

'He does, though you know what Kitty's like, she said she couldn't help but feel sorry for him.'

Jimby rolled his eyes. 'She's too nice for her own good that lass. But as long as she's not upset about it, that's all that matters.'

'Nope, she's not upset. She's well and truly moved on from him.'

'Well, that's good to hear, Miss Smith.' Jimby's smile returned and he went to sit up. 'But I'm afraid I'm going to have to say, after our little session, I've worked up quite an appetite and I need my tea.'

'Just one more minute,' said Vi, holding on to him tightly and pulling him back. 'I don't want this moment to end, it's so perfect. Can't we just stay like this all night?'

Jimby laughed and kissed the tip of her nose. 'Sounds tempting, but I'm starving so I think my stomach rumbles might not quite fit in with your image of perfection. But we should be good for five more minutes.'

'It's a deal,' she said.

## CHAPTER 35

'There, that's the final crystal stitched on the neckline.' Vi sat back and admired her wedding dress.

'Oh, wow, Vi, it looks gorgeous,' said Kitty. 'Are you going to try it on? See how it's fitting around little Pippin?'

'Definitely; I can't wait to see what it looks like now it's all finished. And it was a good idea of yours to lift the waist slightly, with the excess in the seam, it should make it easy to alter as I expand.' Her heart lurched suddenly. 'Oh heck, I've just remembered we're going to be telling everyone about the baby tomorrow; it won't be our family secret anymore.'

'Ahh, everyone'll be so pleased for you both, chick.'

'You're right; it just feels a bit strange, that's all. Anyway, I'll just pop to the loo before I try my dress on, I've been putting off going while I got the last of the crystals stitched on.'

'Okay, while you're doing that, I'll go and lock the door, make sure no one can walk in on us.'

In the small confines of the toilet, Vi's happiness was whipped away and her heart plummeted. There, glaring up at her from her knickers, was a cluster of incriminating drops of dark blood. She clasped her hand to her mouth as tears stung her eyes. *This can't be happening. Please tell me, it can't be happening.*

As soon as she stepped back out into the studio, Kitty clocked her expression. 'Vi, what's wrong, chick?' Her large brown eyes filled with concern and she hurried over to her friend. 'Tell me, what's the matter?'

'There's blood.' Vi's voice was barely above a whisper. 'I'm bleeding.'

Kitty's face paled. 'Oh, Vi, come and sit down. I'm sure everything'll be okay. Are you in any pain? You seemed fine before you went to the loo.' She guided Vi to a seat.

Vi shook her head. 'There's no pain, that's why it was such a shock.' Tears had started pouring down her cheeks. 'I can't tell Jimby, he'll be so disappointed.'

'Listen, chick, try not to worry, I'm sure it's a good sign that you're not in any pain. When I had my mis ... well, you know ... the pain was excruciating.'

'Right.' Vi nodded, wiping her eyes. 'You think it'll be okay?'

'I think worrying isn't going to help. You stay there, I'll call the doctor.'

After speaking to the receptionist, Kitty passed the phone to Vi so she could explain her symptoms to Dr Beth. After a brief discussion, the GP advised her to head over to Middleton Hospital, saying that she'd ring the antenatal department in advance and tell them to expect her.

'I'm happy to take you, Vi, but I really think you should tell our Jimby. He'll want to be with you.'

'Okay.' Vi sniffed. 'But will you ring him for me? I don't think I'll be able to tell him without bursting into tears, and I don't want to panic him.'

'Of course.' Kitty squeezed her tight.

Before Vi had chance to think, Jimby was hammering on the door of the studio. Kitty went to unlock it and he flew in. 'Vi, sweetheart, are you alright?' He scooped her into his arms, holding her close. She rested her head on his chest and sobbed. 'I'm so sorry, Jimby. I'm so sorry. I was trying to be so careful, tried to do everything right to look after Pippin.'

He smoothed her hair, fighting back his own tears. 'I know you did, angel, but try not to think the worst, we don't know what's happening yet.'

She nodded, aware that he was just saying words to make her feel better.

'Right, let's get you to the hospital.' He fished his car keys out of his pocket.

'Good luck, Vi. Let me know how you get on.' Kitty pulled her into a hug, kissing her cheek.

Vi's words had dried up in her mouth and all she could do was nod.

The journey to Middleton Hospital passed in a blur, the sickening knot of worry in Vi's stomach becoming ever tighter. Anxiety hung in the air and she was aware of Jimby glancing across at her. She caught his eye a couple of times and he responded with a watery smile. It wasn't his usual full-on beam, setting his dimples off. That one had been wiped right off his face.

It felt surreal to be back in the waiting room of the antenatal clinic. Vi was called in for an ultrasound scan almost immediately, she was relieved that she didn't have the long, drawn-out wait she had the last time she was there. She lay on the bed as cold gel was blobbed onto her stomach, holding on to Jimby's hand so tightly her knuckles were blanched of colour. She could feel the weight of his concerned gaze on her all the while the sonographer was moving the transducer over her stomach, but she daren't look back at him. *This is my fault. All my fault. If I hadn't got pregnant and lost that baby before, this never would've happened. By telling myself I didn't want a baby all those years ago, I've willed it to happen. I've only got myself to blame.*

## CHAPTER 36

'Baby's heartbeat is nice and strong.' The sonographer's voice sliced through Vi's thoughts, the woman's words making Vi's own heart race.

'Really?' she asked, grabbing on to the glimmer of hope, holding it close. She felt Jimby squeeze her hand as he leaned forward, a flash off relief passing over his face.

'Yes.' The sonographer nodded, not taking her eyes away from the monitor.

There was a knock at the door and a tall woman with a kind face and dark hair pulled back into a sleek ponytail entered the room. 'Hello, Violet, I'm Dr Viva, I'm an obstetrician. I gather you've been experiencing a bit of bleeding?'

An age seemed to pass while Dr Viva scrutinized the screen, her face impassive. Eventually she spoke, pulling out a chair as she did so. 'Okay, I think we've found the source of the problem – and it's nothing to be alarmed about, you're not having a miscarriage, which I think is what you were concerned about.'

Vi nodded, feeling relief flood through her.

Dr Viva continued. 'The scan has showed up a small

subchorionic haematoma, which is basically a fancy name for a type of blood clot that forms between the uterus and the placenta. It's quite common, and we don't really know why it happens but most usually resolve on their own and end up getting reabsorbed into the body. I'm quite surprised yours didn't show up on your earlier scan, but it's only small, so that's probably why.'

'Before I found out I was pregnant, I'd actually come off the pill and I had what I thought was a monthly bleed. I thought it was just while my body was readjusting, but could that have been the same as this?' asked Vi.

'Very possibly.' Dr Viva nodded.

'And is there a risk to the baby?' asked Jimby. 'What can you do to treat it?'

'Well, given that the haematoma is small, has developed in the first trimester, and there are no other symptoms, I can't see any reason why Violet shouldn't carry her baby to full-term.'

Vi turned to Jimby who looked as relieved as she felt.

'However, getting back to your question regarding treatment, James, I'm afraid there is none.' She turned to Violet. 'And, since subchorionic haematoma can mean there's a slightly higher risk of miscarriage – and with your history – I'm going to suggest you take things easy for a bit. We used to call it bed rest, but that's a bit out-dated, we call it activity restriction now, which means, as I said, you should take things easy, avoid any heavy lifting, try to avoid being constipated – so make sure you drink plenty of fluids – and it's best if you avoid having sex until the haematoma disappears.'

Vi nodded, absorbing the obstetrician's advice.

'I'll make sure she does all of those things, doctor,' said Jimby.

'And we'll scan you regularly, just to make sure everything is happening as it should be.' Dr Viva smiled at the pair. 'If you go to the desk in reception, they'll make an appointment for you.'

～

'I'M SO RELIEVED,' said Vi. They were in Jimby's car, waiting in a queue of traffic to leave the carpark. She leaned back into the headrest.

Jimby moved his hand from the gear-stick and gave her fingers a reassuring squeeze. 'Me, too.' He changed up a gear, his car nosing its way out of the junction. 'But you'll really have to do as the doctor says, Vi. I'm not telling you what to do, but if you want my opinion, I think you should give up your burlesque classes until after Pippin's born.'

'Don't worry, I'd already thought about that. There's no way I want to take the slightest risk. I've been feeling too tired to do it recently anyway, it's been more of a chore than a pleasure, so I won't be sorry to have a break from it. And I'm going to stop wearing such high heels, I don't want to risk toppling over in them.'

Jimby looked across at her and smiled a small, "what a bloody relief" kind of smile. Vi mustered one back, feeling suddenly exhausted.

'What do you fancy doing now?' Jimby asked. 'Go for a bite to eat somewhere, or go straight home?'

'Straight home, if that's okay? I just fancy some peace and quiet. I'll text Kitty, tell her everything's okay and that I won't be in anymore today, but I don't fancy facing people – even ones I don't know.'

'That's fine with me; home it is.'

'And can we pick up some more apples from that farm

shop on the way back? They're so lovely and sour.' Vi could feel herself salivating at the thought of taking a deep bite into the crisp flesh.'

'Absolutely.' Jimby's trademark smile returned, bringing his dimples back in all their glory. 'Can't have you and little Pippin going without your daily apple quota.'

∼

THAT EVENING, the couple were sitting on the sofa in the garden at Sunshine Cottage, Jimby's arm flung across Violet's shoulders. The sun was just beginning to slip over the thatched roof-tops of Lytell Stangdale, leaving behind a mellow light and a hint of easy warmth. A solitary blackbird was singing away like there was no tomorrow, sharing his views with whoever was prepared to listen. Evidently, not Jarvis and Jerry who were curled up fast asleep on the matting by Jimby's feet.

'Been quite a day, hasn't it?' He took a sip from his bottle of beer.

Vi had her eyes closed, offering her face up to the last of the sun's rays, her fingers curled around a glass of apple juice resting in her lap. 'You could say. I'm just so relieved Pippin's okay.'

'Me, too.' Jimby pulled her closer. 'I'm just relieved you're both okay.'

She rested her head on his shoulder. 'I'm going to do everything I can to keep this baby safe, Jimby. When I thought I was going to lose it, it made me realise how desperately I want it.'

'Yeah, it somehow really focused things, didn't it? Made it seem more real, if that makes sense?'

'I know what you mean, it does.'

'Are you going to tell your mum and dad?'

'I know I should, but I don't want to worry them. And I don't think I could cope with Mum's fussing. You know what she's like, she can't help herself, and I'd end up feeling even more stressed out. Knitting all those little jackets and bootees has got her all excited – even though the look like they're straight from the seventies – so I think I'll keep her in blissful ignorance for now.'

'I think you're right, you'd probably end up falling out with her, and you don't want that.'

'No, I don't. I want peace and harmony right up until little Pippin's born. I'll have a quiet word with Kitty and Molly so they don't slip up and tell her by mistake.' Vi gave a sudden shiver as goose bumps popped up over her arms; the sun had slinked off, leaving shadows in its place.

'Cold?' Jimby asked.

'Mm.' Vi nodded. 'I think I'll go for a soak in the bath.'

'Come on, Miss Smith, I'll run it for you.' Jimby pushed himself off the sofa, then offered her his hand to help her up. 'I think we could both do with an early night – and not for the usual reasons, after what Dr Viva said.'

'Party pooper.' Vi giggled as they made their way back to the house, hand in hand.

**CHAPTER 37**

'You're looking well, missus.' Molly walked through the door of the Romantique studio armed with three slices of chocolate-dipped flapjack. She was looking over at Vi, smiling.

'Thanks, Moll. I feel it, I'm still a bit tired, but not so bad today, and the haematoma's been behaving itself over the last few days.'

'That's good news.'

'Hiya, Moll. Can you stick the kettle on? I'm just a bit tied up with this fiddly bit of work here, and want to get it finished before I have a break.' Concentration was etched on Kitty's face.

'No problem.' Molly made her way over to the kitchen area and began filling the kettle. 'I just dropped Emmie off at playgroup where all the mothers are buzzing about the calendar. I honestly thought I'd never get away. Then, when I got to the village shop, Lucy and Freddie were full of how they're selling like hot cakes and people are coming from all over just to buy them. Would you believe they've almost sold out?'

'I know, it's mad isn't it?' Vi laughed. 'Who'd have thought anyone would be daft enough to pay for pictures of our blokes half naked?'

'Maneater!' Kitty and Molly replied at the same time and the three women burst out laughing.

'Good point. Apparently she's been drooling over them the way you drool over apples, Vi,' said Molly.

'That bad?' asked Kitty.

'Or you over those biscuits, Moll,' Vi said.

'Touché.' Molly grinned at her. 'I reckon it's going to make our Jimby even more of a bighead than he already is.'

Vi groaned. 'Ughh, don't say that. He's already strutting round like he's a Hollywood star – in a jokey way, you know what he's like?'

'Yeah, till he does something and ends up flat on his face like he did the day of the photo shoot,' said Kitty.

Vi laughed. 'He's still got the scars to prove it, as well. His chin's still a bit red.'

'There's never a dull moment when he's around, that's for sure,' said Molly.

'You can say that again.' Vi rolled her eyes.

'Anyway, I thought we'd better get round to discussing your hen night. Time's running out, you know,' said Molly.

Vi sighed. 'I know, I've been wondering what to do, but with what the hospital said, I think we might have to postpone it until after the wedding.'

'Really?' Molly carried the pot of tea and flapjacks over to the little table. 'Come and grab a cuppa while it's hot, you two.'

'Nearly done,' said Kitty.

'I just don't want to risk anything and, to be honest, I'm just happy to call one of our pamper nights over at Rosie's my hen night. After all, I'd be spending it with you guys anyway.' Vi made her way over to the table and sat down.

'You can't just do that, Vi. There must be something else we can do to mark it.' Molly sat back in her seat, a mischievous smile playing at her lips. 'I've got it.'

'What've you got, Moll?' asked Kitty.

'Judging by the look on your face, I don't think I'm going to like this,' said Vi. 'I hardly dare ask, but go on, spill.'

'Well, *you* won't have to do anything at all, Vi. You'll just need to sit there.'

'Right. Then explain to me why I'm feeling suddenly nervous.'

Kitty was making her way over to the table and giggled. 'You do look a bit like you're planning something wicked, Moll,' she said.

'It's wicked but in a good way.' An impish grin tugged at Molly's lips.

'Oh, bloody hell,' Vi groaned.

'Male strippers,' said Molly.

Kitty, who had taken a bite out of her flapjack, started to laugh, forcing a cluster of crumbs to go down the wrong way. She started coughing and spluttering, spraying chocolatey oats everywhere.

'See what you've done?' Vi said to Molly.

Molly leaned across to Kitty and delivered a series of firm pats on her back, making Kitty's eyes bulge even more.

'I think Kitt's alright now, Moll,' said Vi.

'Thanks.' Kitty grabbed her mug and gulped down a generous mouthful of tea. 'Blimey, Molly. I wasn't expecting you to say that.'

'Well, I think it's a fabulous idea, hiring you a couple of strippers,' said Molly. 'It'll be a hen night you won't forget.'

Vi gave Molly a death stare.

'What?' Molly shrugged.

'Don't you think there's been enough of that in the village, what with the calendar. And there are still people in recovery after seeing our Jimby pelt down the road in just his underpants.' Kitty giggled between a couple more coughs.

Vi looked serious. 'Listen, Molly, if you do anything like booking strippers for my hen do, I can promise you, I will never speak to you again.'

'Promises, promises …' Molly winked at her.

'I'm serious, Molly.'

'I think she's only teasing, aren't you, Moll?' Kitty shot Molly a warning look.

'Of course, I am. I know you'd hate anything like that. Though, we could always give that hunky Zander a shout and tell him that we need him to get his kit off for another good cause. We just won't tell him that the cause is your hen night.' Molly's ensuing dirty cackle brought a smile to Vi's face.

'Since when have you been such a perv, Molly?' asked Kitty.

'Since around the time Camm arrived,' said Vi.

'Mmm. You're probably right,' agreed Molly. 'Anyway, what's Jimby doing about a stag night?'

'Nothing much, really. I can't get him to do anything out of the village. He doesn't want to leave me on my own in case I start bleeding again, so I think he's just going to have a night at the pub with your fellas and Robbie. He was talking to Bea last night and apparently she offered to cook them a special curry. He seemed really chuffed with that.'

'I'm not surprised, Bea's curries are awesome,' said Kitty.

'Maybe we should gate-crash,' said Molly.

'You're just full of trouble today, missus,' said Vi.

~

MOLLY SNIFFED THE AIR, a frown furrowing her brow. 'Can either of you smell burning?'

Kitty and Vi copied Molly, sniffing. 'Yes, I can.' Vi nodded.

'And look, there's smoke blowing along the dale. I'd better shut the window, we don't want it tainting things in here.' Kitty hurried over to the window, closing it quickly.

'It looks like too much smoke for a garden bonfire,' said Molly. 'I wonder where it's coming from?'

The three women looked at one another, each recalling two summers back when their men had had to help tackle a moorland blaze caused by someone having a campfire in the middle of a heatwave. That someone was always believed to be Dave Mellison, though he'd always strenuously denied it.

'It's getting thicker by the minute,' said Vi. 'I wonder if it's got out of hand?'

They ran to the door and along the path, to see people standing outside the Mellison's house, smoke billowing from the rear of it. 'Turn the tap on, Mary!' shouted Gerald, trying to unravel the hosepipe from his garden.

'Here, I'll give him a hand,' Lycra Len called from the roadside. He threw his bike to the ground and ran over to him.

'Oh, thank you, Len, pet. I'll go and set the water away. Make sure he doesn't do too much.' She hurried to the outside tap, calling over her shoulder, 'Be careful, Gerry. Take it steady, we don't want you to end up back in hospital.'

'What's happened, Mary?' Kitty ran over to her, wafting the smell of smoke from under her nose with her hand.

'Dave was having a bonfire in the garden and threw some barbecue fuel on. Honest to God, you should've seen it. The flames leapt so high and caught the washing that was hanging on the line.'

Molly and Vi joined Kitty, their faces etched with concern. 'Does anyone know what's caused it?' asked Vi and Kitty repeated what Mary had told her.

'I don't effing well believe it.' Molly stood with her hands on her hips. 'That sodding family never learn, do they?'

'Seems not,' said Vi. 'I assume someone's called the fire brigade?' She put her hand over her nose. 'Bloody hell, it stinks.'

'Aye, pet. I believe Jonty called them before he started running round asking those with hosepipes that could reach, to help out. The next we knew, people started running to the pond with their buckets and filling them up so they could chuck water at the flames.'

'That sounds like a recipe for disaster,' said Vi.

'What on earth?' Little Mary was making her way from the shop, her usual over-sized shopping bag in her hand and a sun hat perched on her neatly set curls. She stopped beside the friends, taking in the sight before her.

'Garden fire at the Mellison's, got out of hand thanks to Dave's stupidity,' said Molly.

Little Mary shook her head. 'That family ought to be chased out of the village, they've done nothing but cause trouble since the day they arrived.'

'Hear, hear,' said Vi.

'I hope the fire-brigade hurry up,' said Molly. 'With all the thatched roofs, the whole village could go up in smoke in no time.' She frowned, looking round her. 'And where is Dave, by the way?'

'Er, I haven't seen him since he ran down the path shouting for help,' Big Mary replied.

'And Aoife?' asked Kitty.

'I saw her going for a walk with the kids and the dog about half an hour ago. It's hard to miss them, the way they all dress like they're going on some polar expedition. They had them sticks to walk with, you know, like pole-type things?'

'Sounds like Nordic walking,' said Vi, rolling her eyes. As she spoke, the whining siren of the fire engine could be heard making its way along the road from Danskelfe.

'Thank the Lord,' said Molly.

'What the bloody hell's going on?' Jimby appeared beside Vi. 'Should you be out here, breathing in all this smoke? It can't be good for you or Pippin.'

'You're right. I'll head back to the studio and let Molly and Kitty explain what's going on.'

As Vi made her way back, the fire-engine whizzed by and in a moment she could hear the shouts of the firemen telling everyone to keep back.

In no time they had the blaze under control, the acrid smell of burning plastic hanging in the air from the Mellison's wheelie bins that had been caught in the blaze. The rear of the house had been destroyed, leaving a charred skeleton in its place and the uPVC windows melted out of shape.

'What the hell is going on?' Aoife snapped at Harry Cornforth, a volunteer fireman from Oakleyside Farm. She threw down her walking poles and put her hands on her hips. 'What has happened to my home? Who is responsible for this?' Her eyes were bulging wildly. Evie and Teddy were sobbing behind her.

'Your Dave was having a bonfire in the back garden. Let's just say, it got out of hand,' said Gerald. His face was flushed and he was panting.

'Is that right?' asked the local bobby PC Snaith who'd just arrived at the scene.

'My husband wouldn't do anything as thoughtless as that. It must've been a spark from someone else's bonfire.' Aoife jutted her jaw, her body-language screaming hostility.

Big Mary took exception to Aoife's words and marched over to her. 'Listen, madam, that's exactly what happened. And that half-wit man of yours even squirted barbecue lighter fuel directly at the flames – Gerry and me saw it with our own eyes. That's when the flames caught your washing. He's lucky it didn't catch him.' It was unusual to hear the sing-song tones of Big Mary's Wearside Geordie accent replaced with a stern note.

Aoife scowled, momentarily lost for words. She was clearly thinking of some way to wriggle her family out of any responsibility. 'Dave is very aware of the dangers of fire. He wasn't having a fire, and if he was, he would not do anything as stupid as that.'

'I'd like to think that after what happened a couple of years ago, with the blaze on the moor top caused by *someone's* stupidity, that Dave would be more aware of fire hazards,' said PC Snaith.

'Well, well, he is!' Aoife's eyes bulged.

'Mummy,' Evie sobbed, 'Daddy was having a bonfire. He'd started it before he left. You gave him some papers to burn.'

Aoife turned to her daughter, her face distorted with

anger. 'I did not! Why are you saying ridiculous things like that, you stupid girl?'

'But, Mum, you did giv—' Teddy began.

'Shut up!' Aoife screamed.

Big Mary shot her look of utter contempt. She tucked her arm under Gerald's. 'Come on, pet, you could do with a sit down after all that. Not that it's appreciated.'

Aoife stood, shaking with anger, watching as the back of her home smouldered.

**CHAPTER 38**

Later that evening Vi and Jimby joined their group of friends for a quick drink at the Sunne. 'You'll never guess what Aoife asked me earlier,' said Jimby. He picked up his pint and took a deep slug.

'Oh, wait till you hear this,' said Vi.

'I dread to think what that silly cow will come out with next.' Molly pulled a face as if there was a bad smell under her nose.

'She only asked me if her and Dave could rent Forge Cottage.'

Kitty's face fell. 'What? No!'

'You're joking? After what she's done to your family,' said Robbie.

'I hope you told her where to get off.' Ollie pulled Kitty closer to him.

'Oh, you should've heard her. Telling me how we've always got along, and that if they can't rent my cottage, they'll be homeless or have to move out of the village and lodge with her sister, which she said would be unbearable. How the children are devastated.'

'She's a manipulative madam, that one,' said Molly. 'That's where her kids get it from. I hope you weren't sucked in, Jimby.'

'I couldn't stand the thought of her renting your house, Jimby. It'd make her think she'd really got one up on me. You know what she's like, she'd enjoy rubbing my nose in it.' Kitty looked anxious.

'Don't worry, sis. Hell would have to freeze over before I did that woman a favour. Nope, I think the best solution all round is if that whole family buggered off out of the village. They're not cut out for country life, and I'm sick of seeing her looking down her nose at folk, not to mention all the problems they've caused, especially for you and Lily.'

Relief washed over Kitty's face, and Vi gave her arm a squeeze. 'This could be the answer to your prayers, chick. You might finally be free of that woman and her horrible kids.'

'Oh, I hope so.' Kitty sighed. 'The thought of not having to see her glaring at me up at school is very appealing – I actually dread going up there because of her.'

'Well, that's not right, Kitts,' said Vi. 'You've lived here all your life, she's only been here five minutes. She should be the one who keeps out of the way, not you.'

Their conversation was interrupted by Bea who bustled over with a large tray of snacks. 'Here you go, folks. Thought you might like to give these a try and let me know what you think.' The exotic aroma of spices filled the air as she set the tray on the table. Vi felt her stomach rumble. 'Oh, wow!'

Jimby rubbed his hands together. 'Oh, man, that looks bloody good, Bea.'

'It's just a few taster ideas for your Indian meal, Jimby – and I'm actually thinking of adding an Indian taster menu as a regular feature.'

'Fabulous!' he said.

'Oh, and before I forget, did you know we've sold all of the calendars we had here? People keep asking for them, and I think they've sold out at the village shop, too. Do you have any more we could have?'

'Oh, sweet Jesus.' Ollie clamped a hand to his head. 'I still haven't got used to the thought of people seeing me knack-naked in that calendar.'

Bea tucked her sleek bob behind her ears. 'And I still haven't got used to the general public seeing Jonty in the buff. Poor chap hasn't got much meat on his bones,' she chuckled. 'Anyway, I'd best get back to the kitchen. Let me know what you think of the nibbles – and if you can let us have any more calendars.'

Robbie turned to Jimby, who was already tucking into the snacks. 'There's been a load of orders for the calendar on the Facebook business page I made for the committee, too. I've had to put in another order with the printing company to keep up supply with demand. It's gone crazy.'

Jimby nodded and gave a thumbs up as he chomped on his mouthful.

'Sounds like you're going to have more than enough money for the defibrillator,' said Vi. 'What will you do with the extra cash?'

'Air ambulance,' said Ollie. 'We'd already decided that if there were enough people daft enough to buy the calendar and we had money left over, we should donate to that charity.'

Jimby swallowed what he was eating. 'After Pip and Gerald, it's the least we could do.'

Vi noticed a shadow slip over Molly's face. She squeezed her friend's hand and gave her a smile. 'I know I'm being a grass-hopper brain here, but the house is coming along nicely, Robbie.' Sensitive to the slump in Molly's mood, Vi changed the subject. 'I had a peek in earlier and couldn't believe how much has been done in the last week.'

Robbie nodded. 'Yes, I knew Mart and his team were good, but they're actually ahead of schedule. Those frames can go up really quick; it'll be ready for the thatch soon, and they'll be plastering before you know it.'

'Wow, that is good progress,' Camm said.

'I know it's not going to be finished before the wedding, but I'm still pleased that you're project managing it for us, Robbie. It's definitely taken the pressure off. And it's great just having to make decisions on what style bathroom to have, or what paint colour to go for,' said Vi.

'You'd best make sure the shops have plenty of purple paint in stock.' Molly grinned at her.

'Ha, bloody, ha.' Vi couldn't help but smile back.

'Hey, Jimbo, on the subject of weddings.' Molly prodded her cousin with her foot. 'We've been trying to organise a hen night for your future wife here, but she's having none of it.'

'Don't ask what Moll's been suggesting.' Kitty giggled. 'Vi has a good reason for not wanting to go ahead with her plans.'

'I can only imagine.' Camm shook his head.

'I'm not so sure you can.' A memory of what Molly was saying about Zander leapt into Vi's mind. 'But it's not going to happen. I just want a quiet do, if I have to have one at all,'

'Same here,' replied Jimby. 'I can't think of a better way to celebrate it than spending an evening with my best mates, and stuffing my face with a load of Bea's gorgeous food, washed down with a few jars of this nectar.' He held up his pint glass.

'Are you taking note, Moll?' Vi looked at her friend intently. 'Apart from the "nectar" bit.'

'Point taken, I was only teasing earlier, anyway.'

'Kitty, Rosie,' Vi glanced between the two women, 'can you please make sure that Molly doesn't do anything like what she was threatening earlier?'

'Cross my heart, Vi. I'd be mortified if she did.' Kitty crossed her chest with a finger.

'Same here,' said Rosie. 'We'll make sure she behaves herself.'

'Spoilsports.' Molly grinned.

## CHAPTER 39

AUGUST

August arrived in a blast of dazzling sunshine set in a sky so blue, anyone could be forgiven for thinking they were sunning themselves on a Caribbean island and not a tiny village in the middle of the North Yorkshire Moors.

The Romantique studio was stuffy, and Vi was glad of the cool breeze of the fan when it wafted her way. 'I'm absolutely mafted.' She took a sip of her apple juice, her taste buds jumping to attention at its zinginess.

'I know, we've definitely been having some warm summers over the last few years,' said Kitty. 'How do you fancy shutting up shop early and having a run out this afternoon?'

Though Vi was surprised at Kitty's out-of-the-blue suggestion, she quite liked the idea. 'Mmm. That sounds tempting. Where d'you fancy going?'

Kitty shrugged. 'How about a quick nip over to Middleton? We could grab a cup of tea and a cake, if you fancy? I was going to go to the supermarket, so Aunty Annie's already agreed to hang on to the kids a bit longer. And I can do my shopping another day.'

'You're on,' said Vi. 'Shall we finish up about one-ish – after Noushka's been in for her dress fitting – then head straight over there, before anything happens to change our mind?'

'Sounds like a plan.' Kitty beamed at her.

At just after twelve-thirty, Noushka bounded in on a pair of coltish long legs, her wavy blonde hair flying behind her. She was looking stunning in one of the dresses Vi had sent over in the bin bags; she'd teamed it with a pair of sparkly plimsolls.

'Hi, lovie.' Kitty smiled at her step-daughter.

'Hiya, Mum,' she replied. She strode over to Kitty and planted a kiss on her cheek. Vi looked on, seeing Kitty's face flush with happiness. Her heart swelled for her friend; she knew it meant the world to her that Noushka had decided to stop calling her Kitty.

'Hi, Vi.' She hopped over to where Vi was sitting and kissed her cheek, too. 'Thank you so, so, much for the clothes. I like, totally, love them! I know I don't look as glamorous as you, but what do you think?' Noushka held the skirt out and twirled on her tiptoes, her golden hair flying out around her.

'You look absolutely stunning, Noushka, and a hundred times better than I did in it. The jacket and sneakers add a funky, contemporary vibe to the dress, not to mention your long legs and beautiful angel hair.'

'You look like a dream, sweetheart,' added Kitty.

'Thank you.' Noushka beamed happily. 'I literally so can't wait to try my bridesmaid dress on now it's got all the awesome sparkly beads sown on it.'

Kitty stood up and walked over to the rail where the dresses were hanging in clear dust-covers. She pulled the one that was for Noushka, unzipped it and handed it to her. 'There you go, Noushkabelle, it's absolutely gorgeous.'

'Ooh, thank you.' Anoushka took it and hurried over to the changing room.

'Just give us a shout if you need a hand fastening it,' said Kitty.

'Will do,' she called, disappearing in a flick of blonde hair.

Moments later, Noushka pulled the curtain back and stepped out into the room, looking striking in the full-skirted dress of cream ivory satin, that finished mid-calf. 'I just need a hand to fasten the top few buttons.' She scooped her hair up and offered her back to Kitty.

Kitty obliged. 'There, all done.' She patted Noushka's back.

'How do I look?' The young girl skipped across to the full-length mirror at the other end of the room.

'Oh, Noushka, you look like an angel.' Kitty pressed her hand to her chest, and Vi noticed tears glistening in her friend's eyes.

'Wow. Noushka, I think I'm going to be outshone as I walk down the aisle.' Vi smiled fondly at her.

'I doubt that very much, Vi, you, literally, always turn heads wherever you go,' she replied.

'You'll both look breath-taking,' said Kitty.

∽

NOUSHKA HADN'T BEEN GONE five minutes when Kitty's mobile pinged. She scooped it up and read the message. 'Right, Vi, I'm ready when you are, chick.'

'Yep, I'll just clear my table, then I'm good to go.' She

pushed the clutter to one side. 'There.' She laughed. 'All done.'

The fan had obviously been doing a better job of keeping them cool than they realised, and when they stepped out of the studio, the warmth of the sun took Vi by surprise. 'Woah, it's scorchio out here.' She fished inside her handbag for her shades while Kitty locked the door.

'Phew! It is,' Kitty agreed. 'It reminds me of the summers we had when we were kids, running about all over the moors, having a whale of a time.'

Vi smiled and made her way down the path. 'Mmm. Jimby and me were having a conversation about that a few weeks ago. We had a perfect childhood, didn't we?'

'The best. And our kids will grow up thinking exactly the same thing.' She beamed at Vi and squeezed her shoulder.

'Come on, you two, get a bloody wriggle on!' Molly's foghorn voice barged its way into their conversation. She was parked up outside the gate of Sunshine Cottage, the driver window open. Vi looked on askance, she could see who she thought was Rosie sitting in the front passenger seat.

'What does she mean? What's happening?' Confused, Vi looked back at Kitty.

'Don't panic, chick, it's all good. We're taking you on a hen afternoon.'

'A hen ... oh, shit.' Vi's face dropped.

'Honestly, Vi, there's absolutely nothing to worry about, I promise. You're going to have a really lovely time.' Kitty hooked her arm through Vi's, giving it a reassuring squeeze. 'You know I wouldn't let Molly do anything you wouldn't like.'

'Hiya, Vi, honest, you'll love it,' called Rosie.

Vi climbed into Molly's four-wheel drive. 'I'm only getting in because I trust Kitty and Rosie, if it was just you, Moll, I'd run a bloody mile.'

Molly grinned as she put the car into gear and pulled out. 'None taken, Vi.'

Vi grinned back, noting that her friends were dressed smartly – why hadn't she spotted that Kitty was wearing something other than her usual workwear earlier? At least they weren't in the type of clothes that would suggest going to anywhere that would suggest male strippers. *Thank the Lord,* she sighed.

'Right, we'd best get a move on, the strippers will be getting nicely warmed up as we speak.' Molly threw her head back and released a dirty laugh.

'You had better be joking, Moll. Please tell me she's joking.'

'Moll, stop being a daft arse and winding Vi up, it's meant to be a lovely day for her, not one to get her stressed out,' warned Kitty.

'Ooh, I'd better do as I'm told if I've made our Kitty curse.' Molly waggled her eyebrows at her in the rear view mirror and the other women laughed.

'It seems to be coming a bit of a thing, me getting taken to places with no one telling me where. First Jimby, now you lot …' The ping of her mobile phone had her furtling around in her handbag. 'Speaking of Jimby …' Vi paused as she read the text before she burst into laughter.

'What is it?' asked Kitty.

'What's that cousin of mine done now?' asked Molly.

'Oh, you won't believe this.' Vi giggled.

'What's he been up to? I bet it's something to do with that cockerel.' Kitty rolled her eyes.

'The York Gazette have only cottoned-on to the calendar and want to interview him.'

A cacophony of laughter followed. 'Our Jimby'll love that, he's such an exhibitionist,' said Molly.

'It gets better,' said Vi. 'Yorkshire Today want to interview him and his "co-models" – as he calls them – for a feature on the local television news, too.' Hearing this made the women fall into fits of hysterics.

'Oh, my days. Poor old Ollie will hate that,' giggled Kitty.

'I'm not so sure Rob'll be keen, either. It's one thing doing it for a photograph, but a newspaper, or the telly ... it doesn't bear thinking about.'

'Tell you what, lasses, I aren't half glad it's the menfolk that've done the calendar and not us women. Can you imagine that?'

Kitty shuddered. 'Ooh, no, I can't, Molly. Those original ladies were so brave.'

'Too right.' Vi glanced out of the window to see that they were heading down one of the steep banks into Arnthorpe. The frothy heads of cow parsley were swaying idly against the broad, moss-covered stones of the dry-stone walls that lined the fields. The hawthorn bushes had grown so tall, they'd formed an arch above the road, creating a cool, dappled shade. Vi rubbed the goose bumps it had triggered on her arms.

'Not long now.' Kitty smiled across at her.

'So you're still not going to tell me what you've got planned?'

'Nope,' said Molly.

'You don't have much longer to wait,' said Rosie.

A couple of minutes later, Molly pulled up by the village green. 'Here we are,' she said. 'Final destination.'

Vi looked at her friends, still none the wiser, watching as

they spilled out of the car. 'Come on, missus,' said Kitty. She ran around to Vi's side and opened her door. 'Jump out.'

Vi stepped out, breathing a sigh of relief as she followed them across the road to her favourite teashop, Cosy Corner.

'Just wait there for one minute.' Kitty disappeared into the tearoom. Moments later, she was back out again, smiling. 'Right, follow us.'

Vi followed her friends to the tea-garden. 'Ta-da,' they chorused.

'Your hen party is afternoon tea at Cosy Corner,' said Kitty.

Violet felt her mouth fall open as she took in the achingly beautiful scene before her.

In the centre of the tea-garden was a cream coloured gazebo, sumptuously trimmed with bunting and flowers in hues of purple, green and cream. Inside, a table was laid for afternoon tea, the crisp white tablecloth was set with vintage crockery decorated with purple flowers, a large glass jar had blowsy lilac roses and other English country garden blooms spilling out of it, while the gleaming white napkins were tied with lilac silk ribbon. Music from the forties burbled discreetly in the background.

Vi felt her throat constrict as she fought back emotion. 'You've done this for me?'

Kitty nodded. 'Well, we asked Lee and Jools if they'd do it, it's all their handiwork – though Rosie found the bunting in a shop in York.'

'Thank you, girls. I don't know what to say.'

'You don't have to say anything, let's park ourselves while Jools and the crew bring out the afternoon tea,' said Molly.

*The Secret - Violet's Story*

As expected, the food was scrumptious and the chatter incessant. Vi couldn't have wished for a more perfect day.

'If it's okay with you ladies, I think I'll pinch that last slice of Jools's heavenly apple custard tart,' said Vi.

'Dive in,' said Molly. 'We asked him to make it specially for you – we know it's your favourite.'

'Well, if you're having that, would anyone mind if I have the last piece of mixed berry Bakewell, it's divine?' Kitty looked around at her friends who all nodded their agreement.

'This has been the best day ever.' Vi leaned back in her seat and laced her fingers across her stomach. 'Ooh,' she said.

'What?' asked Molly.

'Are you okay?' Kitty's fork stopped halfway to her mouth.

Vi smiled. 'I'm not sure, but I think I just felt the baby move.'

'Oh, Vi. What did it feel like?' asked Rosie, her eyes shining.

'A kind of flutter,' she replied.

'It's a bit early days, but from your description, it sounds like you did.' Kitty beamed at her.

'Sounds more like wind to me,' said Molly.

'You'd know, Moll,' Vi replied. 'Ooh, it's happened again.'

'Ahh, Vi, it's such an exciting time, I can remember it with Abbie,' said Rosie.

'How many weeks are you?' asked Kitty. 'If I remember rightly, about the sixteen week mark is when you can expect to feel something.'

'I think I'm about fourteen weeks.' Vi's heart soared, she couldn't wait to tell Jimby, and for him to feel it, too. She didn't think she'd be able to stop smiling for the rest of the day.

'And how are things with the haematoma?' asked Molly.

'Touch wood, things seem to be settling down there.' Violet reached across and touched the trunk of a nearby rowan tree.

'Oh, that's good news, chick,' said Kitty.

'It is,' agreed Rosie.

'So, are you going to find out the sex of the baby?' Molly poured herself some more tea from the pot.

'Well, I'd quite like to know, but Jimby wants to keep it a surprise, and as I couldn't trust myself to keep it secret – and I don't *really* mind not knowing – I think it's only fair we don't find out.'

'Ooh, yes, if I'd known the sex of the baby when I was expecting Lottie, but Ollie didn't want to, I'd spend the whole time worrying that I'd blurt it out by mistake,' said Kitty.

'Exactly.' Vi nodded. 'It's just easier all round if neither of us know.'

'Yep, we all know how quickly news can spread around the village – true or otherwise,' said Molly.

The others muttered their agreement.

They finished their cakes and squeezed the teapot dry as they soaked up the sunshine and the tranquil atmosphere of the tea garden.

Vi gave a contented sigh. 'Thank you, ladies, for the most wonderful day. I couldn't have wished for a more perfect way to spend my hen do.' She looked around at her friends; she felt truly blessed to have the support of such an amazing bunch of women. She smiled as her heart filled with love for them.

*The Secret - Violet's Story*

~

LATER THAT EVENING, in the cosiness of the bedroom at Sunshine Cottage, Vi was looking at her reflection in the full-length mirror. Jimby was lying on top of the duvet, his hands thrown behind his head, his dark eyes appreciatively soaking up the image before him.

'Little Pippin's making me fill out all over the place, look at the size of my bum and my hips.' She smoothed her hands over her silk nightdress.

In a moment, Jimby was behind her, curling his hands round her waist, settling on the small round of her stomach. He nuzzled her neck. 'I love your curves, always have. You look absolutely delicious, I could devour you whole,' he said huskily.

Vi turned round and wrapped her arms around his neck. 'You could?'

'Mmhm.' He pressed a kiss to her lips that shot a bolt of lust right through her.

'In that case ...' She took his hand and led him towards the bed.

'You're a wanton woman, Violet Smith.'

She squealed with delight as he nibbled all the way up her arm to her neck.

**CHAPTER 40**

'So, you managed to keep yourself out of trouble, did you?' Vi was talking to Jimby about his interview with the reporters from the York Gazette and the Yorkshire Today studio.

'Sure did, it all went very smoothly.' He took a bite out of his slice of garlic bread, stretching out the stringy mozzarella he'd melted on top.

It was the day after Vi's hen afternoon, and the pair were sitting in the small kitchen area of Sunshine Cottage, the patio doors flung open, letting in the early evening air while they enjoyed their evening meal of pesto pasta, salad and garlic bread.

'When's it supposed to be getting aired?' She couldn't help but smile.

'Tomorrow night, I think, and the article's supposed to be in the paper this weekend.' He glanced across at her, feigning an unamused expression. 'And what's so funny?'

Vi pressed her hand against her mouth as she finished her piece of gnocchi. 'I can just imagine what you're going to be like on camera, strutting about with that enormous smile on your face.' She collapsed into a fit of the giggles.

'I was not strutting, I was just being my usual charming self. With me, Ollie and Jonty standing behind the bar in the pub, I can assure you, none of us were keen to strut, we just wanted to stay put,' he said. 'Funny how I couldn't track down any of the other blokes involved in the calendar, though.'

'Yeah, can't think why.' Vi chuckled to herself. 'No cantankerous cockerels to chase in your underpants today, then?'

Jimby batted her comment away. 'So, I'd advise you to enjoy these few moments we have left before my celebrity status kicks in and I'm having to sign autographs whenever I set foot outside the door.'

'Meanwhile, back in the real world, was the new bathroom delivered today?'

Jimby's face was serious for a moment. 'Erm, it was, but it was the wrong one, so it'll have to go back. I wasn't going to tell you, couldn't see the point of stressing you out.'

Vi puffed out her cheeks and sighed.

Jimby reached for her hand. 'Honestly, Vi, it's not worth worrying about, Robbie got straight onto the shop and sorted it out, the new one's already on its way.'

'You're right, I need to stop stressing about things like that, Robbie's doing a great job of making sure everything's running properly.'

Jimby nodded. 'He is. And while we're on the subject of the house, we need to settle on a name for it.'

'I know, I still can't make up my mind.'

'How about Rowan Tree Cottage – a mixture of the places we grew up: rowan from Rowan Slack Farm for you, and tree from Oak Tree Farm for me?'

Vi thought for a moment. 'You know what? I really like that. Rowans are my favourite tree, with their gorgeous berries in the autumn. And there's already one on the plot.'

'My thinking exactly.'

'Ooh!' Vi pressed her hand to her stomach. She looked across at Jimby, a smile spreading across her face. 'It's happening again. Pippin's having a wriggle about. Seems to start whenever I'm eating.'

He reached across and lay his hand on her stomach. 'I can't really feel anything yet.' He leaned in closer to Vi's stomach. 'This is your dad speaking, Pippin, can you hurry up and kick a bit harder for me?'

Vi chuckled and ruffled his curls. 'From what the girls say, it won't be long.'

'I can't wait, I'll feel properly connected to her then.'

'Her?'

'Yep, I've got a strong gut-feeling that we're going to have a little girl,' he said, his eyes shining with happiness.

**CHAPTER 41**

Friday evening found Vi and Jimby crowding round the large television screen at Withrin Hill Farm together with Molly, Camm, Kitty and Ollie, ready to watch the interview on Yorkshire Today. An air of merriment and anticipation floated around the old farmhouse.

'Sorry we're late.' Rosie and Robbie bowled into the living room. 'Robbie had a client we thought would never leave.'

Phoebe jumped up and gave one of her cursory barks, wagging her tail furiously when she saw it was familiar faces.

'Shush, Phoebe,' said Molly. 'Don't worry, it hasn't been on yet. Help yourselves to wine or beer from the fridge, or there's tea in the pot if you'd prefer.'

Two minutes later, the familiar scene of the bar at the Sunne was plastered over the TV screen. All eyes were drawn to Jimby's smile that shone out, just as it always did.

'Look at the state of Jim.' Camm laughed. 'Is your smile big enough?'

'Oh, Jesus, I look as awkward as I felt,' said Ollie.

'And look at the state of Jonty,' giggled Vi. 'I knew he was skinny, but you could play a tune on those ribs.'

'Typical, look at our Jimby, loving every minute.' Molly gave her cousin an affectionate shove.

They listened intently as Jimby took the lead, answering the reporter's questions comfortably, while Ollie attempted to disappear beneath the bar. Jonty nodded so fervently, he almost lost his glasses off the end of his nose, making the interviewer smirk.

'That was brilliant, lads.' Camm clapped Jimby on the back when the piece came to an end. 'There'll be a load of women swooping on the village tomorrow, hoping to buy a calendar, or cop an eyeful of one of you fellas.'

'Please, don't say that.' Ollie shook his head, making Kitty laugh. 'I think I'm going to go into hiding for a couple of weeks.'

'Just as well, we got a load more printed, isn't?' said Robbie.

'Cheers to that,' said Jimby. 'We should have plenty for a defibrillator in no time.'

'Cheers,' they others replied.

'Hey, in the excitement, I almost forgot to tell you.' Jimby took a swig from his bottle.

'Tell us what?' asked Ollie.

Jimby looked across at Kitty. 'You'll be relieved to hear this, sis.'

'Oh?'

'I have it on good authority that Aoife and her toxic family won't be moving back to the village.'

Kitty's eyes widened, a smile tugging at her lips. 'How do you know? Are you sure?'

'Ooh, that's good news,' said Vi.

'Freddie told me. He said Dave had been on the phone

to cancel their newspaper order, and told him that they wouldn't be moving back. He then told him he'd left Aoife, saying he was sick to death of her stuck up ways.'

A murmur of surprise went around the friends.

'And I don't know how true this is, but I heard a rumour Dave had asked Maneater if he could move in with her.' Robbie's news piqued everyone's interest.

'Is that a joke?' asked Molly.

'Apparently not. But she told him to sling his hook. According to my source, Maneater thinks he's bone idle and not worth the effort.'

'I wasn't expecting you to say any of that,' said Vi. 'And I always thought Aoife and Dave were well matched – both equally arrogant.'

'They are – or were – and I'm pleased they're not coming back, but it's a shame for the kids that their parents are splitting up,' said Kitty.

'Don't go troubling yourself with worrying about that after how their youngest treated little Lil. Trust me, Kitts, the village – and school – will be a happier place without them,' said Molly.

'And safer,' said Camm.

No one could argue with that.

∽

As predicted, after the television interview and newspaper article, sales of the calendar went stratospheric. The committee was inundated with orders and were struggling to keep up with demand.

'Mum, Mum!' Noushka came flying into the Romantique studio. 'It's literally gone viral.'

Kitty and Violet jumped up in alarm. Kitty's hand flew to her chest. 'What's gone viral?'

'Jimby's interview. It's, like, literally all over social media; it's everywhere. Honestly, it's going, like, totally crazy. Everyone is saying how totally hot Dad and Uncle Jimby are.' Noushka was practically gasping for breath.

Vi and Kitty exchanged glances before bursting out laughing. 'Jimby's going to love this,' said Vi.

'And your dad's going to absolutely hate it,' said Kitty.

'It's totally awesome. They're calling them the "Hotsmiths".'

'The "Hotsmiths"?' said Kitty.

'Yeah, it's a name they've made up because Jimby's a blacksmith and Dad's a, er … "woodsmith", I guess, or something like that.'

'Woodsmith?' Vi mouthed at Kitty, who shrugged in response.

'I know, totally weird, but anyway, someone literally just came up with the name "Hotsmiths" and it's stuck,' said Noushka.

'What about poor old Jonty,' asked Kitty. 'Haven't they got a name for him?'

'Pubsmith?' suggested Vi, making them all giggle.

'I don't think he's included.' Noushka scrunched up her face.

'I don't suppose he'll be too bothered about that,' said Kitty. 'Though, Ollie will probably wish he could swap places with him.'

'This is going to be absolutely amazing for calendar sales. We'd best warn them to get plenty in stock,' said Vi. 'Though, I reckon that brother of yours is going to be a flipping nightmare to live with for a while.'

'It doesn't bear thinking about,' said Kitty. 'Let's hope it all calms down for the wedding.'

Vi groaned. 'Uh. I hadn't thought of that.

～

THE DAYS that followed saw the committee Facebook page inundated with messages and propositions for Jimby and Ollie – Zander, too. Some harmless, while some were downright obscene. Jimby laughed it off with ease, but Ollie found them terrifying. Jonty wasn't without his admirers either, and there were a small handful of suggestions of what ladies would like to do with him over a beer barrel, which Bea found hilarious.

'One woman said she'd like to lick beer out of his belly-button. Can you imagine that?' Bea was talking to Jimby and Vi, who'd popped into the pub one evening. 'And I won't tell you what she said she'd like him to stir her cocktail with, but he's absolutely tickled pink with the attention.'

'Could've been worse, Bea. She could've asked him to stir something else.' Jimby laughed.

'Jimby!' Vi looked horrified.

'Ughh! On those words, it's time I headed back to the kitchen,' said Bea.

'Ey up, you always have to let yourself down, don't you, Jimbo?' Ollie had just walked in and overhead Jimby's comment.

'I like to think I do my best.' Jimby beamed at him.

～

THANKS to the surge in interest generated by the buzz over the "Hotsmiths", more than enough money was raised to fund a defibrillator. Not wanting to waste time, Jimby had one ordered straight away, and a block of first responder training sessions was booked for anyone local willing to be a volunteer. The number of people keen to sign up for it had warmed Jimby's heart.

'Here's to Jimby, and his bonkers idea for a calendar.' Ollie raised his pint of beer in a toast. The friends, who were at their favourite table in the Sunne, followed suit.

'To Jimby,' they called, clinking glasses.

'Yeah, well done, mate,' said Camm, giving him a sound pat on the back. 'There's a lot of people sleeping easier in their beds, knowing there's going to be a defibrillator close to hand.'

'Hey, it wasn't just down to me, you know. If it wasn't for you lot, it would never have been able to happen.'

'Yeah, who'd have thought a load of old blokes getting their nuts out would've raised so much money?' Much sniggering followed Molly's comment.

'Er, less of the old, if you don't mind, Moll,' said Jimby.

'And trust you to bring nuts into the conversation, Molly,' said Vi.

'Hey, don't blame me for that, it's all our Jimby's fault.'

'I never mentioned them! Anyway, I've just spotted Gerald over at the bar and I just want to check he knows about the defibrillator.'

'In this village? Of course he'll know.' Robbie laughed.

'You're probably right, but just in case …' Jimby laughed as he stood up. 'I'll get some drinks in while I'm there.' He turned and took a step forward, not seeing the black Labrador stretched out on the floor in front of him. 'Arghhh!' he yelled as he went flying over it and landed right in Maneater's arms.

'Well, hello there, gorgeous.' She looked like all her birthdays had come at once.

'Oh, man, what's he like?' Ollie roared with laughter and set his pint glass down. 'I'd better go and rescue him from Maneater's cleavage.'

'Oh, I'd leave him. Watching him wriggle out of her clutches is way too much fun.' Molly chuckled. 'Look, the woman's like a bloody octopus.'

'Thanks for your help, you lot,' Jimby said when he finally got free and dusted himself down.

'Anytime, Jimbo,' laughed Camm.

Vi and the others still couldn't speak laughing. Jimby certainly generated a lot of entertainment, she thought, and he always took his mishaps in good humour. *Life's definitely better for having him in it.*

# CHAPTER 42

SEPTEMBER

The week before the wedding had passed in a blur. The thatcher making a start on the roof meant that things had taken a massive leap forward with the house build. But, best of all, when Jimby had taken Vi to hospital for a scan, it showed the subchorionic haematoma had all but disappeared. Vi was surprised at how much hearing the news had felt like a huge weight had lifted from her shoulders and drifted away; despite all of the reassurances, it must have been bothering her more than she thought. And from the look on Jimby's face she could tell he felt the same way.

The night before the wedding, Jimby had packed a small bag and was heading to Kitty and Ollie's where he was spending the night. 'Come here, and let me kiss you, Miss Smith.' He gave Vi a wide smile as he pulled her to him.

She wrapped her arms round his neck. 'You won't be able to call me that for much longer.'

'True,' he said. 'And I can't wait to call you Mrs Fairfax.'

'Me neither.'

He pressed a lingering kiss to her lips, and, reluctant to pull away, rested his forehead against hers. 'See you in the

## The Secret - Violet's Story

morning, gorgeous. I'll tell Kitty you're ready for her to bob along.'

'Okay. See you in the morning.' She watched him disappear down the garden path and along the trod to Oak Tree Farm, whistling as he went. Her heart swelled with happiness; she doubted she'd be able to wipe the smile off her face for days.

˜

Vi woke over an hour before the alarm was due to go off, her thoughts slowly gathering themselves, realisation dawning as to why it felt strange not to wake up in Jimby's arms. She reached out for his pillow and hugged it close, inhaling his delicious, masculine scent. Excitement curled around her insides, and she wiggled her toes, hardly daring to believe that their wedding day had finally arrived. Such a lot had happened in the short space of time since he'd asked her to marry him, but nothing was going to put the dampers on the day.

Outside, the birds were gradually coming off roost, warming up their vocal chords in readiness to launch into the dawn chorus. There was no way she was going to get back to sleep once that had started. She slipped out of bed, pulled on her lilac silk dressing gown and tiptoed downstairs, not wanting to wake Kitty.

Trying to be as quiet as possible, Vi made herself a cup of tea and took it out into the back garden, savouring a few peaceful moments alone with her thoughts. A gentle haze hung in the drowsy morning air and dew glittered on the rose petals, weighing them down, while the smell of damp earth combined with freshly cut grass tickled her nostrils. Birdsong had begun to fill the garden. Vi gave a contented sigh and gazed out over the dale where she could see the sun beginning to peer over Great Stangdale Rigg, pushing the morning mist out of its way. The previous two days had seen a fair bit of rainfall, which had left the fields and moors looking more vibrant than ever, but the forecast for today was wall-to-wall sunshine, which had come as a relief to Vi, who'd been following it closely.

Sensing a presence behind her, she turned to see Kitty padding down the path in a pair of pink dotty pyjamas, her elfin crop of curls sticking up on end, steam rising from the two mugs of tea she was carrying.

'Here you go, chick.' She beamed sleepily at Vi, before her face was pulled out of shape by a yawn.

'Thanks, Kitts.' Vi set her redundant mug down on the wall.

'Excited?'

'Excited and happy.' Both feelings rippled through Vi, making her stomach flip and butterflies tickle her insides.

'And I'm so happy for you both, too.' Kitty wrapped an arm around Vi. 'To think, in a few hours we'll be sisters.'

'And I couldn't wish for a better one, Kitts.' Vi rested her head on her friend's shoulder.

'Me neither.'

~

AT THE CHURCH, Vi was a mix of nerves and utter happiness. Thanks to a last minute tweak, her satin, ankle-length dress fitted perfectly. 'You look like an angel,' her dad said doing his best to keep his voice steady. 'Your mother and me are so proud of you. And we couldn't be happier that you're marrying young Jimby.'

'Thanks, Dad.' Tears threatened and Vi wiggled her toes

in her satin kitten heels to distract herself. In a moment, the organ struck up, blasting out the wedding march as Little Mary hit the keys with gusto, shooing Vi's tears away in an instant.

'Ready, lass?' asked her Dad.

'Ready, Dad.' She clutched her posy of lilac roses and frothy gypsophila – courtesy of Molly's mum Annie — in one hand and linked her father's arm with the other, and the pair made their way steadily down the aisle.

As Vi approached Jimby, her stomach was a riot of butterflies looping-the-loop, while pure joy joined in, pushing her smile wider and wider. His shoulders looked strong and broad in his new grey suit, while his right leg twitched in anticipation, betraying his nerves. Ollie turned and smiled, before leaning in to Jimby and whispering something. At that, Jimby turned round, revealing a heart-stopping smile and ... *What? What on earth had happened?* Vi felt her smile drop. He was looking back at her with two perfectly matching black eyes.

'Ey up,' said Ken.

Caught off guard, Vi's heart leapt and she stopped in her tracks. 'Oh my God,' she whispered to her dad. 'What's he done now?'

Her father squinted. 'Oh, er, well, unless I need my eyes testing, it looks like he's got a couple of right royal shiners, love.'

'That's what I thought but I wondered if it was the light casting shadows on my veil.'

Ken took a step forward. 'Nope, it's definitely nowt to do with shadows, they're a couple of shiners.'

'Oh.'

Jimby's smile began to slip off his face.

'Come on love, best keep moving,' said Ken.

'Oh, er, right, yes.'

The sheepish look Jimby was wearing when Vi was finally level with him didn't go unnoticed. 'You look absolutely gorgeous,' he whispered to her.

'Thank you. Wish I could say the same for you.' She glanced across at Ollie who was wearing an apologetic expression. 'Did Ollie do it?'

'No!' James shook his head vigorously and laughed quietly. 'There's a perfectly innocent explanation.'

'Thank goodness for that.' Vi couldn't help herself and giggled, which seemed to prompt Rev Nev to clear his throat and begin proceedings.

∼

'Ollie! Why didn't you text me about Jimby's eyes? I could've warned Vi. It must've been a huge shock when he turned round.' Kitty said as she scrutinised her brother's injuries. They were standing outside the church after the ceremony, waiting for everyone to file out.

'You could say,' said Vi.

'I wanted to, but Jimby wouldn't let me. He thought it would worry Vi even more,' Ollie replied.

'Uncle Jimby, can I tell them what happened?' Lucas was leaping up and down, desperate to share the story.

'No, Lucas, I want to. I can tell it better than you.' Lily tugged at her brother's arm.

'I think I'd better do the explaining,' said Ollie. 'I'm not so sure Jimby can remember too much about it, but I saw it happen.'

'Blimey,' said Vi. 'My mind's working over-time now.'

'Well, he was practising his dad dancing in the garden with the kids.'

'As you do,' said Molly.

Ollie smiled and carried on. 'So, he was flying around like a looney in typical Jimby style – as you can, no doubt, imagine.'

'Only too well.' This was Molly again.

'Anyway, the next thing I know, Reg appears in the garden being loud and obnoxious, and Jimbo starts to chase him. He does this massive leap mixed with a twist – Jim, not Reg – and goes flying into one of the posts of the tree house, and ends up flat out on the grass.'

'Jimby!' Vi gasped.

'He was out cold for a few seconds. I think he should've gone to casualty, but he wouldn't hear of it. And, the elusive Reg lives to terrorise another day by escaping over the wall at the back,' added Ollie.

'That bloody bird.' Vi shook her head. 'He's going to have to go.'

'Honestly, Vi, Jimby was, literally, so quiet for like the rest of the night,' added Noushka. 'You totally wouldn't believe it.'

'Now, that I would like to have seen,' said Molly. 'Jimby being quiet is definitely a first.'

Vi touched Jimby's face with her hand. 'Are you sure you're okay?'

'I'm absolutely fine, especially now you're officially Mrs Fairfax.' He scooped her up and twirled her round.

'Mind my dress, Jimby, we've still got to have our photos taken!'

'I don't think a crumpled dress will be the thing people notice, Vi,' said Ollie as they burst out laughing.

## CHAPTER 43

DECEMBER

Two weeks before Christmas, the building work at the new house was finally finished. Robbie had called round to Sunshine Cottage early one evening to officially hand over the keys. 'The carpet fitters have just gone, and I thought you wouldn't want to wait until tomorrow morning to get your hands on these.' He dropped both sets of keys he and Mart the builder had used into Jimby's hand. 'All you need to do now is move your stuff in.'

Vi felt a surge of excitement. 'Oh, Robbie, thank you. That's brilliant news.' She turned to Jimby, to see his eyes dancing with happiness.

'It is, and Vi definitely wouldn't want to wait until morning for them,' he said. 'Thanks for all you've done, Rob, and for keeping things running smoothly for us. We really appreciate it.'

'No problem, it was a pleasure and Mart doesn't need much prodding, he's one of the best builders I've come across.' He smiled. 'Anyway, I'll leave you to it, I'm sure you'll both be eager to go and take a look. Any problems, let me know – not that I think there will be, mind.'

'Cheers, mate.' Jimby patted him on the shoulder.

'You're welcome. I have to say, I've really enjoyed working on the project. I knew it was going to look good, but it's turned out better than I ever imagined.' He smiled. 'Anyway, I'll see myself out.'

'Okay, and thanks again,' said Jimby.

'Yes, thank you so much, Robbie.'

Vi heard the front door click shut and turned to Jimby, barely able to contain her excitement. 'This means we can be in before Christmas.' Already, she was visualising a Christmas tree in the window and one in the front garden, both twinkling with fairy lights as fluffy snowflakes drifted down.

He wrapped an arm around her and pulled her close. 'We can, gorgeous. But I don't want you to do any lifting and lugging.' He smoothed his hand over her growing bump. 'I know the hospital said that the blood clot had all but gone, but I don't want us to take any risks with Pippin.'

'Me neither.'

'Ollie and Camm have offered to help move our stuff across. All you need to do is provide us with plenty of cups of tea and biscuits.'

'Not a problem. Though, do you think they'll be okay to get started straight away, even this close to Christmas?'

'Jimby nodded. 'They've already said they're fine to do it, and between the three of us it shouldn't take long.'

Vi couldn't stop smiling. 'It'll be good to get all of the new furniture out of Forge Cottage, it's so cluttered there.'

'Yep, then we can think about getting it rented out. Not until after Christmas, though. We'll concentrate on making Rowan Tree Cottage cosy with all our stuff.'

Vi clapped her hands. 'Fab. I already know where I want everything to go.'

'Well, that doesn't surprise me.' He smiled, kissing her glossy curls.

'I'm so excited, Jimby, we're going to be in our first home together before Christmas.'

'And before little Pippin comes.' He looked down at her, his eyes shining with happiness. 'Have I told you how much I love you, Mrs Fairfax?'

'Erm, only the five times today,' she giggled.

'Not nearly enough, then.' He cupped her face in his large hands and kissed her.

'Ooh, I knew there was something I had to tell you,' she said, when he released her. 'I was speaking to Molly earlier and she said that she'd mentioned to Tom how my parents were going to retire – at long last – and move in here when we've moved to the new house.'

'Right, I think I know where this is going.'

'Well, she thought he'd been sounding a bit homesick recently and wondered why he was asking so many questions about Rowan Slack. Anyway, the next day, he'd Skyped back and said that he and Adam have spoken to Lord Hammondely about taking the farm on when my parents have left.'

'That's great news. Moll must be chuffed to bits. I know she puts on a brave face and has always said that she was okay with him farming in New Zealand because he was happy, but it's obvious she misses him like crazy.'

'I know, she sounded so happy when she was telling me. And it's a lovely place to live, I was so happy growing up there. Though, Moll said they're probably not going to continue with dairy, but go into rare breeds instead, and maybe even have a farm shop or something; another way to diversify, anyway.'

'He's full of good ideas, he's a chip off the old block; his dad would be proud.'

Vi nodded. 'He would. And it would be nice to think that family are going to be moving in there, too – means I can still pop up for a visit.'

'Have a nosy, you mean.' Jimby smiled at her. 'Fingers crossed Lord Hammondely says yes.'

'Well, from what Molly was saying, it all sounded pretty positive. Everything seems to be working out for everyone, doesn't it?'

'It does, gorgeous.' Jimby pulled her in for another kiss.

## CHAPTER 44

FEBRUARY

February had arrived in a flurry of snow and howling, spiteful gales. Lytell Stangdale was bitingly cold. It was just over a week before Vi's due date and she felt like a house-end. It was becoming increasingly difficult to sleep and she invariably found herself lying awake at night poring over the Kindle Jimby had bought her to help her pass the hours.

'I just can't get comfortable,' she complained to Kitty. 'Pippin's foot or elbow is digging right into my ribs. I wish she would hurry up and decide to arrive.'

'You look tired, chick. Why don't you make the most of the time you've got and try to catch up on some sleep. Trust me, when the baby comes, you're going to wish you had.' Earlier that day, Kitty had bumped into Jimby who'd asked her to go and check on Vi, saying he thought she'd looked a bit peaky.

'Mmm. I might.' Vi sounded distracted.

'Is everything alright?'

Vi wrestled with her thoughts for a moment. 'I don't want to sound like I'm making a fuss, but is it normal for the baby to stop moving?'

'Erm, well, from what I remember, they slow down a bit in the last month. Or should I say, it feels different when they move, more like shuffles and squirms rather than the forceful kicks and punches of the earlier months. There's less room for them to stretch out and wriggle about. Why, are you worried?'

'Pippin just doesn't seem to have moved at all today.' Vi felt panic begin to rise up inside her. She could tell Kitty was trying to act calm for her benefit.

'Okay, well, I think if you have even the slightest of worries, you need to ring Dr Beth. Would you like me to do it for you?'

Vi nodded.

Within fifteen minutes Kitty had whisked Vi to the surgery in Danskelfe and the doctor was listening to the baby's heartbeat pounding away. 'There, sounds good and strong, doesn't it?' She smiled at Vi.

'It does, sorry for making a fuss, doctor.' Relief swept through Vi, leaving her feeling like an over-anxious mother-to-be.

'No need for any apologies, it's always best to have any worries checked out, no matter how small. Though, it is very common for a baby's movements to slow down in the last few weeks. I'll give you a kick-counter chart so you can keep a record of every time the baby kicks – you'll be surprised just how much they do.

Feeling reassured, Vi headed home with Kitty dropping her off at the door. 'Try to get some rest, okay,' Kitty said before she drove off. 'But shout up if you need me.'

THAT EVENING at the dinner table, Vi had barely touched her

food, her appetite having all but deserted her over the last couple of days. Jimby had picked up on it and offered a variety of suggestions, none of which sounded appealing.

'But you've got to eat something,' he said.

'I just don't fancy anything. Not even apples.' She shrugged as she looked out into the garden where snow had begun to settle. 'Snow, that's all we need.'

'Hmm. Hugh Heifer said it's supposed to get quite bad. Hopefully, it'll have gone by Pippin's due date.' He rubbed a hand over his chin.

'The worst of it should be gone by then, shouldn't it?' Vi felt anxiety begin to inch its way up inside her.

'Let's hope so. Don't go worrying about it; we'll get you to hospital when the time comes.'

Though Jimby's words were usually reassuring, when they'd gone to bed Vi had lain awake for hours, sleep eluding her. Storm Helen wasn't helping, howling across the dale and causing havoc in the garden, rocking the rowan tree, making its branches creak eerily. She'd always found the wind unsettling, and tonight was no exception.

Jimby lay beside her, his hand resting protectively over her bump. He'd crashed out as soon as his head had hit the pillow, his deep, rhythmic breathing making her envious.

Try as she might, Vi couldn't clear her mind, there was too much swirling around it. With a sigh, she tried to imagine herself light as air (*that would take some bloody good imagination, the size she was!*), floating on a soft, fluffy cloud, her thoughts drifting away. 'Ahhh,' she breathed out as, gradually, her mind cleared and her eyelids became heavy, and she felt herself slowly succumb to the gentle clutches of slumber.

It felt like she'd been asleep a mere moment when she started as pain gripped her stomach, pushing its way through to her spine. 'Oof!' she gasped. The practice contractions had been getting stronger over the last couple of days, and this one was a real beast. And it was bloody typical that it should interrupt the promise of a blissful sleep. Vi sighed and closed her eyes, drifting off to sleep again, but half an hour later the same thing happened. 'Bugger,' she whispered. Intuitively, she knew that these were no Braxton Hicks; these were the real thing. Her eyes pinged open. *Oh, heck! I think this is it!*

'Jimby!' She shook his arm gently. 'Jimby! Wake up!'

'Wha? What's the matter?' he mumbled.

'I'm having contractions! Pippins on the way!'

'Holy shit!' Jimby flicked on the bedside light and turned to look at Vi. 'Are you okay? Can I get you anything?'

'I'm fine, they're quite far apart, so I don't think she's coming just yet, but will you have a look at the weather, see if the snow's settled much more?'

'Course.' He jumped out of bed and strode over to the window. 'Oh, bloody hell. Looks like it's been snowing nonstop since we went to bed. It must be a good four inches deep, and that's not accounting for any drifting up on the moor top.'

'Oh, Pippin, you've picked your moment to arrive into world. Vi groaned and waddled over to join him, smoothing her hand over her bump. She peered out of the window to see plump, feathery snowflakes swirling from the sky, illuminated by the soft glow of the Victorian-style streetlights. 'Oh no! What are we going to do, Jimby? We'll never get to hospital in this.'

He put his arm around her. 'Everything'll be fine, I have a cunning plan.' He kissed the end of her nose.

'Should I be worried?'

'Not at all, but we'll have to go in the Landie. You go and

get yourself ready, I'll put the engine on, get it warmed up a bit and the windscreen defrosted. We need to set off as soon as possible, we don't know how long it's going to take us to get there.' She watched as he disappeared downstairs.

In a moment he was back, rubbing his hands together. 'Right, that's sorted.'

Vi looked up from zipping her bag on the bed. 'What's sorted? Ouch!' Her face crumpled as she was gripped by another contraction.

Jimby hurried over to her. 'What can I do? Do you want me to rub your back?'

Vi shook her head. 'No, it's fine, it'll be gone in a minute.'

Jimby looked on, helpless, until the contraction passed.

'Phew, that's better,' she said, rubbing her stomach. 'So what is it you've got sorted? And can you help me get these socks on, I can't reach my feet?'

'Course. Camm's on his way, he's fixed the plough to the tractor, and he's going to drive in front of us as far as we need him.' He knelt in front of Vi and rolled her socks over her puffy feet. 'He was going to set out in a couple of hours so the milk tankers could get through, but I told him you'd gone into labour and he was practically out the door before I put the phone down.'

This last winter, Camm had won the contract from the council to plough the local roads in times of heavy snow, keeping the roads clear for farming traffic and the school bus.

'He's a star,' said Vi.

Jimby nodded. 'Yep, he's a really decent bloke. Our Moll's a lucky lass.'

Before they knew it, they heard the scrape of Camm's tractor pushing back the snow in the road.

Jimby held out his hand and pulled her up. 'This is the

last night it'll just be you and me. The next time we come home, we'll be bringing Pippin with us. We'll be a family.'

Vi felt herself well up with the emotion of Jimby's words. 'A family.' She nodded. 'I like the sound of that.'

'Me, too.' He picked up her bag. 'Ready?'

'As I'll ever be.'

Camm waved as they made their way down the snowy path, heads bent, huddling against the nipping wind. He waited for them to climb into the Landie before he set off.

'Do you think we'll be okay, Jimby?'

'We'll be fine,' he said. He released the handbrake and eased the Landie out onto the tracks left by Camm.

They followed him as he made his way steadily out of the village along the winding roads, then up and out onto the bleak, exposed rigg road of Great Stangdale. The snow was falling thick and fast, piling onto the windscreen as soon as the wipers had swiped it away, making visibility poor. Jimby's eyes remained fixed to the road ahead while Vi sat in silence, mesmerised by the snowflakes, breathing through the contractions that had suddenly increased in frequency.

Camm ploughed on, making short work of the deep snow drifts. They were about ten minutes from Middleton Hospital when Vi knew something was happening. 'Jimby, I think Pippin's coming.'

'What? Don't worry we're nearly there.'

'I don't think I can wait.' She gasped as a powerful contraction gripped her stomach, whipping her breath right out of her mouth.

'Oh.' Jimby snatched his eyes away from the road ahead and looked across to see Vi panting heavily, beads of sweat peppered across her brow, glistening in the lights of the dashboard. 'Oh, bloody hell, Vi, hang on as best you can.'

He pushed his fingers through his curls. 'Actually, my mobile's in my pocket, do you think you can ring the hospital – their number's in my contacts? Tell them we're nearly there. Tell them to expect us and it's urgent. Or put them on speaker-phone and I'll tell them. Here you go.' He fumbled about in his pocket and pulled out his phone.

'Okay.' Vi took it, breathing quickly, all fingers and thumbs, she found the number. 'There's signal, thank God.'

By the time they reached the hospital car park Vi was past herself. 'Jimby, I need to push! The baby's coming!'

'Omigod, Vi! Hang on, we're just about there!'

Jimby pulled up behind Camm directly outside the entrance to the maternity wing. Camm jumped down from the tractor and Jimby called to him to tell the nurses they were there. Snow was swirling round as the wind lashed out at anyone brave enough to be outdoors. He shot round to Vi's side and opened the door.

'I can't move, Jimby. I can't move, or the baby'll be born on the floor!'

'Just hang on, Vi.' Jimby's face was wrought with panic.

In a flash a midwife whizzed out of the hospital doors, pushing a wheelchair over the pathway that had been cleared and gritted. 'Come on, Violet, lovie, we need to get you into the warm. We can't go delivering that baby out here.'

'I can't move,' Vi gasped, her face creased with pain.

'Yes, you can. Come on, Jimby'll help you down.'

'Come on, Vi, sweetheart, we need to get you inside.' He leaned in and undid her seatbelt, then took her hand and guided her out of the Landie and into the wheelchair.

Less than an hour later, Vi found herself sitting up in bed in the delivery wing of Middleton Hospital, exhausted,

## The Secret - Violet's Story

but happy. Sitting beside her was Jimby, nursing their little daughter, tears of happiness pouring down his cheeks.

'She's beautiful, Vi. She's just perfect.' He sniffed, shaking his head in disbelief. 'She's got your nose, the same shaped face as you. And look at all that hair, she's got so much hair.'

Vi felt exhausted but happy. Today might have had its hair-raising moments, but after what had happened all those years ago, she never thought she'd be in this position, married to the boy next door, having just given birth to the most beautiful baby in the world.

'Have you still got your eyes glued to your little girl, Dad?' A smiling midwife bustled in with a tray holding two cups of tea and a plate of toast. 'Thought you might be feeling peckish after what you've just been through; it's hungry work, giving birth.'

'Thanks, I'm starving,' Jimby replied.

The midwife looked at Vi and they started to laugh.

Vi's stomach rumbled at the mouth-watering aroma. 'He hasn't stopped looking at her – I don't think he can believe she's real. And thank you, I'm absolutely starving, too.'

∽

'SHE'S A LITTLE CRACKER, love. And her arrival into the world was almost as dramatic as yours.' Vi's father was sitting beside the hospital bed, dressed in his Sunday best and fiddling with the very tie he'd worn the night Vi was born.

'Don't know about that, lovie. At least we all knew this little poppet was due.' Vi's mum cradled her sleeping granddaughter, her ruddy face filled with pride.

'Mind, we never thought we'd see this day, did we, Mary?

You were always so adamant you weren't going to be a mother, Violet.'

'It's because she wasn't with the right man,' said her mum.

Vi looked up at Jimby and smiled. 'You're absolutely right there, Mum.'

An hour later, Vi and Jimby were descended upon by Kitty, Ollie, Molly and Camm. Vi was oblivious, drifting in and out of sleep, while Jimby was nursing their daughter.

'Congratulations, mate.' Ollie spoke softly, squeezing Jimby's shoulder. 'She's beautiful.'

The others followed, whispering their congratulations, being careful not to wake Vi.

'Well done, big brother.' Kitty leaned across and kissed Jimby's cheek which seemed to trigger a new wave of tears from him.

'I can't believe how perfect she is. Look at her little tiny nose, her little mouth, it's like a rosebud, just perfect. And her fingernails, look, she's got fingernails, Oll, they're so tiny.'

Ollie smiled. 'She has, Jim, she's absolutely perfect.'

'I just wish Mum and Dad could be here to see her.'

Kitty reached out and squeezed his arm. 'They're looking down on the three of you, Jimby. And I just know they'll be wearing the biggest smiles, seeing their gorgeous little granddaughter and knowing how happy you all are.'

With a sniff, Jimby nodded. 'You're right, Kitts.'

Vi stirred, a smile breaking sleepily across her face as she became aware that the fuzzy voices she could hear in her dream were her friends gathering round her bed.

'Well done, Vi,' Molly said in a stage whisper. 'I gather you had a bit of a job hanging on.'

Vi rubbed sleep from her eyes. 'Mmm. I nearly didn't

manage. I don't know what we'd have done without Camm's help. I think I would've given birth in the Landie parked up on the moors somewhere.'

'Yeah, thanks, mate. We owe you big time.' Jimby wiped his tears and smiled at Camm.

'Hey, it was nothing. I'd have had the tractor out anyway.'

'So, does this little bundle have a name, or is she going to be stuck with Pippin?' asked Kitty.

'Well,' said Vi. 'We've decided her first name's going to be Elspeth.' She looked across at Jimby.

He sniffed again. 'And her middle name's going to be Helen; after the storm she was born in.'

'Hah! I like it!' said Molly. 'But let's hope it won't be stormy by name, stormy by nature.'

'Looking at that little face, I don't think it will be, she looks so peaceful.' Kitty peered at the bundle in Jimby's arms. 'Ooh, and that baby smell, I just love it.'

'Don't go getting any ideas,' said Ollie. 'We've already got a houseful with our four.'

'I'm sure another one wouldn't make much of a difference.' Molly cocked a playful eyebrow at him.

'I think I'll leave that to you and Camm, Moll.' Ollie's reply had the desired effect and knocked Molly off her stride.

Oblivious to the banter, Jimby beamed down at his little daughter who had just opened her eyes and was gazing up at him. 'Welcome to the world little Elspeth Helen, and welcome to your family.'

# EPILOGUE

Vi was sitting in the cosy living room of Rowan Tree Cottage, sipping a cup of tea as a wave of happiness surged through her. *Somebody pinch me,* she thought. She couldn't believe how lucky she was, sitting here in her dream home, looking on as the man she'd been in love with probably as far back as her teenage years cradled their daughter – who just so happened to be the most beautiful baby in the whole world – in his big, strong arms, feeding her a bottle of expressed breast milk.

It had been quite a year, and to think she'd nearly lost it all because of a stupid secret. And not exactly the worst secret in the world, either – she hadn't killed anyone, or stolen anything or brought down a government, for heaven's sake. Though the way she'd felt at the time, anyone would think she had. But the longer she'd kept it to herself, the bigger it had grown in her mind, slowly obliterating her happiness, making it harder and harder to share. How could she not have realised that the fact she hadn't shared it with Jimby would hurt him more than the secret itself? He was such a decent man. But Vi had learnt an important lesson from it, to look at things from more perspectives than just her own; to look at the bigger picture.

She'd changed in other ways, too. So much so, her business friends and colleagues from her former life didn't recognise her – some even sneered at her choice. Where, they wondered had Vi, the hard-nosed, ball-breaking, career-driven businesswoman gone? Vi knew the answer to that: she'd never really existed, she was simply the veneer that covered the woman who'd had her fingers burnt by a manipulative older man.

As if reading her thoughts, Jimby looked up and smiled, the sort of smile that still had the power to make her heart flip and her knees turn to jelly.

'Love you, Mrs. Fairfax,' he whispered.

'Love you, too, Mr. Fairfax.' Her heart flooded with love for her husband and their little daughter.

Vi had the happy-ever-after she'd always wished for.

THE END

# AFTERWORD

Thank you for reading The Secret – Violet's Story, I hope you enjoyed it. If you did, I'd be really grateful if you could pop over to Amazon and a leave a review – if you Google the links below they should take you right there:

Eliza J Scott – Amazon UK – The Secret – Violet's Story
Eliza J Scott – Amazon US – The Secret – Violet's Story

It doesn't have to be long – just a few words would do – but for us new authors it makes a huge difference. Thank you so much.

If you'd like to find out more about what I get up to in my little corner of the North Yorkshire Moors, or if you'd like to get in touch – I'd love to hear from you! – you can find me in the following places:

Amazon author page: Eliza J Scott – Amazon UK or Eliza J Scott – Amazon US

Blog: www.elizajscott.com
Twitter: @ElizaJScott1
Facebook: @elizajscottauthor
Instagram: @elizajscott
Bookbub: @elizajscott

## ALSO BY ELIZA J SCOTT

**The Letter – Kitty's Story** (Book 1 in the Life on the Moors Series)

**The Talisman – Molly's Story** (Book 2 in the Life on the Moors Series)

**A Christmas Kiss** (Book 4 in the Life on the Moors Series) – publication day: 4$^{th}$ November 2019

All available on my Amazon author page:

**Eliza J Scott - Amazon UK**

**Eliza J Scott - Amazon US**

## YORKSHIRE GLOSSARY

The Yorkshire dialect, with its wonderful elongated, flat vowels can trace its roots back to Olde English and Old Norse, the influences of which can still be found in some of the quirky words in regular use today. As a few of them crop up in The Secret – Violet's Story (as well as The Letter and The Talisman), I thought it might be a good idea to compile a list of them for you, just in case you're wondering what the bloomin' 'eck I'm going on about. I do hope it helps!

Aud – old

Aud mucker – old friend. Used in greeting i.e. 'Now then, me aud mucker'.

Back end – autumn

By 'eck – heck

Champion – excellent

Chuffed to bits – very pleased, i.e. 'I'm chuffed to bits with my new coat'.

Diddlin' – doing – i.e. 'How're you diddlin' means, 'How are you doing?'.

Ey up – hello/watch out

Fair capt – very pleased

Famished – hungry
Fettle – fix/put right
Fower – four
Gander – look, i.e. 'Have a gander at this'.
Hacky – dirty
Jiggered – tired
Lops – fleas
Lug/lug 'ole – ear/ear hole
Mafted – hot
Mash – brew, as in a pot of tea
Mucker – friend
Nithered – very cold
Now then – hello
Nowt – nothing
Owt – anything
Raw – cold, in reference to the weather
Reckon – think
Rigg – ridge
Rigwelted – word used to refer to an animal that has fallen over and got stuck on its back
Rum – odd/strange
Snicket – an alleyway
Summat – something
Yat/yatt – gate

## ACKNOWLEDGMENTS

It's been great fun getting to know Violet; she's a colourful character, and not without her contradictions. One minute, she's a driven, ball-breaking business woman with a cool exterior, the next, she's content to settle down with the boy-next-door and start a family in the village where she grew up. It may have taken Vi years to accept that she was in love with Jimby, and would be more than happy to move back to her home village of Lytell Stangdale, but it was truly heart-warming to see her get the happy-ever-after she'd been secretly yearning for. It was also good to revisit the friendship group she's part of; three very different women who've grown up together and who are fiercely loyal to one-another, though aren't afraid to welcome others in – Rosie springs to mind here! Indeed, it's this powerful friendship that's been at the core of the first three books in this series.

As ever, there are several people I'm indebted to for making this book possible. Top of the list has to be my family for the usual supply of Yorkshire tea and ginger biscuits – not to mention their unwavering support of my writing. Oh, and for putting up with the heaps of my writing 'mess' on the dining table (my writing room still isn't ready; maybe by book four…!).

Special thanks are owed to Alison Williams for her fabulous editing skills and words of wisdom. Alison is a joy to work with – I've learnt such a lot from her – and I always look forward to getting stuck into her edits.

Huge thanks to book cover designer extraordinaire Berni Stevens for designing an absolutely delicious cover for Violet's Story; it goes beautifully with Kitty and Molly's. It's always exciting to get Berni's ideas back and I can't wait to see what she has in store for my first Christmas book!

Rachel Gilbey at Rachel's Random Resources – aka Wonderwoman of the book world! – also deserves a great big thank you for so many reasons. Not least for organising such fantastic cover reveals/blog tours, and for being totally organised and making sure everything stays calm and orderly on the run-up to the said cover reveals/blog tours.

I owe an enormous thank you to all of the book bloggers who have taken part in the Cover Reveal and Blog Tour for The Secret – Violet's Story, for taking the time to read it and for sharing it on their fabulous book blogs.

And I can't go without saying a massive thank you to the wonderful people I've got to know in the book community; your kindness and support over social media has been amazing.

THANK YOU!

## ABOUT THE AUTHOR

Eliza has wanted to be a writer as far back as she can remember. She lives in the North Yorkshire Moors with her husband, two daughters and two black Labradors. When she's not writing, she can usually be found with her nose in a book/glued to her Kindle, or working in her garden, battling against the weeds that seem to grow in abundance there. Eliza enjoys bracing walks in the countryside, rounded off by a visit to a teashop where she can indulge in another two of her favourite things: tea and cake.

Printed in Great Britain
by Amazon